SEAHORSE

JANICE PARIAT

A NOVEL

The Unnamed Press
Los Angeles, CA

The Unnamed Press

1551 Colorado Blvd., Suite #201

Los Angeles, CA 90041

Published in North America by The Unnamed Press.

1 3 5 7 9 10 8 6 4 2

This book was originally published in 2014
in India by Random House India.

Copyright 2014 © Janice Pariat

ISBN: 978-1-939419-55-2

Library of Congress Control Number: 2015956690

This book is distributed by Publishers Group West

Designed by Scott Arany
Cover design by Jaya Nicely
Cover illustration by Patsy McArthur

For Luigi

———

"My songs, lords of the lyre,
which of the gods, what hero,
what mortal shall we celebrate?"
—PINDAR

SEAHORSE

1

AND SO I BEGIN WITH NICHOLAS' DISAPPEARANCE.

The moment I discovered he was missing. I remember like it was yesterday.

Although perhaps that isn't an accurate way to phrase it.

Yesterday may be further away than two years past, than seven, or ten. I can't recall my supper a week ago, but that morning remains palpable in my memory—like the touch of sudden heat or tremendous cold. It's a wine I've sipped, and sipped so long it colors everything else on my palate.

It was July, but early enough in the day for the air to still be mild, sunshine glimmering white around the edges, warning of the warmth to come. I'd arrived at the New Delhi railway station at dawn; even at that time clamorously crowded, with hustling coolies and families recumbent on the platforms. I hurried back to my room in the north of the city in a taxi, the roads clear and quiet. Through Old Darya Ganj, along the wide length of Raj Ghat, the pale fury of the Red Fort. Everything, I felt, was touched by unimaginable beauty. After only a quick shower to wash away the grime of a two-day train journey, I headed to the bungalow on Rajpur Road. I was in a hurry, I took the shortcut through the forest. When I reached, the security guard wasn't at the gate, and the wicker chairs and table on the lawn nowhere in sight. Around the fringes of the garden, flower beds glowed with early-blooming African daisies and hardy summer zinnias.

I remember, as I walked up the porch, dusty and littered with leaves, how it crept into my heart, a rush of something like love.

When I tried the door, it opened easily. The bungalow lay still and silent, everything in its place. The dining table set, as though for ghosts, with plates and cutlery, the drawing room tidy with cushions, neatly brushed carpets, an arrangement of dried flowers. I headed straight for the bedroom, expecting to find Nicholas sleeping, tangled in a sheet, dream-heavy. Above him, the patient creak of the fan, swirling. The smell of him in the air, sweet and salty, the tang of sweat.

He wasn't there.

The bed was made in neat, geometric precision. His things—an extra pair of glasses, a fountain pen, a comb—missing from the bedside table. I walked down the corridor to the study; in all my months at the bungalow I hadn't ever seen it so uncluttered, loose papers swept off the floor, the table relieved of tottering piles of books. I looked for a painting, the one that had stood on the table, of a woman holding a mirror, and it was gone.

Only when I reached the veranda did something splinter, and it rushed in, the fear that had been waiting in the wings. In the corner, the aquarium, that bright and complete universe, was empty.

———

Nicholas disappeared in the summer of 1999, when I was twenty, and in my second year at university. Although perhaps I need to rephrase that as well. He didn't disappear.

He left.

Who's to say they're not the same?

At first, I searched wildly for a note, some sort of written explanation—taped to mirrors, or doors, or walls. Weighted down by books or bric-a-brac so it wouldn't be blown away.

Behind me, a shelf bearing a small seashell and stone collection, to my right, a spacious divan covered in a densely embroidered bedspread. Next to it, a tall areca palm, its leaves sharp as knives, quietly wilting. The day's heat seeped ferociously through the jaali screen, the light turned bleached and blinding. I didn't switch on the fan, or retire inside for shelter and shade.

Later, around mid-day, when the silence grew deep and thick around me, I left.

This time, I took the long way round, back to my room in a student residence hall in Delhi University, along the main road, willing the noise and traffic to somehow jolt me back to life. That this, as clichéd as it may sound, had all been a dream.

At first, it felt similar to the time I heard about Lenny. Many months ago, my sister's voice faint and grasping on the phone. *I'm sorry... there were some complications...*

Yet this was not death.

For death leaves behind modest belongings, the accumulated possessions of people's lives, their books and jewelry, a hairbrush, an umbrella. Lenny had been my friend, I had his letters, his VHS tapes, his cassettes, and folded away in the recesses of my cupboard back home, his faded leather jacket.

With Nicholas it was as though he had never existed.

No life can be traceless, and leave behind scarcely any imprints. Yet his hadn't. A great rushing tide had swallowed the shore and wiped it clean.

That day passed as all others do. In my room, I worked through my unpacking slowly—socks in the drawer, books on the shelf, slippers under the bed—filled not with anger or despair, but faint, lingering anticipation. Something else had to happen, this couldn't be all. This wasn't the end. I'd receive a letter. Nicholas would return. Someone would come knocking on my door, saying there was a phone call.

A message. An explanation.

That night I went to bed in hope.

And even now, I sometimes awaken with it wrapped around my heart.

We are shaped by absence. The places that escape our travels, the things we choose not to do, the people we've lost. They are spaces in the trellis on which we trail from season to season.

———

Perhaps this is why people write.

And this careful arrangement of lines is a way of saying "Let it always be there."

Everything held still and held together—radiant, everlasting.

A way of defying memory, shifting slide-slippery thing, that refills as much as it empties. When I lay down these words, this is what I'll remember.

I first saw Nicholas in a room that reminded me of an aquarium.

The lights dimmed, a projector flickering like an old movie reel. Sunshine seeping through the curtains into green semi-darkness. The air cold and muted; somewhere the hum of an air conditioner serving as the underlying rhythm of breath and life.

A talk was underway.

"What are the possible consequences?" asked the speaker. "If Alexander had succeeded? If he had swept unchallenged across the Indian subcontinent in the fourth century BC? Huge social and political ramifications, to be sure. But I'd say the most spectacular influence would lie elsewhere..."

I was struck by the shape of him. The shapes of him. A figure carved in light, growing as he walked nearer, diminishing when he edged away.

He smiled. "In art."

I attended the talk by slim coincidence.

It was one of those drifting days on campus, the afternoon mirroring the sky—vast and empty. I'd left my roommate Kalsang, standing by the window, smoking a joint. Like the trees outside, he too was all twigs and arms and branches. A long-limbed Tibetan with a slow languorous voice that sounded like lazy Sundays. Around college, he was called "Rock", an abbreviation of Rock of Gibraltar, a title he'd earned after repeatedly attempting, and failing, his undergraduate exams in

Chemistry. It made him oddly out of sync with the world, and considerably older than me.

"Are you sure you don't want?" He held out an elegantly slender spliff.

I was certain. I had a lecture to attend. On Samuel Beckett and symbolism.

That, he demurred, offered even greater pretext to join him.

For reasons I cannot remember—perhaps the class was canceled?—I found myself aimlessly wandering the college building. Through red-brick corridors divided by slabs of sunlight and shadow, passing rooms desolate as churches, their wooden benches and tables drawn and empty. To my left, through the arches, unfurled a length of grassy lawn, speckled, in winter, with sitting, sloping figures. Occasionally, squirrels scurried across to the stone-path edges, or mynas alighted for a quick walk-about, but now it lay empty, shimmering cleanly in the sunlight. I curved against the length of a pillar. If I leaned out and glanced up, I'd see a cubical tower rising into the sky, bearing, at the top, a cross and a star. On both sides, the wings of the building spread long and low, like a bird in flight. Beyond the hedged borders of the college campus, past the road trilling with rickshaw bells, stood the Ridge Forest, growing on gentle hills running all the way to Rajasthan. The lifeline of Delhi, its rainy, gasping lungs, its last remaining secret.

"In a forest," Lenny once told me, "all time is trapped."

In retrospect, I should have taken up Kalsang's offer. He was usually in possession of stellar weed, not the kind that drove people crazy. I'd heard the stories, of course, about various drug-fueled antics in the residence halls. Oral folklore shared year after year among students, old and new, amounting to a grand collegiate archive, embellished by time and generous imaginations. The one about a boy who uttered his name, persistently, for three days—*Karma Karma Karma*—for if he stopped, he believed, he'd cease to exist. Or how a lethal blend of the green stuff, cheap glue and cheaper alcohol, convinced a certain economist he could fly. He flung himself off a balcony and landed in a flowerbed, emerging more mud-slain than maimed. Another ate three dozen omelettes at a nearby roadside dhaba. (The owner, Mohanji, said the rascal still owed him money.) More recently, a particularly potent brand of Manali cream had persuaded a historian on the floor above mine that he could see ghosts. "They hang around at the foot of our beds," he said, "watching us as we sleep."

Against my arm, the stone pillar burned gently. As respite from the weather, I usually slipped into the library, a cool basement level space where I'd find a corner, read, or more often, nap. That afternoon, when I checked, the library was "Closed for Maintenance"—although there didn't seem to be any work being done inside. I walked away, mildly disappointed, but further down the corridor, the door to the ambitiously named Conference Hall was slightly ajar, acquiescing a stream of startlingly cold air.

The speaker's voice was low yet clear—a strange, deep birdsong—carrying the clipped crispness of a British accent.

"For centuries, the Buddha was represented through aniconic symbols... his footprints, a Bodhi tree, a riderless horse, the dharma wheel, an empty throne... how could the infinite, the boundless, be apprehended? Early Buddhist art was shaped by non-presence. Devotees were face to face with a "no-thing". Certain scholarship states it wasn't until the Greek presence in South Asia that anthropomorphic representations of the Buddha emerged..."

The speaker gestured at a map projected on the wall, a rectangular window glowing white and unearthly.

"In essence, the art created in the Gandhara region during the Hellenistic period derived its content from Indian mysticism while the form was that of Greek realism. It could have been purely for economic reasons, of course. Gandhara was ruled by the Kushan kings and it was a wealthy region, thanks to its position on the Silk Road... So with the luxury goods traveled the monks and missionaries, and with them the Buddha, in human form, perhaps because an image aids in teaching across language barriers. Yet is that all? What is this desire to human-ize our gods? To make them in our own image..."

In the shimmering darkness, I watched him closely.

He had a face I wanted to reach out and touch.

Broad, yet not indelicate, with long, chiseled cheeks shaded by stub-ble. A nose that sloped straight and high between deeply-set eyes. I leaned forward, hoping to decipher their color—but with his glasses, and from that distance, it was impossible to tell. Only his hair gleamed dense and dark, framing his forehead, his temples, his ears, in waves.

He was never still.

A ripple here, a touch there, a step forward, a few back.

With anyone else this might be a mark of anxiety, of nervous, undis-peled energy, but his movements were—I can think of no better word—silent. Seamless. Precisely elegant, a tall, sinewy man on a wire, whose gestures swept gracefully through the air.

I had never seen anyone like him.

Or dressed like him.

In a mandarin collar shirt of lightest grey, rolled up at the sleeves, and tailored hazel trousers, belted smartly in black leather. I was cer-tain he'd never set foot outside an air-conditioned room; otherwise impossible to appear, in Delhi, in summer, that immaculate.

The map on the wall flickered, replaced by the image of a stone fig-ure, fractured and antique. "One of many works that French historian Alfred Foucher acquired on his expeditions to Shahbazgarhi between 1895 and 1897..."

The figure was decked in the accoutrements of religious ritual—robes, fluid as real cloth, twisted around a slender waist, falling to slip-pered feet. Carved ornaments crossed its bare torso, and its turbaned head was framed by a full-moon halo.

"We tend to decipher figurative sculpture instinctively... employing a tool we use everyday... subconsciously perhaps, but, in fact, almost all the time in our waking lives."

The speaker stepped closer to his audience. "Can anyone tell me what it's called? The study of body language..."

"Kinesthetics." It was Adheer, a final-year history student. With a pale, artistic face, and, even though he was no more than twenty, peppery grey hair.

"That's right... you may have heard this before, that figurative sculpture aspires to one thing—to arrest the body and capture life. True, but not always."

He turned, appraising the image.

"Scientifically, we may determine Foucher's bodhisattava is over a thousand years old... carved in light grey-blue schist, from an area now in northern Pakistan... But how would you *read* him?"

A few observations were proffered—the figure was serene, princely, in prayer, the right hand raised in blessing.

"All accurate, no doubt, but at the heart of it, the key to truly unlocking an image is iconography... it comes from the Greek *eikón*, "image" and *grafein*, "to write". If literature depends on the slower rhythm of the word, iconography relies on the swifter rhythm of the eye. The artist takes an elaborate temporal succession of events, and condenses them into an image... it holds everything."

Each element, from the flaming halo down to the carved base, served as a clue.

"The bodhisattva's hand, for instance, is fixed in *abhaya mudra*, a gesture of fearlessness. And this," he pointed to the fingers, which—I hadn't noticed—were webbed, "is not an amphibian motif, but an indication, some say, of supernatural power. If you look carefully at his turban, you'll see it contains a small figurine... of Garuda, a mythical bird-like creature, carrying a naga."

"Why is that?" asked Adheer.

The speaker shrugged. "The motif is most likely related to a Greek myth... the abduction of Ganymede by Zeus in the form of an eagle. It appears widely in ancient south Asian art, but in this context its significance remains a mystery."

I remember, at the end of the talk, I waited while the hall emptied, flooded with stark-white tube light. The speaker glanced around the room and I wondered whether he saw me—slouching in the corner in my faded jeans and t-shirt. He stashed away his papers in an old-fashioned briefcase, and joined a professor waiting by the door. They headed out. I caught snatches of conversation. Laughter. Someone flicked the lights off and once again the room sank back into watery darkness.

Later, I saw a poster pinned on the college notice board announcing—like a prophet of the past—the event I'd accidentally attended. Organized by the Department of History. A talk by art historian Doctor Nicholas Petrou.

———

While Nicholas was an art historian, Lenny was the artist.

Or so I like to believe, even if it probably isn't a label he'd have claimed for himself. In our hometown, as in hundreds of small towns in India in the late 1980s, there was little room for the imaginative and abstract. The elusive and intangible. Our options indelectably confined to medicine, engineering, or government service—safe, sturdy careers, long, narrow ladders leading to a future ostensibly improved. A quest always for security, hardly for meaning—or what the Greeks called eudaimonia, a human flourishing—and, especially within the puritanical Christian circles our families moved in, rarely for enjoyment. Lenny wasn't devoted to an artistic profession, but I remember how effortlessly creativity alighted on him, the startling deftness of his hands. He'd sketch portraits of strangers while sitting at roadside teashops, on scraps of paper and napkins. A quick, light touch, each one taking him less than a minute. Or fold paper into birds, which he'd place along his window sill, longing for the sky. Strum the guitar, casual and easy, singing low and tuneful.

A month ago, I was at the National Portrait Gallery in London, for a retrospective on Lucian Freud. The man who only painted portraits. Room after room of faces, distraught, humiliated, indifferent, tenderly in love. A lifetime spent in attempting to capture all of humanity—its myths and frailties—with unrelenting intensity. I followed the eyes, and the eyes followed me. Paintings are always once removed, but not on this occasion. Each canvas raw and visceral. Turned to skin, loose, marked and scarred.

The people he painted, he took their soul.

There's a sketch Lenny sent me before he died that looks as though it could have been drawn by Lucian Freud. That's why I like to believe he's an artist, and that if he'd lived longer, perhaps he'd have come to realize it too.

Instead, he was enrolled, through his parents' persistent coercion, in a science degree—zoology? biology?—in a college in our hometown. Except, I never saw him attend class, or complete assignments, or venture near an academic building of any sort. He did what all parents found impossibly infuriating—he drifted.

I knew Lenny all my life. We grew up in the same neighborhood, although he was older and we became friends much later, when I was fourteen. Unexpectedly, at the side of a basketball court. One of those dilapidated public sports grounds where youngsters congregated in the evening for lack of anything else to do. Mostly, I hovered around the edges, invisible, pretending to follow the match, watching the big boys play, the ones who jumped like they had wings on their feet.

One day, Lenny showed up and declared it the silliest game he'd ever seen.

"Is this what you do?" he asked. "Sit around watching these guys fight over an orange ball?"

"Sometimes."

"Do you play?"

I thought it pointless to lie. "No."

He lit a cigarette, and threw his head back. His face pieced together by an irreverent sculptor—an uneven nose, slanting eyes, a rough chin, and sharp plane cheeks. He smelled of smoke and pine forests, of something wild and unexplored.

He said nothing until he'd finished the cigarette, until he threw it to the ground and it flickered and died, burning itself out.

"Come."

And I followed.

Before Lenny, I was unattuned to much else apart from my parents' precise clockwork regime. Weekdays stretched taut between school and homework, punctuated by weekend visits to my grandparents, and church service on Sunday. When I was with him, though, time dissolved into insignificance. It lost its grasp, and loosened, unfurling endlessly as the sea. He'd rent VHS tapes from a movie parlor in town, and watch one after another—it didn't occur to him to stop if it was late, or dawn. Or he'd walk, for hours, winding his way to unfamiliar neighborhoods on the other side of town. Often, he'd ride his old motorbike out into the countryside, beyond the furthest suburban sprinkle. He ate when he was hungry, slept whenever he happened to be tired, awoke at odd hours between early afternoon and evening. He was out of time. Removed from it like a modern-day Tithonus, existing at the quiet limit of the world.

I'd hurry over to Lenny's room after school, or on weekend afternoons. It was a basement level space, down a narrow flight of steps accessible only from the outside of the house. Dimly-lit, oddly shaped, with jutting walls and sudden corners, and quite bare apart from a single bed, a writing table, and cupboard. In the corner stood a wooden shelf sinking under the weight of books, some so old they'd turned brittle, riddled by silverfish. They once belonged to a tenant upstairs, an elderly Bengali gentleman who died on a cold winter's night, leaving Lenny's family in the awkward position of having to pack up his belongings and giving them away to charity—for he had no family, here or elsewhere, that they knew of. Lenny persuaded his parents to let him keep the library—an eclectic collection, ranging from the obscure (*The Collected Letters of Henry J Wintercastle*) to the mildly collectable (an 1895 edition of *A Tale of Two Cities*). I remember how they lay thick and heavy in my hands, slightly musty, the smell that makes me think of Lenny when I walk into a secondhand bookshop.

In the afternoons, we'd go for walks in the pine forest behind his house, and smoke cheap cigarettes, seated on mossy rocks or, if it was a dry month, lying on the ground.

In between the roots of trees, the spines of the earth. Everything suddenly inverted, an upturned silence, grass behind my neck, a tilted view of patchy sky through crazy tangle of twigs and needle-leaves. We'd talk, or rather he'd talk and I'd listen. His voice murmuring like a stream. A book he'd read. This movie he'd seen, about a man wrongly sent to prison. A line he liked. *You know what the Mexicans say about the Pacific? They say it has no memory.* A poem by Auden. His favorite. *All we are not stares back at what we are.* Or we'd be quiet. And if we were quiet and unmoving long enough, the forest would flourish over us. They would return, like slivers of sky, a pair of long-tailed blue jays. Elsewhere, a cluster of playful sparrows ventured closer. The clouds seemed to stop and linger. I'd feel heavier and lighter, quieted by the fall of pine needles, feeling their smooth silkiness under my hands. The prickle of tiny black ants clambering over my fingers. For them, I was tree root and stone. Here and there, the sudden fickle flit of yellow butterflies. We were woven, all at once, into the fabric of a spring afternoon.

On other days, colder and shorter, Lenny would take me to tea shops, scattered around town, near bustling markets, on busy main roads. We'd dip slabs of rice cake into small chipped cups of bitter tea, and watch the crowd swell and thin around us. Folk who dressed rough and spoke rough, butchers and builders who worked with their hands. (Of whom my parents would have disapproved, saying they were not "our type.") Sometimes, we headed away from the clamor of the centre, past the car parks and newsstands, the bakeries and pharmacies, and slipped into a narrow lane flanked by a sludgy canal and the bricked back of a building. Its smoothness interrupted by a chink, an opening that led into a triangular one-room tea shop manned by a lady with an aged face and young eyes. She served us heaped plates of food, brimful cups of tea and called Lenny "my butterfly." I couldn't quite follow their banter—their language wrapped in lively innuendo.

"How many plums have you eaten recently?" she once asked Lenny.

I reminded them it wasn't yet the season.

But it pleased me to be with them, to feel part of something adult and amorous.

More often, deterred by relentless rain, we'd stay indoors, in Lenny's room. Reading, or playing our own version of darts on an enormous map of the world on the wall—a patchwork of colors amid posters of longhaired musicians in white vests and tight leather pants. Lenny would aim for South America—because he said he loved that vision of wildness—and land mostly in the Pacific or Atlantic. I'd aim for England—he'd call me boring—and end up in North Africa, or the deep blue Mediterranean.

We'd fling the darts from across the room, lazily lying on his bed, and then I'd scurry over to gather them.

"I have to get out of here, Nem," he'd tell me, as he aimed for Brazil.

"You will," I'd say loyally, because I truly believed he could achieve anything.

For the longest time, I placed it there—the reason for Lenny's rest-lessness. His plummeting moods and sudden disappearances. Those afternoons when he wouldn't permit me to accompany him out. "But where are you going?" I'd ask and he wouldn't reply, sending me home instead. "Go finish your homework." Those evenings when he didn't return to his room at all. Later, the unexplained mud on his motorcycle wheels, his shoes, the frayed edges of his jeans.

I placed it there.

The smallness of our small town, its bland familiarity and quiet, ter-rifying dullness.

Yet how are we to truly map others? To fully navigate the rooms they carve in their hearts. The whispers they alone understand. What is love to their ear? The crevice it fits into is different for each of us. We are separate worlds illuminated by strange suns, casting unrecognizable shadows.

In the end, we follow spirits only our eyes can spy.

I have to get out of here, Nem.

Eventually, I suppose, that's what Lenny did. In a way that left him with no hope of return.

A few weeks after I found out about Lenny, Nicholas and I went to a bar in Model Town, a neighborhood near the university, comprising circles of apartment blocks built around a lake. We took an autorick-shaw, weaving through the traffic, between lumbering DTC buses, honking cars and pedestrians who'd spilled onto the road from side-walks choked with garbage and abandoned construction material. In certain places, Delhi swayed in a perpetual state of chaos, and that night I was glad for the tumult. The bar was located in the unsavoury side of Model Town, just off the imaginatively named 2nd Main Road. Clusters of men loitered around, hovering close to a paan and cigarette stall. How they stared at us—this strange duo, a tall white foreigner and his small-built companion who looked as much an outsider.

Inside, a low smoke-cloud hung over the room. The clientele, middle-aged and solely male, dotted the tables, seated with their drinks and plates of glistening murg tikka masala and seekh kebabs. I don't remember what we were drinking, but it was different from the usual stuff we swilled in college—foul Haywards 10,000 for a cheap, quick high or a blindingly acidic whisky called Binnie Scot. It wasn't long before I lost count of the refills. The bar transformed into a warm cocoon. A small planet spiraling into free fall, plummeting through space. The lights were brighter and dimmer all at once, the air pulsing with a musical beat that arose from all corners.

I know who killed Lenny.

I thought I heard myself say those words; I wasn't certain.

Nicholas placed his hand on my arm. He wasn't killed, he said.

He was.

"Your sister explained... there were complications..."

No, he was killed.

In my head, I was adamant.

"Why do you say so, Nehemiah?"

I stayed silent.

He asked me again.

Much as I wanted to confide in him, at the time I couldn't bring myself to explain.

———

If art is preservation, it is also confession.

Few lectures stay with me from my university days—a class on DH Lawrence's language of synesthesia, Woolf's complex layering of time, Ismat Chughtai's seething denouncement of the world—and those that do were mostly delivered by Doctor Mahesar. A professor of petite yet rotund build and razor-sharp articulation. His tutorial room was atop the college building, on the open, flat roof, overlooking the lawns and trees, where in the evening, squawking parrots came to roost. In the summer, it was unbearable, a compact, vicious furnace, with only the rare, welcome visitation of a breeze.

One morning, we discussed "The Love Song of J. Alfred Prufrock."

We watched beads of sweat form on Doctor Mahesar's forehead, and stream gently down the contours of his face. Before him, bent over our *Annotated T. S. Eliot*, we similarly perspired—the smell of sweat, pungent as a sliced onion, hung in the air. Last year, under identical sweltering conditions, Doctor Mahesar had thrown his text on the table. "I give up." He said he couldn't teach "Shall I compare thee to a summer's day" without crumbling under the weight of irony.

Naturally, he was everyone's favorite professor.

That day, everyone in the room hoped for a similar tirade, seeing there was mention of fog and cool winter evenings, but no such shenanigans took place.

"How does the poem begin?" he asked, holding the text up to us like a mirror.

There was a mumble of voices—*Let us go then, you and I... when the evening is spread out against the sky...*

"That is incorrect."

Small circles of confusion spun around the room. Finally, a girl in the front row spoke up, "It begins with an epigraph."

"Thank you, Ameya. Yes, it begins with an epigraph."

"You mean the part we can't understand," said someone from the back.

"Yes, Noel. The part in Italian, which, *if* you've heard of it, is a Neo-Latin Romance language spoken mainly in Europe."

The class sniggered.

"*S'io credesse che mia risposta fosse, a persona che mai tornasse al mondo...* Now, I'm sure there's someone here who can recite it for us word for word in translation."

There was deep and resolute silence.

The professor spoke the lines softly.

"If I but thought that my response were made to one perhaps returning to the world, this tongue of flame would cease to flicker... But since, up from these depths, no one has yet returned alive, if what I hear is true, I answer without fear of being shamed. So you see, the poem begins with the promise of a secret between the soul of the dead... and you."

He placed the book on the table and mopped his forehead with a large white handkerchief.

"Why do you think this is poised as a confession?" The class stared back, blank as the blackboard behind him. "Because that's the psychology of secrets," he explained. "People have a primitive or compelling need to divulge their emotional experiences to others. Confessions can be written as letters, notes, diaries, or in this case, an entire poem..."

For a long time I couldn't tell Nicholas about who'd killed Lenny.

I felt it was the promise of a secret between the soul of the dead and me.

It may have been a coincidence, as these things usually are, but after the talk in the conference hall, I frequently noticed Nicholas around campus. It wasn't all too difficult to spot him, since he was one of few Caucasians around, although admittedly Delhi University had seen its fair share of white folk, most of whom eccentric. A French sociologist who cycled around wearing a Vietnamese nón lá (some say that's how he'd traveled to India from Paris), an Anglo-Indian professor of literature who couldn't ever remember who'd written what, "Shelley's Ode to a Nightingale", and a visiting biologist from Germany who brewed his coffee in intricate laboratory apparatus. Nicholas, though, was more object of fervent curiosity.

Often, he'd visit the senior member's common room, mingling with the other professors, obtrusive for his youth—the rest were mostly grey-haired gentlemen and a few prim salwar or sari-clad ladies—and attire. Pale shirts of impossibly fine cotton, pressed and pristine, sharp-cut trousers, stylish loafers. Simple yet hard to imitate; everything I could afford in the market looked—there's no other way to say this—cheap. Sometimes, he'd lounge in the college café, drinking endless cups of tea, writing in a black notebook, picking at a serving of mince cutlets and buttered toast. Or he'd read, on the fringes of the lawn, under the generous canopy of peepal trees.

I'd watch him, follow his movements, keep a lookout for when he'd visit the campus.

As, I suspect, did many of the other students.

It wasn't only because he was a white stranger.

There was something thrillingly mysterious about him.

Or so everyone liked to believe.

From here and there, I caught snatches of rumor.

That he was a new lecturer who'd recently joined the faculty, that he was a visiting scholar from Cambridge. Someone else said he was here on fieldwork, conducting research at the National Museum.

Among the students, the girls in particular, he was of special interest; they sought him out and jostled for his attention. Some claimed to have befriended "Nick", saying he'd paid keen attention to their theories on the earliest figurative representations of the Buddha.

Occasionally, in the corridors and lawns, I saw him with Adheer.

And strange as it may sound, I was stung by jealousy. That Adheer was marked out from the rest. That it wasn't me. Although then it seemed impossible, unthinkable even, that I could be similarly acquainted with the art historian.

I was in most ways unremarkable.

I'd always felt so. Once, I read about Italo Svevo, a nineteenth-century Italian writer whose characters are often referred to as *uomini senza qualità*... men without qualities... people whose qualities are ambiguous, dilute... perhaps in some ways even inept with the world.

And I thought that could be me.

When I looked in the mirror, I always wished I occupied more space, that my reflection was less inconsequential. In college I wasn't painfully thin, or scrawny—I played football often—just... slight. And I'd examine my face, in the time it took for me to splash it at the sink, knowing they were there to stay—the eyes, a shade slanted, that diminutive nose, a full stop rather than an exclamation mark. My mouth. Like squashed fruit.

Above all this, I had no reason to approach the art historian. Even if I did, I was certain I'd be unable to muster up the courage. And why shouldn't it be Adheer? Marked out from the rest. From a royal family in Indore, I'd heard. With his elegantly tailored kurtas, long and light, flowing like a breeze around him. Adheer was the most sophisticated of us all (though, at the time, we preferred "pretentious"). While we listened to Led Zeppelin and The Rolling Stones, rich and tragic ragas drifted out of his room. While we thumbed through Salinger and Camus—like every generation before us we held *Catcher in the Rye* and *The Outsider* intimately and preciously our own—he claimed to have read all of Krishnamurti, all of Kabir.

"Perhaps," I'd offer, "they didn't get along."

I'd be met by incredulity. And a look. *You're an idiot.*

One thing I was certain of, though, was that Adheer wasn't unremarkable.

A month into term, I tried to let my interest slip. Although it was difficult to ignore the whispers and hushed discussions swarming around Nicholas, alighting on him like bees. Once, outside the college café, where students usually gathered to smoke, I caught his name in conversation. Two girls, chatting, holding glasses of nimbu paani. I'd seen the one with short hair and a nose ring in last term's college production of A Midsummer Night's Dream. She'd played Titania, the fairy queen, and scandalized the senior members, and thrilled the rest, with her Biblical choice of costume—little more than flowers and leaves. Her companion, a willowy girl with sleek, straight hair and a pale almond-shaped face, came from my part of the country. A "chinky," as they called us here in the north. She was studying English in the year below mine, and even though I hadn't ever spoken to her, I knew her name was Larisa.

I bought a samosa from the makeshift snack stall nearby, one that also dispensed lemon juice, and didn't stray far, keeping them within eavesdropping distance.

"He's British, but of Greek ancestry," said Titania. "That's what he told Priya, apparently."

I hadn't known, but it explained the olive skin, the dark hair.

"Talk about a Greek god," giggled her friend.

"You think? He's tall and all that... but not really my type..."

"Yes, because you prefer skinny struggling artists."

They both laughed.

I bit into the samosa—the shell came away in my hands, loosening the soft potato and peas filling. It steamed gently on the paper plate, while the tamarind sauce pooled darkly around the edges.

"You should invite him to a house party..." said Titania. "I'm sure someone's planning one soon."

Her friend lifted a dainty eyebrow. "Why not? I don't think he teaches here. Maybe we can get him drunk... although, I'm not sure he'd come."

"We could ask Adheer to invite him."

"Adheer?"

"They spend a lot of time together... don't you think?"

"What are you saying?" laughed her friend.

"Don't be an idiot, Lari, you know what I mean."

"What do you mean?" She sounded genuinely confused.

"I think they're... you know..." She must have mouthed the word for I couldn't hear her. What I did catch was Lari's cry of repulsion.

"That's disgusting... you really think so? It's so *gross*."

Titania sipped her drink, and stayed silent.

What I observed, over the weeks, was that Nicholas didn't pay special attention to anyone in particular. He was indiscriminately charming. When in the mood. Or resolutely cool. He remembered people's names, or at least had a way of requesting them to remind him so they weren't slighted. He appeared attentive, if not deeply interested. Mostly, I think, he enjoyed the attention. And tired of it just as easily.

People have fickle memories though. And often they mainly remember the agreeable, latching on to the winsome details. A wave across the lawn. At the café, a round of tea at his insistence and expense. A recommended book. His smile. Rare, precious gesture—that in an instant swept you into his closest, most secret circle.

Yet the lines were drawn long before we imagined, who would be allowed in, how much, how far, always keeping, inevitably, to himself. Intact. In his own hands, he was porcelain.

I see that now.

If he spent more time with Adheer, it was because Adheer sought him out more persistently, and successfully, than all the others. Hurrying after him in the corridors, waiting, nonchalantly, by the gates, reading on the lawns. Accompanying him to university talks and seminars. And while Nicholas escaped unscathed, for it didn't strike anyone to mock him, people called Adheer a "bender" behind his back. Others employed their words more delicately: "Look at him," they whispered, "that poo pusher."

———

In college everything was sexualized.

And looking back now, I realize, that was one thread that stitched us into some kind of collective. The mystery of sex, and (mostly) its lack.

Living in residence halls fueled by male camaraderie, regarding the close co-existence of girls, their mighty distance. In there, we were swamped by complex hierarchies and communal fissures, trapped in an intricate system of jurisdiction—where the Jats were feared, the Punjus scorned, the northeasterners ignored, the Gujjus mocked, the Tam Brams held in mild amusement, the Bongs quietly tolerated, the Mallus generally liked by all and sundry. Then came the broader divisions of sports quota folk and special reservations, the slackers and endless Civil Service sloggers, the cool and uncool, the artsies and sciencees.

All entwined in the general joyful wastefulness of youth. And something else.

We'd move from room to room, swapping cigarettes, alcohol and lies. Talking, skirting the issue, the act of, plucking euphemisms from insecurity—do it, bang, beat, bone, bugger, screw, bonk, go all the way, home run, old in-out, pound, bed, shag, slay, mount, boff, bugger, cut, dance, dip, doink, scuff, fire, fubb, fuck, fug, do the nasty, get any, get it on, get lucky, give it up, hit it raw, hit skins, have a go, grease, hose, knock, make the beast with two backs, woopie, nail, ram, rock and roll, score, shine it, slap and tickle, smack, smash, lay, hump, plow, quickie, romp, ride, roger, *you know what.*

It was endless, and language the sheet with which we all hid our nakedness, and longing.

⸻

On most weekends, the residence halls emptied, as students headed out to South Delhi or Connaught Place—the ones who could afford to drink at newly opened bars or watch movies at shiny multiplex cinemas. I'd been to South Delhi a few times, traveling there on a long bus ride from the Inter State Bus Terminal at Kashmiri Gate, filled with vehicles spewing smoke, roaring like metallic monsters. Past the green expanse of Raj Ghat alongside Mahatma Gandhi Road, the perpetually chaotic ITO, and the gated distance of Pragati Maidan. Slowing down once the bus cut into the city, passing through Lajpat Nagar with its labyrinthine market, the calmer environs of Siri Fort, Delhi's second city, bourgeoisly concealing its brutal origins—founded by Ala-ud-din Khilji on the severed heads of eight thousand Mongol soldiers. From there, it wasn't far to our destination, to Saket Complex, lined with air-conditioned shops, a colorful new McDonalds and TGIF, and, its crowning glory, a royal blue-gold PVR cinema.

Others made their way to neighborhoods clustered around the college campus, to flats and apartments rented by their outstation friends, for parties fueled by cheap booze and marijuana. There were some, who stayed in, from not having been invited, or propeled by the fear of an unfinished assignment.

A Sunday night spent mustering inspiration to discuss *Waiting For Godot* as an existentialist text. *The essence of existentialism focuses on the concept of the individual's freedom of choice, as opposed to the belief that humans are controlled by a pre-existing omnipotent being, such as God. Estragon and Vladimir have made the choice of waiting, without instruction or guidance...*

After a few insipid attempts, I'd usually sneak down to the common room in the residence hall. In the dark, the television screen burned tense and bright. Muted souls sat on the ground; one close enough to change channels expertly with an outstretched leg. The set had recently been hooked to Star TV and moved effortlessly from one channel to the next. Music followed by sport followed by the news, by movies and back again, in a dizzying circle. A ring of sacred, ancient rocks, surrounded by solstice worshippers. Often, I'd sit at the back while the others argued over what to watch—highlights of a tennis match between Pete Sampras and Andre Agassi, last year's Bollywood blockbuster *Hum Aapke Hain Kaun*, or endless MTV, where Nirvana and Pearl Jam displayed incredible angst and apathy.

Invariably, the dissent ceased at eleven. When the adult films aired.

Movies for which no one cared about the plot. A psychiatrist who fell in love with his troubled patient. A professor with his student. A young boy with his older neighbor.

Hisses and whistles broke out each time the girl's dress dropped, or the lead ran his hand up her thigh. The images unfolded in a montage of flesh and desire. Nobody bothered to follow dialogue, waiting mostly for the scenes in the pool, the shower. In a room that looked like a picture from a magazine, filled with plush leather sofas and pristine glass tables (did people really live like that?), where they (always a man and woman) fell in a heap on a spongy grey carpet. And then moved seamlessly to a wooden bed with rumpled blue sheets. Her bare breasts shiny and heaving under his hand. With a twist he'd grind into her from the back, while she clung loosely to the head board. Another time, in a Jacuzzi, lathered and wet, the water soapy in strategic places. She'd climb on top and arch against him. Scene change. And they'd be in a room filled with light streaming in from tall windows. On a table, he'd cradle her back and lean in towards her. Then the image splintered—caught in a kaleidoscopic reflection of bodies writhing in pleasure. When the credits rolled, few would leave. We waited, breathless, to watch the next offering.

In college, everything was sexualized, yet it was impossible to talk about sex.

On rare occasion, though, they took place, those conversations that cut cleanly through the euphemisms. When I returned to Delhi in mid-July for my second year at university, I found I'd been shifted into a room with someone new. A spindly long-limbed Tibetan. Kalsang, I was relieved to find, was minimally intrusive. He didn't talk all that much, he didn't pry, or ask me questions about my life in my hometown, or why I wrote letters to Lenny. We shared joints and lives of mutual exclusivity.

Yet sometimes, late at night, when it was marginally cooler, we'd keep the window open, our room filling with the fragrance of something sweet, a distant flowering saptaparni. The pathways outside cobbled and vacant, bathed in yellow lamplight. We had conversations that, at that hour, people usually only held with themselves. Entirely plausible, of course, that this was intimacy occasioned by weed or alcohol, but I like to think it a special exclusion.

"I lost my virginity to my cousin," Kalsang once told me. "I was fourteen, she was seventeen. We were visiting them in Kathmandu... I was sleeping on a mattress in the sitting room and she came downstairs... I was so scared someone would walk in. You know, my parents were sleeping in the next room... if they'd caught me..."

"What would've happened?"

"I don't know... they would've killed me."

"Do you still see her?"

A long, errant silence. "Sometimes."

On another night, even though I was terrified, I admitted, "I've never, you know..."

"What?"

"You know..."

I could see him, in the darkness, his outline upright on the bed.

"Never done anything?" he asked.

It didn't count, I suppose, the boy from my class in school, who I'd "accidentally" meet in the toilets or a corner of the empty library. The one in Math tuition, who sat beside me, his hand below the table, on my thigh, unconcerned by the mysteries of trigonometry. In my hometown, I'd hang out with Lenny, and he hardly talked about girls, or to girls. So I didn't tell him about my sister's friend, how she'd lean over while I was at my study table... *"Such a good boy, always reading"*... her neckline dropping low and open. How she'd casually brush against my arm, my shoulder, if we happened to cross paths in the kitchen, the corridor.

In college, I stayed away. Uneasy. Apprehensive. Unsure. There were too many invisible, unspoken rules to navigate. I thought of Adheer.

Poo pusher. What would Kalsang do? If I told him. Would he shift out of our room too?

"So... nothing?" he reiterated.

"No."

The silence lay rich and deep.

His voice broke through the darkness. "That's okay, man. They say the longer you wait, the better it feels."

This wasn't, couldn't be, true, not in this world or the next, but that's the reason I was fond of Kalsang. He was exceptionally cheerful.

He began inviting me to parties outside college, probably in a bid to alter my chaste circumstances. But in vain. These were mostly large gatherings—immense crowds of strangers, friends of friends of friends—and I shied away. I could see, though, that it was a liberation. Outstation students who lived in the city harnessing a new, unbridled freedom. It couldn't have always been this way, but the country was changing. Opening its arms—multiple, like pictures of all those Hindu goddesses hanging in auto rickshaws and shops—to the world, embracing the policies of tomorrow. The ones that had brought Coca Cola and Hallmark into our markets, MTV into our homes, and stamped Levi's across our asses. Allegedly, this was "freedom of choice". And it filtered to us, in our student room, with its wobbly wooden tables and bare lamps, rumpled sheets and uncushioned chairs, all coated in a layer of undisputed dust. We could head elsewhere, if we preferred, somewhere brighter, more glittery. Where everyone dressed like the people on TV, and danced to the latest music, and believed that somehow, because of all this, they were unbelievably lucky.

"Want to come?" Kalsang would ask.

"Alright, let's go."

The night awaited, brimming with possibility.

I never did find out whether anything happened between Nicholas and Adheer.

Despite the rumors.

In all our time together, I hesitated to ask.

(In all our time together, I hardly needed to think of Adheer.)

They made me think of Adheer.

I suppose it's an alliance that calls for some explanation.

One morning, in late September, I headed out the college campus into the Ridge Forest. Trying, fervently, to avoid thinking of a news item from a few weeks ago—a corpse had been found, hastily hidden in the undergrowth. For days, newspapers plied their choicest headlines: "Mystery Body"; "Mutilated beyond recognition"; "Advanced stages of putrefaction."

Apparently, this happened here with disconcerting frequency.

And if it wasn't the discovery of a corpse, the Ridge, as with most ancient places, seethed with other stories. Of unhappy spirits that lived in its trees. Of a strange creature, similar to a white horse with a very long neck, which could often be sighted at night. Of a ghostly woman and child weeping. It was well known too that amorous couples found shelter here behind the cover of shadow and leaves.

In all honesty, I might have preferred coming across a ghost.

My journey through the forest proved quiet, and disappointingly, uneventful.

Beneath my feet, the ground squelched, softened by months of monsoon rain, and the air carried the smell of damp, decaying things. Here and there, a high-rising gulmohar, now green and unblooming, and the sparse babul with yellow summer blossoms. Hidden amid the others, the petite ber, with drooping, glossy leaves, and, of which I was fondest, the golden amaltash, when it was radiant against a blue April sky. I hadn't ever spotted any yet, but the forest was inhabited by gentle chinkara and blue-coated nilgai. Once or twice, I thought I'd glimpsed a tiny leaf warbler, and the sudden scarlet of a rose finch. Over the years, this place had remained unaltered while the landscape around its fringes transformed rapidly—on one side the university buildings, on the other, the Civil Lines neighborhood, demarcated from imperial-era military zones, a remnant of the British Raj. In comparison to the south of the city, though, the north was relatively static.

The South, if you'll forgive the hyperbole, was our generation's brave new world.

Heaving with suddenly wealthy neighborhoods, its roads peeling under the speed of foreign cars. Everywhere the fresh scent of money, the incredible hum of movement.

It all seemed terrifically heady and exciting, but here, in the north, beyond the Dantian circles of Connaught Place, the tangle of crowded markets in the old walled city, the hulking sandstone loneliness of the Red Fort, life was still somewhat slow and untouched.

And that afternoon, as I tread on a slushy dirt track, listening to the sounds of a forest, I could have been miles away from a city of many millions.

"In a forest," Lenny once told me, "all time is trapped."

Admittedly, tramping through the Ridge wasn't a preferred pastime. I was on a journalistic mission. In my first year in college, I'd been accosted by Santanu, a lanky Bengali with the (still) faint beginnings of a mustache and wispy long hair.

"Would you like to write an article?" he asked.

"For?"

"The college newsletter." Of which Santanu was the often despairing, yet resilient, student editor.

"I'm not sure I'm the best person for this."

"You're in English Lit, aren't you?"

I nodded.

"Everyone in the Lit department can write. Or at least has some secret ambition to be the next Rushdie or something."

Accustomed to persuading reluctant contributors, Santanu wasn't one to give up easily—"I'll give you plenty of time"; "You'll see your name in print", and finally, "I'll buy you beer."

Okay, I said, suddenly convinced.

Since then, I often wrote for the newsletter—a piece on the oldest academic bookstore in Kamla Nagar, a commercial area near the University, interviews with visiting lecturers, a book review as though penned by Chaucer: *But thilke text held he nat worth an oistre.*

That day, I was trudging through the forest looking for a story.

Soon, I came to a clearing. And there stood a four-tiered tower, atop a stepped platform, built of fire-red sandstone, capped by a Celtic cross.

Santanu wanted me to write on the Mutiny Memorial.

Apart from solemn, elegiac monument to the dead, it also served, for years now, as a frequent nocturnal hangout for university students. For gatherings of the least expensive and un-glamorous kind. Usually, the birthday boy spent the money his parents sent him to buy "something nice" on a neat half dozen bottles of whisky. Now, though, the place was vacant, strewn with the remnants of revelry, cigarette butts, broken bottles and greasy bits of newspaper.

The tower glowed warm and fiery against the sky. Over a century ago, it had been built by the British to commemorate the soldiers who died in the Mutiny of 1857. (Or as Santanu explained, more appropriately "India's First War of Independence.") It rose above the trees in solid, symmetrical lines, tipped by elaborate Gothic adornments. On the walls, white plaques carried the indecipherable names of the dead. An arched doorway led to the upper tiers, although a thick, rusty chain was slung across the entrance and a signboard, in English and Hindi, warned against using the stairs. I peered inside; the rubble floor was choked with weeds and plastic bags. It was moving and absurd all at once—this promethean bid for remembrance. Its faithfully distilled recording of history. I looked around wondering if this was the only one in the forest. What other monuments were there, rising from the ground like giant tombstones?

In the stillness of the evening, I heard a distant echo of voices, the slap of footfall. It might have been students, gathering to drink or smoke weed. Perhaps a courting couple, looking for some privacy. Through the trees, I caught a glimpse of two figures. One in a long blue kurta. Peppery grey hair. The other in a pastel shirt. In his hand, an old-fashioned briefcase.

I was caught in inexplicable panic.

In that instant, I could have jumped into the shrubbery—but the noise might alert them. What would I say if I were seen? It was too late to flee down the path leading out of the forest to the main road.

Perhaps it was better to stay where I was.

Unless, it suddenly struck me, they'd come here to be on their own.

They were getting closer; I could hear laughter, the sharp crack of undergrowth.

On impulse, I jumped over the chain strung across the doorway and ducked inside, fumbling up the stairs that spiraled into darkness. Loose rubble scattered from under my feet, and a queer stench clung to the air, a mixture of urine and moldy dampness.

Their footsteps grew louder, hitting stone. I could hear the art historian's voice.

I imagined them gazing at the tower.

From here, his could be the only voice in the world.

"Architecturally, there's nothing quite like it in Delhi." Adheer was speaking. "It's built in a high Victorian Gothic style..."

Did he really need to explain this to an art historian?

"Why this particular place, though?"

I didn't know, but Adheer hazarded a guess. "It was the site of a British army camp, I think, during the rebellion... Of course, back then, this whole area was forest and marshland..."

They were circling the tower slowly. The art historian pieced together the few still-visible names into a curious mantra—*DelamainChester NicholsonRussellBrooks*. He pronounced them carefully, as though the chant would somehow keep their memory alive.

Adheer went on to explain how in 1972, the twenty-fifth year of India's independence, the monument was renamed Ajitgarh, Place of the Unvanquished, and the government had a plaque put up with corrections—"That the 'enemy' mentioned on the memorial were immortal martyrs for freedom..."

The art historian stopped by the doorway. Blocking the patch of light pooling on the floor. Would he hear me breathing? Or somehow sense I was there.

"Does this go all the way to the top?"

I was tempted to inch up further, but was afraid I'd dislodge some rubble, or worse, have a stair give way under my feet. For now, where I was, they couldn't see me.

"I don't think so... it's like at the Qutub Minar. They've closed the stairway for safety reasons."

In the silence that followed, I could hear the art historian deliberating. The stench around me grew stronger.

"See..." I imagined Adheer pointing at the signboard. "It says it's unsafe. Better not risk it..."

I was thankful for his caution. The art historian stepped aside.

The pool of light emerged whole, intact.

I shifted imperceptibly, in relief, and wished they'd walk back into the forest, leave me with my ruin.

"It doesn't smell very inviting." I could hear their laughter, then as though in obedience, their voices and footsteps faded.

At first, I couldn't move. My limbs caught in a grip, still tight and motionless. Above me rose a strange, secret rustling. Was it an owl? A squirrel? Perhaps I'd disturbed the creatures that inhabited the tower.

Under my feet, a silver-green masala-flavoured chips packet glistened, long empty. I wondered who else had strayed there, and when, and dropped it at that spot. And why?

I began descending. I should leave. It was getting late. I'd prefer to be out of the forest before dark. When I'd almost reached the bottom, Adheer and the art historian drifted back. They'd probably only moved to the edge of the platform. I stopped short, pressing myself against the curved stone wall.

Even though they hadn't been gone long, something had shifted, their voices oddly tense.

"I know what it is," the art historian was saying, his voice clear, ringing through the air. "I know why... that's why we're here... and it's alright."

I was uncertain what Adheer said, if he said anything at all.

"I don't see how it could happen..."

"Of course... I-I don't know what... I mean... I didn't mean..." It was the first time I'd heard Adheer stumble over his words.

"It's not like I don't understand."

"I know... I didn't mean..."

"It's alright." There was a brief, tight pause, before he continued. "Why don't you show me where the plaque is?"

"Yes... yes, it's here. This way..."

Again, their voices, and footfall, died away. This time they didn't return.

———

In our time together, I thought this was one of few details hidden from me about Nicholas. The strangeness of love is it tempts you to feel you haven't met a person at a particular moment in their life, a mere sliver of time, but that somehow you've embraced it all. Their laden pasts, their abundant present, and (you hope so much) their undiscovered future. I did try and enquire, occasionally, as elliptically as I could—

whether he'd been for many walks in the Ridge, if he'd heard some of the stories about the place, the ghosts, the strange creatures, the couples and parties at the monument.

He'd furrow his brow. "Yes... Myra and I explored it a few times too..."

Myra was his step-sister, who'd visited him in Delhi over Christmas that year. I wasn't keen to discuss her, bring her into our conversation; while she was around, I hardly stayed at the bungalow, and Nicholas and I were never alone.

Had anything odd ever happened? In the Ridge.

I had to leave it at that; I wouldn't like to try his patience.

I never confessed what I'd overheard, him and Adheer, and how.

Once, though, I asked if he knew about the pond.

"In the forest? Are you sure?"

I was certain.

When he asked me where, I couldn't explain its exact location.

I found it the afternoon I ducked into the tower.

By the time I emerged, it was early evening, and in the twilight, the forest had thickened, hiding its paths under leafy shadow. Suddenly, it wasn't a place to be alone. I tried to retrace my steps, but must've taken a wrong turn. The track disappeared and the ground hollowed into a pond. The water green and solid, clogged with lotus roots and leaves. I stood at the edge, the woods around me glistening with hidden light. I turned back, my breath heavy, a trace of fear on my tongue. Something struck at my shoulder, a dead, heavyweight branch. As panic rose like a dark thing from my chest, I caught a glimpse of the mud track leading out to the main road.

When people leave unexpectedly... Nicholas, Lenny... you are left only with unanswered questions; they travel long with you, looping their way into your thoughts, becoming your intimate companions.

"But where are you going?" I'd ask Lenny, and he'd offer no reply. On those afternoons he wouldn't permit me to accompany him, on those evenings he didn't return to his room. The mud, unexplained, splattered on his motorbike wheels.

Maybe on one of those excursions he met Mihir.

The stranger.

The solitary backpacker who drifted into our hometown, winding his way from the northern tip of the country, down the wild mountains, across wide rivers and into our sloping streets. He had coal-dust eyes, and mercilessly sun-darkened skin. I remember he carried the scent of bonfires, of nights spent out in the open, of old wood-bone. He spoke softly, hesitant for you to hear what he had to say.

While I was working on somehow getting through my final exams in my last year in school, Lenny took Mihir for bike rides out of town, to all the secret tea stalls he'd shown me. To the forest. The lady at the one-room tea shop called them her butterflies.

I met them infrequently—between tuition, extra classes, and paranoid parents, I had little time—yet when I did, I could sense Lenny was secretly, silently reanimated. They would travel together, it was planned.

"Where?" I asked in wonder.

And Mihir, in his twilight voice would tell us where he'd been. To Varanasi, sitting at Assi Ghat at dawn, to Sandakphu from where you could see the Himalayas, and four of the highest peaks in the world. To a hidden, abandoned fort along the Konkan coast.

For a while, it was alive, the map hanging on the wall, glowing with promise.

Yet living is all loss.

And time, or rather the passage of time, doesn't bring understanding. Only invention, appropriation. A wild attempt to prop up the past before it slides out of sight. Often, I feel I haven't truly left the forest. That I'm still there, astray on an endless evening. Stumbling around in the darkness, looking for a clearing, where anything is possible.

If Kalsang's parents would have "killed him" if they discovered he was sleeping with his cousin, mine would have done the same if they suspected the slightest deviance. So I was careful, making sure I was in my room every second Sunday when they called on the common telephone in the corridor. It rang loudly and often, when it worked, that is, or hadn't been set on fire for fun, or stolen by someone looking to make some quick, easy money.

On any given day, it was difficult to carry on a conversation with my father.

I remember once, when I was still in school, he brought home a sapling from the market, a delicate green thing wrapped in plastic and soil. He planted it in our garden thinking it was a flowering hydrangea, but it grew into something else. A great tangling creeper with dark leaves and rare orange blossoms. And he'd stand in front of it bewildered.

What is this?

Sometimes, he looked at me the same way.

It didn't help that, more often than not, the corridor erupted in riotous distraction. At the far end, boys played "indoor cricket" with a tennis ball, someone else danced around in a towel and little else. Music blared from many rooms, spanning various eras and genres. Kishore Kumar from one, Black Sabbath from the other.

Our conversations proceeded the same way each time, as though we were working meticulously through a checklist.

"Hello."

"Hello... can you hear me?" My father always asked.

"Yes... hello pa."

I can still imagine him now, walking out the house, down the sloping road to the market, to a PCO round the corner, a small shop with a telephone booth attached to it like an afterthought. A black and yellow signboard dangling over its door. Nine o'clock was late for my hometown. Its streets would be empty, filled only with a flimsy mist and nippy breeze. My father would be tired, after a day's work at the hospital, but he'd wait until the crowds were gone to escape the queue at the PCO.

"Howwwzzzaaaaatttttt!" the cricketers would shout.

"What's that?" My father's voice would ripple, like he was speaking underwater.

"Nothing, pa."

"What was that noise?"

"Nothing."

"Okay. How's everything?"

"Fine."

Conversations were a staccato recital—short, abrupt, awkward.

"How's ma?"

"She's here... she wants to speak to you."

"And Joyce? How is she?"

"She's fine... busy with her work."

My elder sister was a nurse in Calcutta. We wrote each other occasional letters, but moved in different worlds, which barely touched apart from when we both happened to be home.

At times, with my father, I'd feel more expansive.

"I'm writing an article for the college magazine."

"Is it part of your course work?"

"No... I'm just writing it..."

"When are your next holidays?"

And I'd tell him. Pujas. Diwali. Christmas.

"For how long?"

"About two weeks... I think."

"It's better you stay in Delhi then... it's too short..."

"Yes." There were other reasons my father preferred that I stay away from my hometown.

"Here, speak to your mother..."

This would be a relief. My mother was easier, more affectionate.

She'd run through all her concerns—food, cleanliness and the heat.

"I'm fine, ma, don't worry."

"Your sister is thin as a stick; I told her how can she nurse other people if she won't look after herself."

I could imagine Joyce's face, the way she'd click her tongue in exasperation.

I smiled. "I'm sure she's fine."

I'd allow my mother to chatter on—a cousin having a baby, a grand-uncle in hospital, an aunt visiting over the weekend. The news was as distant as I felt about my hometown, standing in the corridor, cradling the receiver against my cheek.

"Alright, dear... we'll speak to you again soon..."

Sometimes, I'd slip it in. "Ma, what news of Lenny?"

A sharp breath, the beep of the machine. Beep. And then a few seconds more.

"Nothing, as yet. He's still there..."

"For how long, ma?"

"Until he's cured."

And there was nothing left for me to say but good night.

Sometimes, I tried to imagine Lenny.

From the hints in his letters, the tiny details he slipped in without noticing, or assuming them to be of importance. In the room next to his, a young boy drew picture after picture of a black sun. Over and over, in infinite, untiring circles. "Why don't you draw something else?" they'd tell the boy. And he would. A forest, a house, a line of mountains. Then he'd finish with a black circle, coloring it in until the crayon broke. On the other side, the room to his right, a girl would silently play with stones—five pebbles that she'd toss in the air and scatter on the ground. Picking up each one carefully as though they were jewels.

Nem, I am wedged between the earth and sky.

In the evenings, if he looked out the window, through the patterned grill, he'd see the silvery gleam of pine trees, and far away, the uneven shape of hills, the brittle disc of the moon, precariously balanced. *From where I am, the town lights are too distant to be visible.* Night after night sleep would not come. For sleep, he said, was pressed into small white pellets, chipped away from the moon. Arranged neatly, like his night clothes, in a row, washed with clear, spring water, in which it dissolved like star dust, and swam to the tips of his fingers, his toes, somewhere to the crown of his head.

I wondered when he started gathering sleep—the pellets dispensed after dinner. The lady in white was meant to watch him swallow, but she was careless, a little impatient. She had many sleeps to give away. He stored them in a pen he'd hollowed, throwing away the cartridge. He'd have collected enough when it was full. Enough sleep, so he wouldn't need to wake up to the brightness of this room. This square cell. The world that was too green and hurt his eyes. So he wouldn't need to see the way they looked at him. Wracked with this sickness. Under his breath, he murmured lines from memory. He'd read somewhere that when an earthquake buried an entire city, people underground kept themselves alive reciting poetry.

But now all these heavy books are no use to me any more, for
Where I go, words carry no weight: it is best
Then, I surrender their fascinating counsel
to the silent dissolution of the sea
which misuses nothing because it values nothing.

He too would do the same. Recite from memory, each syllable marking the passage of time.

But for how long? And why?

How slowly time passed in the dark.

See, barely a minute.

Here we are, still waiting.

For something to drop.

In his hand, I imagined, sleep lay in neat clusters, in the centre of his palm. He unscrewed the pen cap and filled it up, a boy collecting treasure.

Did he remember dark skin, how it quivered below him? Hair a thousand shades of dusk and light. *It was a thing of shame.*

Out the window, the moon would be wakeful. The trees hushed in the breeze. How he longed to be beneath them, to curl his hand into the earth. He said he often thought of all the times we'd done that, him and I, his young friend. Going to the forest behind his house, smoking cheap cigarettes, lost among the trees.

Once, in the deepest part of night, when darkness had unfurled to its full, long length, he stepped out of bed, and moved to his desk. A small table by the window. In the light of a milky pre-dawn, mingled with the last sprinklings of the stars, he drew faces. His mother, when she was most vulnerable, when she checked on him at night in his room and thought he was asleep and couldn't see her face as she looked into his and tried to fathom what she had brought into the world. His father, always twisted with rage. Such a deep and secret anger. The stranger. But this one he crumpled. Then he smoothed it out and filed it away.

Me. His friend, with a face that looked to him with love.

He sketched each portrait with care and precision. Emptying his memory of them on to paper. Marking his name at the edge of the page, over and again—*Lenny, Lenny, Lenny.* He would send them away, his memories. So he was lighter. So sleep would take him easily and lay him down with her in a dark and hollow place where he could rest for all time.

———

Of all the parties I attended in my years in university, there's one I remember in particular.

For many reasons.

The venue was in Hudson Lines, a neighborhood of tottering multi-story houses, packed tightly together, close to a wide, sluggish canal choked with garbage. On still evenings, the air was ripe with the sickly-sweet stench of decay. No one seemed to mind. The kids playing badminton on the sidewalk, the aunties wedged around the vegetable cart, prodding papayas-cucumbers-tomatoes, the pot-bellied men lounging in their vests and lungis, demurely dressed young ladies walking home from tuition. Living with the perpetual smell of decay. Perhaps it is possible to get used to anything.

Kalsang and I rattled along the potholed road on a cycle rickshaw.

"Bas," he said. We stopped in front of a biscuit-colored house, with a narrow unlit staircase. We climbed, stumbling over sleeping dogs and garbage bags, to a flat on the fifth floor. From behind the door came the dull leaden thud of music. Even now, before I enter a party, when I'm standing outside the entrance, listening, I wish, for an instant, I hadn't come. I feel I'm intruding on some secret ritualistic practice of a tribe I don't belong to.

We stepped into a large terrace space, dotted with people sitting in dark corners, standing with glasses against the railings. It seemed everyone, apart from my roommate, was a stranger. People called out to Kalsang, saying hello, asking him if he had any "maal".

A stereo in the corner spilled tunes into the warm night air—*But it's just a sweet, sweet fantasy, baby...* several voices sang out, rising from a mesh of bodies swaying to the beat... *When I close my eyes you come and you take me.*

I stood by the bar—a rickety wooden table strewn with glasses and bottle tops—and watched the others dancing. *There's no beginning and there is no end.*

"I'll be right back," said Kalsang, and disappeared for the rest of the evening.

I poured myself a drink. Cold, frothy beer. Behind me, the lights of the city flickered between tree tops and wires. I wondered whether I could see the mutiny memorial from here. Rising above the treetops. Far below, bathed in orange-yellow lamplight, the road was beginning to empty. A few couples marched by, intent on an evening walk. A man selling chuskies did brisk business. Stray dogs circled each other in suspicion.

"Hey, do you have a light?"

"What?"

"Got a light?" She swiped her forehead with the back of her hand; her bracelets tinkled.

"No, sorry." But I wished I did.

Someone close by threw her a lighter.

"Thanks," she yeled. I could smell her perfume mingling sweetly with sweat.

"You were very good..." I blurted.

"I was?" She exhaled, and her face was lost behind plumes of smoke.

"In Midsummer Night's Dream..."

I expected her to be pleased, but she rolled her eyes. "I'm beginning to think that's the only theatrical role I'll ever be remembered for..."

Of course, I should have known. What a ridiculous thing to say! Haltingly, I apologised.

She waved it away, with a cool, careless hand.

What should I do next? Perhaps offer her a drink...

Our conversation, aborted as it already was, swiftly came to an end as Lari danced up to her, skirt swirling. She pulled Titania, laughing, back to the dance floor.

It was almost a relief. I wondered whether they'd ever invited the art historian to a house party. They probably didn't have the nerve. And this wasn't the kind of place where we were likely to find Adheer either. I poured myself another beer; it would be, I was certain, a long evening.

After several pints, I stumbled indoors, looking for the bathroom. The flat was mostly empty, probably because it was uncomfortably hot inside, and ceiling fans swirled around warm, sticky air thick as soup. I walked through, what was presumably, the drawing room, strewn with thin, folded mattresses, a battered TV set, dirty cushions, slippers, and tottering bamboo shelves holding brimming ashtrays and old magazines.

Eventually, I found a bedroom. The mattress placed on a rickety foldout bed, with a sheet tugged hurriedly around it. A pile of clothes spilled over a chair. The posters on the wall—Scorpions, Guns "n" Roses and Mr Big—reminded me of the ones in Lenny's room. The first door I tried, hidden behind a curtain, led not to the loo but a small covered balcony strung with washing lines and littered with old newspapers and empty bottles. I liked it there; it was quiet, away from the crowd.

Suddenly, I heard the bedroom door open.

"Here, just lie down for a while..."

I recognized the voice.

I peered inside, through a small dusty grilled window.

Lari held her head in her hands, giggling about how the world was spinning, while Titania helped her across the room to the bed. She pushed some clothes off, and smoothed it out.

Her friend lay down, placing her arm over her face. "Ooh, that's so bright."

Titania switched off the tube light and turned on a lamp in the corner. The light spilled out in a soft, golden glow.

"Better."

"Would you like some water?"

The girl shook her head.

Titania knelt on the floor, beside her. They spoke in whispers; I caught fragments, they were talking about the party—*drink, who was that... the music... strong joint...*

Until Lari asked, "Will you do that? What you did the other day?"

Titania reached out, stroking her friend's forehead.

"This?"

Her friend nodded, smiled.

Titania began with her face, caressing the contours in slow, delicate swirls. Through her long, silky hair. Untangling. Unknotting. Her fingers found Lari's neck, the ridge of her shoulders. The girl closed her eyes. She traced her way down her arms, interlaced their fingers. Then slowly over her chest, over the flimsy chiffon top. Around the curve of her breasts, cupped in a black bra.

All the way across the flat, smooth plane of her stomach, to the top of her skirt. Her fingers ran over her waist, her thighs, the dip in between, down the length of her legs. She did this over and over again, making her way down, then back up to the top. Lari stirred, turning her face slightly towards Titania. Their faces moved closer, meeting in silence.

I waited behind the wall of glass.

There's no beginning and there is no end.

When I left, the neighborhood was empty and quiet; interrupted only by the watchman's beat, his walking stick rapping the ground. Somewhere, a gong sounded. It was three o'clock. Too late to find a rickshaw. I had no choice but to walk back to the residence hall. The roads emptied of all vehicles, save for some night creatures. The homeless, the stray, the forgotten, the lost. I hadn't intended to stay out so long, but I couldn't get away until Titania and Lari had left the room. They'd touched, and swept, and caressed, lying side by side, until they fell into a silence that I thought was sleep. Eventually, they'd risen, switched off the lamp, and stumbled out in the darkness. Now, the knot in my stomach, that hot, dense mass of desire, was slowly unraveling; I was tired, and sleep pressed heavily against my eyes. The walk took almost twenty minutes, down broken sidewalks and stretches where there was none. When I reached, the campus seemed haunted. Emptier than I'd ever seen it. The cross and tower outlined in a dark silhouette. I switched on the lights in my room. Kalsang hadn't returned. Someone had slipped a note under the door. A phone call. From Joyce. "Please call back."

———

The next day, at noon, I walked to the PCO on the main road, outside campus. It had rained earlier, for the air carried a rare freshness, and the dust had settled on the sidewalk. It was odd that my sister had called, for no apparent reason. We wished each other on birthdays and Easter, were usually home together for Christmas, posing for an annual family photograph in front of the tree. But apart from that, we didn't usually reach out and make contact. I hoped all was well with my parents. No, I was quite sure about that; they weren't the type to shy away from telling me they were ill, or that I should come home. This was sudden and strange.

At the PCO, I waited for a bulky gentleman in a striped shirt to finish a call. Outside, a man with a parked cart dispensed banta from a thermocol container filled with ice.

"Special," I requested.

The man plucked out a thick, squat bottle and popped the stopper. It fizzed gently as he poured it into a glass, and stirred in a teaspoon of rock salt and a squeeze of lime. The drink tingled at the back of my throat, washing cold down my chest. Finally, I wedged myself into the stuffy booth, and dialed the number—this too was a common phone at the hostel where my sister was staying. I hoped she was in.

"Hello," answered a young female voice.

"May I speak to Joyce, please?"

"Hold on, let me check if she's there."

The line beeped, and the machine numbers climbed higher. After what seemed ages, my sister came on the line.

"Joyce, you called?"

"Hello Nem." Her voice sounded strange and distant, as though she was very far and very small.

"Is everything okay?"

"It's Lenny," she said.

"What do you mean?"

"I heard... actually, mama and papa rang me... they said they didn't know how to tell you."

"Tell me what?"

The line beeped, like a heartbeat.

"Lenny passed away."

The words hung on an invisible thread, stretching from her to me.

"I'm sorry... there were some complications with his medication, Nem. He went to sleep and didn't wake up." After a moment's silence, she added, "It would have been painless."

I placed the phone back on the receiver—my sister's voice sounding sympathies into the air—and leaned against the door. Someone rapped against the glass, hard and impatient. It was the same man in the striped shirt. He'd returned to make another call. I paid and fumbled out. On the road, a DTC bus passed by exhaling a thick plume of grey smoke—it hit my face and burned my eyes, the sick, unhealthy smell of exhaust.

I lurched towards the uncovered gutter, and threw up. The liquid sweet and empty in my mouth. When I straightened up, it didn't return. The breath we ease into and out of, the rise and fall of our chest. That unnoticed, that necessary. It remained in some dark tunneled space in my chest. Filling with the stench of decay.

———

A week before, someone had come to my room with mail. A glance at the handwriting, long and looping. Lenny's. I hadn't heard from him in a while. Lately, he didn't write often, and even when he did, his letters were brief, sketchy, responding to mine in an oddly absent way. The last thing he sent me was not a letter.

The envelope sat thick and secretive in my hand as I carried it to the lawn. I wanted to open it outdoors, as though whatever it may conjure could not be contained within walls. It was sealed neatly with cello tape; I opened it carefully. The paper inside was folded to a compact square. A sketch, a pencil drawing and a scribbled line—*As I remember you.*

It was remarkably good, even if I felt Lenny had been rather generous by gently proportioning out my features—the eyes a tad larger, the longer, straighter nose, the slimmer, more chiseled face. In his strokes, Lenny had infused something I hadn't ever seen before in the mirror. It was a myth of me.

Nicholas found it once.

He was rummaging through a pile of books—his and mine, gloriously mixed together, like our lives over the past few months—and a folded paper fell to the floor.

He picked it up.

"We should have this framed..." he said, holding it out, smiling.

"No." I tried to snatch it back.

"Why? It's marvellous..."

I plucked it from his fingers and tucked it into my pocket.

The sketch was the only thing I denied him.

"It's from Lenny."

I remember Nicholas watching me, his eyes, dark and attentive, taking in my gestures.

We were in the study, lounging on the sofa.

"You told me somebody had killed him..." he said softly. "Why did you say that? What did you mean?"

The stranger with the coal-dust eyes, and sun-darkened skin. Who carried the scent of cold nights and bonfires. Lenny took him for bike rides out of town, to all the secret tea shops he'd shown me. To the pine forest. One afternoon, Lenny took him to his room, when everyone was out. But his father happened to return early and, for some reason, did something out of the usual. He walked downstairs to the basement.

"He found them there..." I told Nicholas.

In bed, entwined, skin on skin.

And while I have spent many years thinking about that, conjuring endless scenarios, this is one moment I cannot bring myself to imagine.

It is merely darkness. A blank spot. An open grave.

Did his father shout? Did he retch? Did he storm up to Lenny and slap him across the face? Pull him away in his nakedness and shame? Did he stare at his son in the stranger's arms and walk out silently?

"They would've killed me..."

Everything else remains pristinely clear in my mind—the oddly-angled room, the air tinged with the smell of cheap tobacco and old books. The map on the wall. The bed. The bed. Lenny's family tried to keep it quiet.

"Can you imagine," I asked Nicholas, "how fast news spreads in a small town?"

Where everyone knew everyone else. And whispers grew as tangled gardens, abandoned in their wildness, words flitting like butterflies from tongue to tongue.

"Did you see him again?" asked Nicholas.

I shook my head. "I only wrote him letters."

At the time this happened, I had just finished high school. My final exams a week behind me. I had no clear plans for after, the thing everyone called the future. And so I thought that's what my father wanted to discuss, one evening, when he called me to his study. Except, when I walked in, there was something in his eyes I'd never seen before—embarrassment.

"I wanted to talk to you about..." He stopped. Hesitant. He needn't have said any more. I knew that the words about Lenny, whirling around town, had reached his ears too. I expected clamor and curses, rebukes and reprimands. *I told you... I told you... I told you... I told you... he was a disgusting boy.* To stay away. Instead he spoke with surprisingly timidity.

"Did he do anything to you?"

I was much too taken aback to reply.

"Tell me, did he?"

"What do you mean?"

It grew, the look in his eyes. Twisting on his tongue.

"Did he... touch you?"

His words hung in the air, cleaving the space between us.

I shook my head.

Perhaps then it changed to relief. He sat back in his chair.

"It's better you don't see him again."

"But why?"

"It is better."

I had my hands on the table, clenched, my knuckles white.

"Right now he needs to be left alone with his family. You see, Lenny is suffering from—a disease. Your mother and I don't want you around him..." *It's contagious.*

I held my silence.

My father was done. "I think I've made myself clear."

It wasn't enough to keep me from seeing him.

My parents sent me away to Delhi. They thought it for the best. They'd heard of a college there, founded on good, wholesome Christian principles, where students lived on campus, which had special seat allocations for people like me who came from places and communities far from the capital, marked as underprivileged and marginalized. I was sent away. I was offered to Nicholas on a plate. Something like fate.

If time is measured in a god's blink, I didn't emerge from my room for a million years. I don't know if it was the next day, or the next week—or had a month passed?—after I heard about Lenny. At some point, on some day, before dawn, when the murmuring voices were silenced, and darkness glowed with a light that seemed to come from nowhere, I walked out of the residence hall, down the brick-lined path, away from the campus and into the forest. I picked my way through stone and undergrowth, the leaves glistening with dampness. Somewhere, perhaps, a moon. Ancient, watching through the branches of charcoal trees. The air still and silent, pulsing with unknown things.

I came to a tower. A tall sandstone tower, which I entered, and climbed, because from the top I'd be able to see all the reasons why. The air would be fresher, and filled with promise. From there, I'd be distant, removed from the clutches of this great and quartering heaviness. I'd almost reached the end when suddenly there was no ground to stand on. Like stepping on water. Falling through the air.

I lay curled at the bottom of the spiral staircase, the floor stone-cold and grainy against my skin. Hours later, a figure appeared at the doorway, and stood in a pale rectangle of light. His brows furrowed, his hands hesitantly reaching out to stop a fall that had already happened.

I didn't look up, didn't ask why or where, as I was half-carried and led out into the forest, the trees green and reverent around us. Something ached but I couldn't tell where the pain arose from, it seemed to surround me, dense as the humid late summer air.

After a while, we reached a wide road lined by Gulmohar trees, bathed in a rich and luxurious silence. The slow, persistent purr of a passing car. The faint jingle of bells. We stopped at a gate where a man rushed out to help us. The exchange of words between them was brief and muted. Soon, I sensed we were indoors, in a cool and high-ceilinged corridor, the creak of doors, the slap of footfall, the voice of a woman. Hands, gentle as cotton, lifted me over, suspended me for a second in mid-air like I'd been only just before, while falling, and then a sudden release onto a soft, smooth plane that stretched endlessly like a field of snow. The unmistakable smell of fresh linen. Of something sharp and lemony. The warmth of wind and sunshine. A heated touch swept over me, a cloth struck at my skin, rough, spongy and damp. Something peeled, layer after infinitesimal layer. And then the deep, dark mercy of sleep.

II

IN ALL THESE YEARS, I'VE come to learn that the greatest lie is the face of a clock.

Time doesn't hang on a wall. It doesn't tick by on a wrist. It's infinitely more secretive and intimate. Time, contrary to all notions, does not flow. It's not beautifully fluid, a murmuring river passing under a bridge. In our heads, it hastens and halts and stumbles. On occasion, it dissolves. It ceases to exist.

Nicholas disappeared in the last century.

(*Ni. Cho. Las.* How easily his name trips off my tongue even after all this time, when I'd broken up the syllables and stashed them like three shells in a box).

Just before it rolled over, the calendar glistening with zeroes, three in a row, portals looking over the endlessness of the sea. What would it bring over the horizon? Everything new. Much of the same.

I graduated, and studied again. A Master's in English Literature, and then moved to the south of the city. My hometown became a place of sporadic visitations, Christmas, the death of a grandparent, the birth of a niece.

I settled for the usual options, open at the time to someone cropped from the Humanities—editorial jobs at newly-opened publishing houses. Although never television. Or the newspapers. Somehow, I found them categorically unappealing, with their terse daily deadlines, their massive, unrelenting production of images and text. Eventually, I joined a magazine as copy-editor. It was steady, if unexciting, until, because of an absent colleague, I started handling the arts pages. I did it for an issue, then two, and more. The absent colleague moved to Bombay. And my editor took it for granted I'd continue, and so I did. If the Delhi of the previous decade had sowed the seeds of capitalism, this one saw its rampant flourishing. Only now was it possible to lay out six pages of a magazine dedicated to art. And as many to shopping, gigs, eating out, nightlife, cultural events. In South Delhi, a new gallery opened almost every month—in wealthy neighborhoods of marble-brick houses and leafy streets, Golf Links, Panchsheel, Defence Colony, Neeti Bagh, in previously unfashionable Lado Sarai and industrial Okhla. We were inundated by an outpouring of installations, video art, photography—I attended shows, and interviewed artists, I sat in un-crowded galleries on early weekday mornings, looking at art that I sometimes loved, sometimes detested.

I did this for three years, until my absent colleague returned.

Nithi didn't take her job back, of course. She offered me one instead.

To work for a new art and cultural journal, at their small yet not immodest office in Delhi. It was an exciting venture—the publication offered the space to write long-form, exploratory pieces. "To encourage insight, experimentation," she said, dragging on her cigarette in short, abrupt puffs. "Why should art writing be relegated to a last-page column? Clubbed with 'Entertainment' like sordid Siamese twins."

We published monthly, which, after working for a weekly magazine, seemed an immense luxury. It gave me time to focus on idea and craft. I found a book by Marjorie Munsterberg, a guide to writing about visual art. John Berger's *Ways of Seeing*. Joshua Taylor's *Learning to Look*.

I don't know whether I turned to art or whether it turned to me. Perhaps we were pulled to each other by similar longing. You see, I've always thought that people write, paint, compose music, for remembrance. Like what Philip Larkin said—that at the bottom of all art lies the impulse to preserve. Lest we forget. Works of art are beautiful scars.

Over the last few years, our journal did sufficiently well. Receiving favorable attention, a few journalism awards, and harnessing steadily growing subscriptions. At work, a promotion. Deputy editor.

I moved from a cramped one-bedroom flat in Malviya Nagar to a reasonably more comfortable one-bedroom place in East of Kailash. On some nights I had company, those who stayed over, some who didn't— else I read, played the radio, or drifted through the vastness of the Internet, page upon page, swallowing up the hours. Once, I brought home a stray cat, and it stayed a while, sometimes falling asleep on my lap while I wrote. Wandering the rooms, un-restful, at night. Then it wandered out one evening and didn't return.

More often, rather than love, there were fleeting encounters.

For most of us, the years pass with few markers.

And we are surprised to find that the events in our lives—that meeting with a friend, that trip to Cairo, that casual reunion—took place so distantly in the past. "A couple of years ago," you begin, and then correct yourself, "No, *six* years ago now."

And we move along, mired in memory. Although the paradox of memory is that it gives you back what you had on condition that you know it has been lost. To regain it, you must remember it has gone; to remake the world, you need to first understand that it has ended.

So it rolls on until over a decade since the century turned—and I'm not quite certain whether the world is now amazingly smart, or incredibly foolish. At the edge, there were the two towers, yet I prefer not to count the years by war, on terror or otherwise. Somewhere in-between, the tsunami. Unlike hurricanes, tsunamis have no name. Just the Tsunami, a word that rolls off the tongue like a wave. Towards this end of the decade, the great crushing economic catastrophe. And it lingers, how it lingers. For this too, there is no name.

The problem is with reappearances. It's not what isn't there that shapes us as much as what might return. I suppose it all might never have happened if I didn't move to London.

When I told acquaintances in Delhi I was leaving for a year, they said they were thrilled for me. "Ah, if you are lucky enough to have lived in London as a young man, then wherever you go for the rest of your life, it stays with you, for London is a moveable feast."

"Paris," I corrected. "That's about Paris."

But, I realized, it didn't matter. All these cities were identical, cloaked with the same shiny, glittering appeal, pronounced with reverence, like a hushed prayer. I haven't been to Paris, but I found that London was filled with old light.

Since I landed, it was shifting into autumn, and I wanted the trees to stay that way forever. Flickering with fire. Dropping flames onto people's shoulders, at their feet. People usually make their life's discoveries when they're young—their first kiss, sex, alcohol, drugs. I was in my early thirties and I'd discovered a new season. An entirely new season. I felt self-congratulatory. It was a revelation. The world was ending, and also somehow being renewed.

———

With the crisis, financial and otherwise, the journal almost folded. My colleague considered moving back to Mumbai. She called herself the human yo-yo, constantly swaying between two cities. And I? I was lost. Not that I had no options—many galleries still stayed open, people still bought and sold art (in fact, this was a good time to in-vest, said one shrewd acquaintance, when the prices were low. "Warhol for a pittance.") There was talk also of a major private, not-for-profit art centre opening on the fringes of Delhi, amid the towering steel and glass structures of Gurgaon. They'd definitely be looking to hire.

At first, I fell into a flurry of activity, sprucing up my CV, trying to fix up meetings with all the right people... and then? And then, I stopped. Not only because the journal miraculously survived—but I was weary.

The city was a heavy place. Full of incestuous circles and petty rivalries. I felt I had escaped one small town and landed in a city that had tightened around me like a noose.

Delhi's vast, mighty spaces felt so *reduced*. Evaporated into something as thick and wretched as what floated down the Jamuna.

And so, I was in London.

Yet wouldn't it be more gratifying to attribute this stint to reasons higher and more majestic than that of diversion? To offer it the weight of chance or predestination. In Greek mythology, the Moirai were three white-robed sisters who controlled man's fate. Clotho, the spinner, who spun the thread of life, Lachesis, the allotter, who determined its length, and Atropos, the unturnable, or the cutter. If our lives are thread, thin and silvery, it's easy to imagine them entangled across the globe, sometimes parting, never to touch again, or else unexpectedly meeting, re-entwining.

That's what happened with Santanu and me.

We'd kept in touch infrequently after our university days. All of us scattering like a handful of seeds. I stayed on. He left Delhi for elsewhere. He wasn't around for the few college reunions I attended. I wasn't there for the others. Boozy get-togethers on and off campus, where old acquaintances and adversaries exchanged numbers and pleasantries.

Last year, I decided to send him an email.

I'm not sure you remember me... I wrote for the college magazine while you were editor...

He replied far more promptly than I expected—*Nem, you were the only one who turned in articles on time. How could I forget you?*

It was a promising start.

So I explained how I was interested in a fellowship from the Royal Literary Fund programme at the college where he was senior lecturer. At the Centre for Cultural, Literary and Postcolonial Studies. I was eligible to apply for a grant, but I required, what they called, a "formal nomination". The fellowship ran for a year; it was prestigious, both for the Centre and for him. And for me, a tidy stipend too, considering all I needed to do was keep office hours a few days a week, and offer students writing support, and foster "good writing practice" across all disciplines.

Santanu's reply was suitably succinct. *Sure.*

After that, only matters of procedure and paperwork remained.

I handed in a request for a sabbatical from my job. Which was rejected.

"There's something called the Internet," said Nithi. "You can work from home."

And then the longest plane ride, a move, timeless and suspended.

On most evenings, Santanu and I met at a bar across the road from where he worked, close to an old Faber & Faber building where, I learned, T. S. Eliot had once been an editor. From 1925 to 1965. If the bar had a name, I don't remember it. Run by a student union, it was a Spartan place, of white melamine counters and silver-grey metallic tables. A standing blackboard announced the day's special offers—jugs of sangria, extended happy hours, Belgian beer fests. Basic, unfussy, dependable. It was, as Hemingway had written, our clean, well-lighted place. Santanu had been a stubbly, longhaired student in perpetual open slippers, slip-sliding down the corridors, clutching a sheaf of papers and folders. He'd changed—neater clothes and smart closed shoes—but didn't seem to have aged, his bony, sculptural face still boyishly unshaven, his hair still at a length that evoked gentle rebellion. As people hinged by the past are bound to do, we often spoke of old acquaintances—life stories bordering on the tragic, and the illuminating. The ones who'd married, had children, had moved away, or remained. The ones missing from memory. *Do you remember... ? What happened to... ? Did you hear... ?* Names were conjured and discarded—apart from one. Nicholas.

On one occasion, we stood outside the notably fancier Marquis, at the end of Marchmont Street, a quiet, unobtrusive road in Bloomsbury. Decked out on the simpler side of art nouveau, with a pale blue and white façade, and sweeping arches over the door and windows. The awning, striped gaily like a fairground tent, stretched taut and bright over the sidewalk, sheltering a row of empty benches.

We were dressed in dark winter coats and looked like a pair of birds.

"It's a gastro-pub," said Santanu, "Where the potato wedges are hand-cut and everything's organic." He didn't sound impressed. Nevertheless, we stopped for a quick drink. Inside, I had the impression of vast amounts of wood, smooth and polished, like the interior of a ship. Scattered with low chairs and tables, while quilted maroon leather couches lined the edges. The lights, low and inviting, cast a rich glow on paneled walls and parquet floors. We headed to the bar, a walnut-topped counter lined with beer pumps standing in a row of shiny golden armor.

"What can I get you?" The young lady behind the counter looked remarkably cheerful for someone who'd had to ask that question a hundred times a day. Her autumn-red hair was twisted into a bun, but some of it had escaped, falling around her face in rebellious wisps. If she wore it open she'd look like a Pre-Raphaelite virgin. (Or, since the artists were Victorians, a lovely penitent prostitute.)

"Pint of Guinness, please."

I would've preferred whisky, but perhaps it was somewhat early in the day. "I'll have the same..."

We tipped our glasses.

The stout was deliciously cool, drifting into a lingering aftertaste.

I'd grown to enjoy this ruby-rich drink laced with bitter dreams.

Admittedly, one of the less strange libations Santanu had prompted me to try. He was on a self-appointed mission to sample every available ale in the country—and had made me his willing accomplice. Each new one we came across was recorded in a small black notebook.

"Hooky Bitter, Old Ember, Harvest Pale, Worthington White Shield, Old Speckled Hen... and my favorite... Sheepshaggers."

One day, he declared, when he was done teaching the evolution of Bengali culture from the seventeenth to nineteenth century, he'd write a book on the anthropology of brewing.

"Beer culture and the politics of identity."

It was, I concurred, a worthy follow-up.

Through the large windows, on the sidewalk, I could see people out on their evening run, mothers pushing baby strollers, shoppers with bulging Waitrose bags, students wandering past to and from one of the many colleges clustered near Russell Square, corporate workers in their suits and air of self-assurance. The city of London I imagined as a giant clockwork being, fueled by souls. By Santanu. By the Pre-Raphaelite bartender. Even, somehow, myself. Every interaction, a ripple, moving beyond our sight.

Santanu, who was checking his phone, said, "Eva's coming, but she might be a little late." He added, "We're invited to drinks at her place this evening."

Eva was his English-Japanese friend; she worked at the institute, organizing events, conferences and festivals, showing up always meticulously attired in slim pencil dresses the color of peacocks.

"My grandmother sends me silk from Osaka," she told me once. "I never buy clothes in this country. The English only wear beige."

Santanu downed the last of his Guinness. "Another?"

I hastened to finish my pint. "No, not if you prefer I didn't slur during my reading."

Inside, the room was carved into niches by bookshelves running all the way up to the low ceiling, neatly divided by geography. Nations—Japan, China, India—and the more all-encompassing Middle East, South Asia, Africa. Up front, a space had been cleared for chairs and tables, armed with glasses and bottled water. While Santanu greeted people, I quietly lost myself in the crowd. I was good at this, being as inconspicuous as a corner chair or a potted plant. Besides, it was difficult to feel out of place in a bookshop, where I could pretend to browse, slipping books off the shelves, carefully tracing my fingers along their spines. For a while, I studied the Chinese woodblock prints on the wall, intricately lined figures on cool peppermint-blue paper. And the Islamic calligraphy of Bihnam Al-Agzeer, whose words become pictures.

I stood at the edge and studied faces, none of whom were recognizable or familiar. Looking back now, I'd attribute the pre-event hum with an air of serendipity. Something, I was certain, was about to happen. In a corner, I spotted a pot of fragrant rosemary. And rosemary, as we all know, is for remembrance. *Pray, love, remember.*

At the shelf, it slipped from my hands to the floor, a book of Cavafy's poems.

An echo of the days of pleasure.

Even if it could merely have been my nervous anticipation of the evening.

We were gathered for a literary reading, part of the Kaagaz Series organized twice a year by The Asian House in London. Their guest "curator" this time was Santanu. I held the pamphlet in my hand—the cover carried a composition, explosive and colorful, of a contemporary mandala, ringed circles of delicate floral patterns, fantastical beasts, glimpses of the cosmos. I flipped through the pages, thick and inky, marking my name, *my* name would be reading a "work in progress". Scrawled hastily in a notebook, a last-minute print out thrust into my pocket. The words seemed unfamiliar, as though a different self had set them down.

"Which one would you like?" I'd asked Santanu, holding out my literary offerings.

As RLF Fellow at the institute, he'd invited me to contribute.

He was unfussy. "What do you have that can fill three pages?"

Around me, the crowd had swelled, and the bookstore buzzed with the murmur of conversation. White faces, and brown, a man in a turban, a woman wearing a shade of pink lipstick I could see from across the room. Another in an embroidered kaftan. Someone hastened through the door, the color of her coat catching my eye—fitted and belted in stil de grain yellow. Eva. And following close behind, a lady I'd sometimes seen around the institute. She was dressed more demurely, in a navy top coat, and a petite felt-corsage beret. Two familiar faces and no other.

That's when I noticed him, a solitary golden-haired youth.

Perhaps because of the birds.

He was standing under a flight of red paper swallows hanging in the corner, swaying slightly, touched by an invisible hand. Tall and slender, he wore skinny jeans and a tweed coat he hadn't taken off indoors. Settled over his features, finely etched as they were, was the unmistakable mark of boredom.

Soon, we readied for the event; I followed the other writers taking their places. People shuffled around choosing seats, the back rows filled up while the front remained stoically empty. A few chairs away to my left, Santanu tapped the microphone—"Good evening, everyone... important things first, there *is* wine after..."

The room rippled with laughter.

The next half hour was filled with small speeches and readings—a poet from Taiwan, a writer from Hong Kong, the Nepalese artist who'd contributed the cover art. Soon, I heard my name—"our Royal Literary Fund Fellow from India...", the title of the journal I worked for in Delhi.

"Thank you, Santanu." My voice was soft, too soft. Louder next time. I didn't want to lose everyone to whispers. While I read, the room fell silent, apart from a sudden car horn outside, and a jangling cell phone. The person stopped the ringing, but stepped out to answer the call.

I stumbled over the word "obfuscate" and wished I'd never used it in the first place. Perhaps this was the wrong piece to be reading. I'd picked something I'd written on a photography exhibition of Delhi in the 1970s, inspired by a review I'd read on Rembrandt that spoke of "reversing the gaze." The reviewer imagined the painter's self-portraits coming alive at night, in the quiet of the gallery, and I did the same—

I can see them, those grainy black-and-whites frozen on the wall, prisoners of paper and light. They are ghosts—the people in the photographs, the city, the photographer herself. These multiple selves spill from the frames, and the rooms, though empty, fill with shadows...

The writer endowed Rembrandt's paintings with sight, envisioning how they had watched the centuries move past before them, the faces they, in turn, had seen. When I reached the end, I read slower, lingering on my treasured line: *As you stand looking at them, they look back. Sometimes, a photograph reviews you.*

I glanced up. It was disconcerting, to see everyone's eyes turned to me. I was glad I'd finished. Eva and her friend were quietly conferring; I caught Eva's eye and she smiled.

The blonde youth at the back was checking his phone.

My reading was followed by one more, and then it was over.

The wine was brought out in gaiety and an impromptu bar set up in a corner. People walked around holding long-stemmed glasses, seeming to know each other so fondly and casually. Clusters gathered around Santanu and the Nepalese artist. Out of nowhere, Eva appeared at my shoulder. "Nem, you were marvellous."

Compliments tend to made me nervous; I laughed. "Well... thank you," I said, trying to salvage some degree of graciousness.

"No, really. Tamsin thought so too..." She turned to make quick introductions. Tamsin was the in-house designer at the Institute. "She makes all those beautiful posters and programmes for our events." Her friend, like Eva, had dark hair—though longer, falling loose over her shoulders—and she was taller, her frame more voluptuous. Something about her made me think of the British women's magazines my grandmother collected from the '60s. The Russian-red lips and cat-eye make-up, the slim-fit cigarette pants and beaded top. I thanked her for coming; charmingly she said it was quite alright in an accent, slight but noticeable, that I couldn't place.

"Are you"—I plucked it from out of thin air—"Scottish?"

"Close." Her mouth tilted into a smile. "I'm from Cornwall."

"You're coming over later, aren't you?" asked Eva.

I hesitated.

She placed an arm on mine. "Do come... it'll be a small crowd."

I said I'd see her there.

Eva reached out in a way few people did in this city. Nobody had told me London could also be terribly lonely.

Heading to the bar for a refill, I was accosted—the blonde youth stood before me. He was still wearing his winter coat. Perhaps he just couldn't wait to leave.

He held out a copy of the pamphlet, and a pen.

"Could you sign this for me, please?" He was holding it open to the page with my excerpt.

A strange request, but who was I to argue? Isn't this what writers do?

"Who shall I address it to?" I asked.

The boy's skin was delicately pale, and reddened where it had been touched by the cold.

"Nicholas, please."

My pen stayed poised above the page.

"Is anything the matter?" the youth asked. He looked faintly amused.

"Not at all." I wrote it out. Nonchalant.

"And could you sign it "From Nehemiah?""

I was about to sign "Nem"—it was brief, convenient, and no one called me Nehemiah.

Apart from one person.

"Did he send you?"

The boy cocked his head, like a bird. "I'm afraid I don't know what you're talking about."

"Who are you?"

Instead of a reply, he handed over a slim white envelope.

I stood speechless as he darted back into the crowd. By the time it struck me to follow, the fleet-footed messenger was at the door. He pushed it open and was gone.

———

I remember the first time Nicholas took me swimming.

One afternoon, we walked out the bungalow and headed away from the Ridge Forest, onto Raj Niwas Marg. We edged closer to the city, the roar of traffic and cycle bells growing louder, until we crossed the wide expanse of Sham Nath Marg.

"Where are we going?"

"Almost there."

The road was narrower, and to the left rose a white, colonnaded building, set away from the street, sheltered from the onslaught of the city by a sprawling lawn and rows of palm trees. Only when he turned in at the gate did I realize where we were headed.

A five-star hotel. One of those places I couldn't imagine stepping into—Delhi was like that, set into levels of wealth and access.

"Are you sure..." I looked down at my jeans, my sandals. Nicholas was in a plain white shirt, but it was pristine and expensive.

"Of course..." He touched my arm. "We'll walk round to the back from the lawns. They know me here... they won't make a fuss."

The place was strangely empty—perhaps, because it wasn't yet high tourist season, or the newer hotels in south Delhi were proving more popular. We crossed manicured lawns, and walked through a small latched gate.

The pool lay clear and blue and shimmery.

I'd never seen anything more beautiful.

I changed and showered, and carefully tucked my hair under a scalp-tight swimming cap, straightened my trunks. I looked ridiculous. My legs too long. My stomach flat but un-sculpted. But I could do this,

I told myself, looking away from the mirror. I was grateful to Nicholas for so much, and I could do this.

For him, almost anything.

When I emerged, he was already in the pool. And like all good swimmers, he made it look easy. Each movement perfectly timed—the push, the lift, the breath of air, the turn. I too would learn how to glide through water. I was certain of it, up until the edge of the pool.

"Come on in... you're in the shallow bit." Nicholas was on the other end, hanging on to the edges with his arms up on either side, smiling.

The steps quivered underwater, playing tricks on my sight. They changed shape and position. They weren't really there. Sculpted only by shadow and light. But my feet found them, and I sank, lower and lower, until—a moment of panic—there was seemingly endless space before I touched the bottom.

The water was warm, it rose up to my chest, below my shoulders. I laughed.

I tried walking, it was like pushing through something far thicker than I'd imagined, solid and liquid at the same time. I kept my arms up, like a bird, to push myself forward. I could tell the ground was dipping lower, but I ventured forward, keen to impress. To show I was as comfortable as he was in this space.

He leaned back, his face to the sky. In a moment I would reach him.

But the world suddenly fell away beneath me. All I needed to do was heave myself up and move behind to safety, but I didn't know, I hadn't learned yet. I flung my hands out instead, reaching for something concrete; they slid through water like air.

I lurched back, trying to throw the water off my face, my eyes, my mouth, but there was so much of it. Surrounding me endlessly.

Underwater, something stops. There is no time. No sound apart from a low roar of silence. I remember feeling—not thinking—that this would go on forever.

Until hands grasped me under my shoulders, driving me up and back, pulling me across to the edge, propping me against the side. The infinite safety of solidity. The bar, the blue tiles. The gritty, firm cement.

"It's okay... you're standing..."

"I can't..." I gasped. The water was a living, breathing thing. "I'm sorry..."

"We'll do this slowly..." His voice was low and soothing, close to my ear. His breath warm as life. "See, you're fine..."

He was right. The water only reached up to my chest now. It had retreated.

Nicholas moved closer, his skin studded with drops. "The first thing we need to do is teach you how not to drown."

He didn't. For on all occasions after, I pleaded not to return. I made excuses. I was busy. I wasn't well. I had a pressing assignment to complete. Myra accompanied him joyfully when she visited Delhi; they went to the pool almost everyday despite the winter cold. I never did learn how to swim.

———

Time is tricky. You organize it into days. You break it down to a second, and build it up to a century. A millennium. You shift, and stack, hoarding time into holidays and long weekends. You peel away the calendar pages. Carry it around in smartphones and computers. It has a shape. A design. Hands and digits. Glowing figures. And yet, it can't be tamed. Constantly in our grasp. Constantly out of reach. All it takes is a tremor to bring it down, the carefully staged arrangement. Precarious as a falling leaf. Time is riddled with fault lines. Slim as paper. Delicate as swirls of ink.

In the bookshop that evening, after I read Nicholas' note, I tried to drag myself back into the present. But there's a reason why time is likened to water. It is viscous. It resists. I drank more wine. Suddenly exhilarated. I think I conversed with strangers, my voice louder than usual, my laughter more urgent. Everything seemed heightened. It lasted even when I was in the tube with Santanu, when we were making our way to the south-west of the city, to Eva's place. Above the carriage door, we spotted a Shaadi.com advert—*The smart way to find your life partner.* Neha, 25, Model, Loves modern art and boxing. Sanjay, 29, Businessman, Loves Stallone and wildlife.

"Santanu, 34, Recalcitrant Academic, Detests everything," I offered.

"Nehemiah, 32, Wastrel."

After we'd run out of colorful insults, he told me, "By the way, when we get to Eva's flat, look at what's on the dining table…"

"What?"

"You'll see."

That evening, I'd have preferred to settle for fewer surprises. "Tell me…"

"I will. Later."

And I couldn't get any more out of him as we jostled along. At the next stop, a man stepped in and stood in front of me, sporting a military-style haircut and a shiny black leather jacket. On his neck, below his jawline, a shaky tattoo of a pair of dice.

Eva lived in Wimbledon, close to the Buddhapadipa Temple, in a compact yet quietly expensive flat. Filled with neat, contemporary furniture, stylish industrial lampshades, and edgy urban photo art—a series of images of a woman in a glass box placed at bridges, cliffs, at the edges of skyscrapers. Santanu told me her father was a wealthy entrepreneur in Tokyo—"There's no way anyone can afford *this* on a normal salary."

There were fewer than a dozen people in her drawing room—friends from Tokyo studying in London, a colleague or two from the institute including Tamsin, a few writers and artists from the event at Wilhelmein, and a Palestinian woman with a solemn face and dark shiny

hair that spilled over her shoulders in coiled ringlets. Eva opened the
door to us; she was on the phone, and gestured she'd only be a minute.

"Sorry about that," she said, coming over to us after. "Stefan called...
sorting out some dates." Her eyes, I noticed, were bright, unusually
shiny. Stefan was her boyfriend or, as was the customary title in this
country, her partner, currently in Paris, or Geneva. Posted there as...
she'd mentioned, but I'd forgotten. "Foreign correspondent" came to
mind. I asked Santanu.

"He's a journalist, I think...."

"By the way," I said, lowering my voice, "there's nothing unusual on
the dining table." I gestured across the room.

"Do you see the flowers?" he asked.

Standing in the centre was a vase of long-stemmed white lilies.

"No matter where he is, he sends her a fresh bouquet every week."

The room was filled with their fragrance, strong as the scent of longing, rising above the murmur of conversation, Ani Difranco on the
stereo, the tinkle of glasses.

Later, Eva introduced us to her Palestinian acquaintance.

"Santanu, Nem, this is Yara... she's warned me not to introduce her
as a poet."

The girl standing beside her smiled.

We asked her why.

She had the face of a Modigliani painting. Perfectly polished and
oval, with a sharp, pointed chin, and long, prominent nose; only her
hair and eyes were more feisty than anything he ever captured on
canvas.

"Because people look at me with pity. Like poor child... it will be a
tough life." Her voice was pleasantly gravelly, and her words rounded
and deepened over the vowels.

"What do you usually tell them?" asked Santanu. I'd never seen him
look that... delighted by anyone.

She laughed. "That I teach... but it usually elicits the same reaction."

Yara worked as an Arabic tutor at a language centre in the city, where, she said, most of her students were diplomats. Weeks later, she gifted us copies of her chapbook—*How to Survive Breathing*—bound in neat bilingual order, her lines dropping on the pages, visceral, exquisite.

"Is Yara an Arabic name?" asked Santanu.

"Yes, it means small butterfly... but my name seems to belong to everyone... in Brazil yara is a water goddess... for aborigines, a seagull... for the Incas a song of love and death... in Sanskrit, a bright light... I think in Hindi, it means..."

"A friend..." completed Santanu.

"That's right... but my favorite, and I don't know if this is true, is the one from a Native American community..."

What was that, we asked.

"The line of the horizon that separates the stars from the ocean."

That's because you're a poet," teased Eva. "I prefer water goddess... although that also makes you sound like a swimwear model."

Yara said if all else failed, which considering her calling was entirely possible, she'd give it a thought. She turned to Santanu, her eyes charcoal-black, tainted with silver light. "And your name?"

"Hardly as poetic, or as multifarious, I'm afraid... Wholesome..."

"Like porridge?"

Santanu had the grace to laugh with the rest of us.

"And you?" she asked. Her lips were stained with wine.

"Me? It's a Biblical name..."

"I know." Her stare was disconcerting.

I hesitated. "It means builder of new worlds."

Through the evening, we mingled, weaving our way around the room. We settled into informal clusters. Then broke away, refilled our drinks, picked at plates of canapés. Some rolled their Golden Virginia, and stepped out into a tiny balcony that barely fit more than a person at a time. Tamsin smoked too, neat little menthol cigarettes, and I could see Eva keeping her company outside, dark heads bent close together. Laughing, looking at each other in delight. At some point, I found myself next to the writer from Hong Kong—a slight girl named Xia, who reminded me of a sparrow. She was working on a PhD in creative writing at the University of London, and had recently published a collection of short stories. "They span over a hundred years," she explained, "from the 1830s to the handover in 1997."

And what were they about?

As you know, she replied, that's the most difficult question to answer.

We laughed in artistic camaraderie.

"And you?" Her eyes were very dark and very shiny, like polished beads. "I mean, do you also write fiction?"

"No, not really."

"Why?"

I told her I didn't write fiction because I couldn't find the words.

She was quiet—expecting me to elaborate.

That at some point in my life they were taken away from me. By Lenny. By Nicholas.

Just then, we were joined by the Nepalese artist, a shaven-haired youth wearing a paisley-pattern shirt and vintage lunette glasses.

He introduced himself as Nayan, his British accent clear and crisp.

"Have you lived here all your life?" asked Xia.

The artist was drinking whisky, and something about the way he sipped from his glass made me want to touch his lips.

His grandfather, he explained, had served with the Gurkhas; his parents migrated to the UK before he was born.

"When I visit Nepal," he said, "I tell them about autumn. They don't have autumn there... do you like it? What it does to the trees."

I said I too loved the lost season. Was that one of his inspirations? For the artwork on the journal's cover.

He laughed. "Yes. As well as everything else." Mandalas, the cosmos, cells, lace, brocade. The long tradition of geometric and floral patterns of the Far East, the Middle East, the Byzantine and the Baroque.

"How," he slung back the remaining whisky, casually, "is it possible to separate?"

Later, I was alone with Eva in the kitchen. Helping her uncork more wine. It was neat and superciliously clean—white tiles and counters that looked like they'd never seen a grease stain, or spillage of crumbs. In short, a kitchen in which nothing much was cooked. When Eva opened the fridge, I could see why—shelf upon shelf of ready meals from Waitrose, delectable tubs of prepared food. *Tea smoked salmon. Tagliata with rocket and Parmesan. Sea bass filets with samphire and vanilla butter.*

She plucked out a bottle of white wine. A clean, elegant Calvet Pouilly Fumé.

"Who was that man earlier?"

"Which one?" I fumbled with the opener, sending it spinning across the counter.

"Earlier... at the bookstore."

"I don't know." And that, at least, was the truth.

"He gave you something..."

"That—well, I'm not sure really."

"A secret admirer! What did he give you?"

The envelope lay folded in my pocket. I couldn't feel it, but it was there, heavy as stone.

"A note."

"A note?"

"Just an old friend. Nothing important." I hoped I conveyed a nonchalance I didn't feel.

Eva laughed, her hair catching the light. "Alright... I won't pry. Now, will you come with me this Saturday? To see a show by this British-Indian artist..."

I was thankful she hadn't persisted. I wouldn't have liked to be rude, not to her, especially since she seemed to have taken me under her wing, concerned I might feel lost, out of place. Although, now that I'd heard about Stefan, I wondered whether there was something more, that I was filling a gap in the shape of a figure who was always elsewhere.

———

Later that night, I went home with the Nepalese artist.

To his studio flat in Hammersmith. On one side, a hurricane of paper, brushes and paints, on the other a neatly arranged cupboard and double bed. Without his glasses he kept his eyes closed, his lips parted, as I touched him. His fingers dug into my arm, a faint moan, pulling me closer, lifting himself so I could reach easier, quicker, to the softness underneath. While my mouth stayed on him, a silky grip, he laughed at the quick nip of my teeth. I remember his slim shoulders, his burnished seashell-skin, the light from a lamp smoothly slanting off his chest. Above me, he was weightless as a leaf, shaped as one by his ribs, rising and falling. Then we scissored ourselves together, slick and moist. Urgent, clumsy hands. Entangled limbs. A deep-shallow breathing that ended in long, uneven gasps.

He fell asleep, with his hand between my thighs, as though to feel me even in his dreams. Somewhere in the darkness along the edge of the room, a boiler wept and gurgled.

I too was restless.

On the ceiling, I watched fleeing shadows, falling through the window. Outside, on the road, there were shouts, I couldn't tell, of playfulness or anger.

It was past two when I left. I rode the night bus until Embankment and walked the rest of the way home. All along I followed the river; it was high tide and the Thames had swelled its banks, ripe with the sea.

I passed steadily docked boats, lamps burning holes of light into the sky, and solitary figures who vanished like smoke into the night.

When Nicholas wrote the note he was in a place by the sea.

That's what I liked to imagine.

A place by the sea where memories cawed at him as seagulls.

Like him for me, they were alive yet they were ghosts.

I leaned over the railing for a moment; the Thames lay still and seamless. At the horizon, stitched magically, invisibly to the sky. A narrow yet empty expanse, a curiously inverted world. In the summer months a deep twilight lingered long into the night, the sky turning the darkest shade of blue, but never black. It had changed, though, from the end of September, when a certain hardening came over the days. Everything around me chill and brittle.

As I walked, the wide road, with its Victorian houses and avenue of trees, soon morphed into something smaller, less charming, until I lost sight of the river altogether. Eventually, I reached the white and green expanse of Trinity Gardens, and its lofty memorials, bearing the lists of lost ships and sailors. The streets in this part of the city, lined with high-rise glass buildings, were empty. In the evenings, pubs here swarmed with carousing revelers in suits.

I reached a particularly desolate stretch, passed a closed Pret A Manger, and finally came to the small studio flat I was renting, opposite a church. On some evenings, I'd hear bells, and they reminded me of my hometown, the call of worship filling an empty sky.

My room was on the fourth floor, up a musty, narrow flight of stairs lined by an ugly wheat-brown carpet. The room was dark when I entered; I'd forgotten to leave a light on when I left earlier that afternoon. In the corner my bed was wedged between two cupboards, a small couch against a wall, and a writing desk beside a window that overlooked the street. It held a low table lamp, my laptop, a pocket guide to London, and a piece of bric-a-brac, incongruous simply because it was the only one there—a small carved oxen of mottled jade, no higher than a finger. The layout was unelaborate. One door led to the kitchen, a tiny space of shelves and counters fitted like a Rubik's cube, and another to a bathroom with the single most luxurious feature in the apartment—a deep, creamy tub.

I hung up my coat and emptied my pockets. I placed the envelope on the table, and walked into the kitchen, turning on the electric kettle. There was wine in the fridge, but I would settle for tea. The air had cleared my head a little, but the evening's drinks still ran deep and strong. My fingers smelled of the artist.

I paced the room, slipping off my shoes, my jumper. I stood by the window and lifted the blinds—the shape of the church rose up before me, and behind that I imagined the city, carved from shadow and light, rising and falling, an endless tide.

All the while, I tried to ignore it. The white rectangle, light and innocuous as a feather, but it kept pulling me back. An unstoppable ocean current. I glanced at it. Touched to see if it was real.

I'd opened it earlier in the bookshop, while people milled around, drinking wine. Casually, I'd stepped out, and returned before anybody noticed, just in time to be called over by Santanu—"Nem, I'd like you to meet..."

Outside, it was raining, drops slashing into the ground beyond the awning, in silver sideway streaks. The sky had darkened and vanished, and the air glimmered with hidden light. They say looking at a painting is like watching the artists' immediate gestures.

Nothing is more immediate than a handwritten note.

Dear Nehemiah,
My builder of new worlds.
I hope you find your chariot of winged horses.
NP

And if that wasn't cryptic enough, something else fluttered out of the envelope to the ground. A rectangular piece of paper, thicker than the note. I picked it up, wiped it clean—it was a ticket. To a musical performance in London, over a month away. I switched on the laptop on the table. It hummed into life, the screen filling with bright, sudden light. A window within a window. I could search for anything in the world, apart from what I was looking for. I typed the words carefully. "The Orpheus String Quartet", then hit delete and entered "Lauderdale House London" instead. This is where Nicholas wished me to go. Perhaps that's where we would finally meet again.

———

If you visit the Galleria dell'Accademia in Florence, and walk into the hallway where David is displayed, it's difficult to look at anything else. When you enter, he's to the right. And you are suitably entranced. They've positioned him beneath a glorious dome, and he's bathed in natural light. He is an angel. You circle him slowly, gazing up, casting your eyes over his limbs. Studying the shape of perfection carved out of a nineteen-foot block of marble. Your thoughts are sparse, limited by awe. Somehow, words and emotion seem inappropriate, inadequate, out of place.

Yet if you enter and turn left, you encounter something else entirely. Michelangelo's "Prisoners." Placed in a dark corridor, rows of figures commissioned for the never-completed tomb of Pope Julius II. They are unfinished, perpetually wrestling with stone. Unlike most sculptors who built a model and then marked up their block of marble to know where to chip, Michelangelo always sculpted free hand, starting from the front and working his way back. These figures emerge from stone as though surfacing from a pool of water. They will not stun your mind into silence, rather they rouse it. You are moved by their frailty, their endurance. They are endless metaphor. And infinite possibility. Much the same as anything unfinished in our own existence.

We treasure the incomplete, for it lends us many lives—the one we lead and the million others we could have led. We are creatures of inconsistency. Passionately partial. Unexecuted. Unperformed. Undone. Unaccomplished. And un-concluded.

David will only be David.

———

At first, I was gripped by nothing less than exhilaration. The clutch of excitement at inexplicably arbitrary times. While paying for oranges at Tesco's, or waiting to cross the street. Questions flying out like small sharp arrows—Why? How? What did he mean? What would happen now?

And then it faded.

The note transformed into a paperweight. While I wasn't looking, it changed shape.

We are perpetually chained. Compelled to want and not want. To complete and leave incomplete. Eventually, though, the note conjured annoyance. Somehow, even a trace of fear. By meeting Nicholas at the concert, I'd finally acquire what was called a verifiable outcome. It could be changed from the poetic to the quotidian. The lushly imagined to disappointingly real. There would be a continuation. Possibly even an ending.

Quod erat demonstrandum.

What if it couldn't compare to everything I'd imagined all these years?

What if that was all we ever wanted? The things that didn't happen.

As though that was the only way to free ourselves from the responsibilities of the real.

And yet. And yet there was the tug of it.

The sudden proximity of the threads of our lives. Perhaps they'd been running closer than I ever fathomed. Perhaps, in the way that we like to believe these things are fated, we were meant to always touch.

It was a constant swaying. The pendulum-gut feeling of it.

Over many nights, I don't know how long I lay awake in the darkness. Moving fitfully into the hours most deep and silent. The bed soft and warm beneath me, the quilt cast aside. In the distance, the sounds of a police car, an ambulance. The startling emergencies of the night. At some point, I would drift away, without knowing, into the black void of sleep. The next time I opened my eyes it was morning, I would hear the sound of rain. Water. That's what usually woke me. I was searching for water, holding in my hand a blue and silver fish, running through a building that could only appear in dreams—stitched together from many others, familiar but difficult to place. In my dreams, I was looking for a room with an aquarium.

After my fall in the forest, I awoke wrapped in near darkness.

It was a long disorientation, stretched out, those seconds, wondering where you are, when the familiar is veiled momentarily by strangeness. This time, the veil didn't lift. I was in a place I'd never seen before.

The curtains hung thick and voluminous, shielding me from daylight. I reached to my left, touched a bedside lamp, and fumbled to switch it on. It was a large room—easily twice the size of the ones back at the student residence—and the furniture, all heavy, polished wood, looked quietly, confidently luxurious. Both Kalsang and I could probably fit into the cupboard in the corner, a beautiful piece, carved around its edges into something elegant and floral. The full-length standing mirror next to it tilted upwards, reflecting the plain, clean geography of the ceiling. In the centre, a low table held a cluster of carvings—an elephant, a fish, an ox—and a pile of magazines. Not the ones I usually saw in people's homes and my own, Femina or India Today, but thick, glossy foreign publications. Everything struck me as tastefully subdued. The only clemency of color came from a row of paintings on the wall, which now I would recognize as intricate madhubani. At the time, though, the peculiar figures only seemed to amplify the alarm I was beginning to feel.

I'd awakened in a stranger's house, in a stranger's room.

Then I remembered the hands that had lifted me, their careful benignity. They hadn't hurt me last night; nothing would harm me now. The silence was commiserative. In here I was safe.

My clothes, like my surroundings, were also not my own. I'd been stripped of the jeans and t-shirt I was wearing—they were nowhere in sight—and clad in a white shirt, loose yet soft and light as smoke, and a pair of long pajamas that pooled around my feet. Who had changed me? How much, I wondered, had they seen?

I stepped out of bed and stood in front of the mirror.

A dull ache ran down my arms, spreading across my back, my thighs. I was in pieces. Somehow held together by skin. When I peeled away the shirt, I saw it—a deep, greenish-purple bruise on my right shoulder. At the very crest, a finger-width of scraped flesh that had been cleaned, carefully bandaged. Eventually, it healed, but I carry the scar, a flat, lightened reminder, a sliver of white.

Today, I'd awoken. Lenny never would.

If I could, I would have stayed in that room always. The room with no calendar, no clocks. To confront no one. The people whose voices I'd heard. My family. My loss.

From the window, through the leaves of an overhanging neem, I could see a patch of grassy lawn, edged by a sprinkling of flowers—cosmos and begonias. The kind my father planted back home. I would have liked to stay there, swaddled in the comfort of the unfamiliar. The utter newness of things. All around me a blank slate, the fantastic lightness of the unknown. It was a relief. These clothes, this room, the furniture, the paintings, the table, all bearing imprints not my own.

There wasn't any requirement to leave; I could stay here until someone came looking for me. But how long would that be? I supposed I mustn't overreach my welcome.

Yet if I could, I'd climb back into bed, its own kingdom, and pull the covers, cool and smooth, over my head, and pretend, for days, and years, to be asleep.

Finally, I pushed the door open and stepped into a corridor.

To my left, an empty dining room, with the table set for ghosts. On my right, an archway that opened into a spacious drawing room.

This is what I would do: I'd find my host, say thank you, and leave. And ask for my clothes, of course. I couldn't walk away in these.

Yes, I'd say, I was fine now, thank you.

Yesterday... well, I'd come up with an explanation when asked for one. Something probable if I could manage it, fittingly credulous. I ventured into the forest for a walk, and decided to explore the tower. No, I hadn't noticed the sign. How silly of me.

Feeble, but I wasn't sure I could do any better.

I greatly appreciated their kindness, I'd add, the much needed rest, and now I must be on my way back.

Out the door, through the lawn, and the gate. Down the wide, quiet road. The forest. At the other end, the college building. At the back of the campus, the residence hall in which I shared a room with a boy from Tibet. No one else need to know. I'd attend classes, sit for tutorials, write my assignments, speak when spoken to, drink and eat, get into bed and out, one foot in front of the other. Like I was doing now. Like I'd keep doing until I missed a step, or found, like yesterday, that there wasn't any ground to stand on.

I wandered through the bungalow, larger than my house or Lenny's back in my hometown, and different in almost every way—the high ceilings, the bare, cool stone floors, the large, airy windows. Our houses were braced against the weather, long rains and cold winters, everything compact, sternly economic.

Perhaps my impression was reinforced by the emptiness.

Where could everyone be?

Was I the only one there?

It didn't feel right to walk around someone else's house—even if it wasn't done in stealth and secrecy. So instead, I decided, I would wait, politely, in the drawing room, until someone showed up. Surely they'd remember they had an unusual, unlikely guest?

The drawing room windows overlooked the lawn, where a gardener wielded a shovel in one hand and a wicker basket in the other. The length of a large wall was crammed with knick-knacks—souvenirs, I presumed, from journeys around the world. Miniature windmills and wooden clogs. Wooden carvings of human figures. A replica Fabergé egg. Sunny, smiling matryoshka dolls. A pair of Indonesian laughing-weeping masks. A snow globe—the only thing I lifted and shook—with miniature figures of skaters on a pond.

For a while, I sat on an armchair, examining, during my wait, a set of paintings opposite, large canvasses dabbed with flat blocks of rich earthy shades and intense whites.

They hadn't struck me as extraordinarily remarkable then, but some years later, I attended a retrospective of Amrita Sher-Gil's work, and left wondering whether the ones in Rajpur Road were by her hand.

What also drew me was a writing table, littered with letters, written in a long, rounded swirls, each line slanting up at the end. Without willing to, I caught a few phrases—*tonight, I long for you... how many months apart... these trees they only show me your absence...* My eyes moved, inordinately, to the end of the page, where it was signed *All my love, M.* So was the next one, and the next.

They were all from the same person.

I want you in me.

I flushed, placing them back, trying to remember the order in which I'd found them, and moved away from the table. I walked to the oppo-site wall, covered by thick velvety curtains. What would I see from there? A view of the back garden? I drew them aside to reveal a sliding glass door opening into a sheltered veranda.

And there he was, the art historian, bent over an aquarium.

Standing barefoot. His hair falling over his face. The sleeves of his navy cotton shirt clinging wet and limp to his wrists.

He was trying, carefully, to net a fish.

(How vulnerable a person who doesn't know they're being watched. Even the air around them shifts to accommodate their unguarded gestures.)

When I pushed the door open, he looked up, startled, and almost dropped the net. Something leapt out, and slid across the floor. It was a fish, lying there, flapping, gasping for breath it couldn't reach.

"I'm sorry..." I rushed to pick it up.

Silver and blue, on my palm, with eyes like shiny raindrops.

"Come over here, quick." He held out a glass bowl filled with water.

I dropped the fish in; it darted around in fright.

He turned to me. "You're awake."

His eyes were light grey, flecked with silver—or gold?—a peculiar color. Once, I had traveled with my family to Puri on the coast, and we rose early to catch the train back to our hometown.

His eyes were the color of the sea at dawn.

"How are you feeling?" he asked.

"I'm well now, thank you."

"That was quite a fall..." I tried to decipher the expression on his face, but it was cryptic, like the tone of his voice.

"It was stupid of me... to go up."

"Despite the warning."

"Yes, despite the warning." I could feel the warmth climb up my neck, my face.

"I thought I'd take you to the hospital, but you seemed more dazed than hurt. Nothing broken."

If he only knew.

"Thank you... for bringing me back here."

"That's alright." The art historian laughed. "I wasn't sure where else to take you."

"I live close by..." I told him where.

"You're a student there? I hope you aren't thinking of going back for classes today."

Our October term holidays had started, I said, but didn't offer to explain why I hadn't traveled home.

"Good, so you're free to help me clean this..." he gestured to the aquarium. "I think our friend in the bowl may have an infection... I hope it hasn't spread..."

I peered at the tank, at its carefully orchestrated landscape. "It's beautiful."

The fish, with delicate lacy fins, were edged in red and blue. They darted through the water plants, hiding in the nooks and crannies of an arrangement of rocks.

"Firefish. Terribly shy... but, as you just saw, with a surprising propensity to leap when startled."

The water was pristinely clear, and sliver-leafed plant ribbons swayed gently in an invisible current.

I pointed at a creature hidden behind a swirling conch shell. "And that? Is that a..."

"A seahorse."

It was the first time I'd seen one, real and alive. "I didn't think they'd be so... small." Its delicate swerving body, a punctuation of orange-gold, could easily fit in the palm of my hand.

"Yes, deceptive creatures. There should be two in there somewhere..."

"I can't see it."

The art historian leaned over beside me. He smelled of faded musk, and something else, for which, at the time, I had no name.

"There." He pointed to the back. The other seahorse was hidden among the plants, its tail curled around a leaf.

"My sea monsters," he said. "From the Greek *Hippocampus*..."

"These belong to you?"

He nodded. "This aquarium was lying around, unused and empty... so I thought, why not get some fish? Amazing what you can find in the alleyways of Chandni Chowk." He laughed. "This man, who owned the shop, told me he could get me any water creature in the world. So I thought I'd test him. 'Seahorse?' he said, 'No problem, sir. I get for you next week.' And what do you know, he did." He shook his head. "I have no idea how... or from where. Perhaps it's better not to know."

I think it was at this point—despite the bungalow's other sights— that I felt I'd discovered a new world. Entirely unfamiliar, removed from anything I'd known before. Looking at the firefish, the seahorses, I felt a low, electric thrill.

"I could watch them for hours."

The art historian leaned casually against the door. "You're most welcome to."

Was it, could it be, an invitation to return?

Something like joy weled up inside me. Then I thought of Lenny, and it subsided.

"Devi might think you're crazy, but she's patiently put up with all my eccentricities." Devi, he explained, dropped by on weekdays to help with the housework. "If you sit—" he gestured to a chair, "and keep very still... you might see them better..."

I followed his instruction.

Soon, the firefish emerged hesitantly from their hidden places, darting like miniature arrows. The seahorses remained unmoving, patiently watching, their patterned skin intricate and ancient.

All this while I was also keenly expectant, waiting for the art historian to ask a question. He'd want, I was certain, an explanation.

Why I'd been in a tower in a forest, at that time of day.

"I was wondering..." he began, "if you'd like some tea."

"I—yes, please."

He called for Devi, and a woman glided into the drawing room, clad in a floral salwar kurta, loose and comfortable. She carried the authoritative air of having worked there for years.

"Ji, sahib."

It was her voice I'd heard last evening when they brought me into the house. I wondered whether it was her hands that had bathed me and changed my clothes.

"Could we have some chai, please, Devi? Over there..." He pointed to the garden, to wicker chairs under an umbrella.

She nodded and disappeared through the doorway.

After tea, I was resolved, I'd change and leave.

What can I tell you about that morning?

It must have been sunny, for I remember him, for a moment, shading his eyes.

Was I staring? Inadvertently. It might make him uncomfortable. And I, deathly embarrassed. I looked around, pretending that the rest of the lawn's aspect offered as much of interest. In the far corner the gardener coiled a hose pipe; at the gate the watchman dozed.

I wondered who'd rushed to help us yesterday.

What a peculiar sight it must have been.

A disheveled stranger half-carried by the sahib of the house. No odder than now, though, me sitting there in my oversized pajamas, holding a teacup, nibbling on a biscuit.

I was most aware of it at first.

This strange, abrupt unreality. My anomalous presence. The vastness between worlds separated by the Ridge Forest.

"Devi will have them washed for you... although I think your tee-shirt might be ruined."

"Oh."

"You can keep mine if you like..." He glanced at me; my cheeks burned. "The one you're wearing."

I protested, it was kind but I couldn't possibly.

"Why... don't you like it?"

I did, of course, I did.

His mouth flickered in amusement. "Then it's settled."

Was he being kind? Or did he feel this piece of clothing might somehow be... tainted?

"Besides," he added, "it looks much better on you."

I sipped my tea and burnt my tongue again.

"Now"—he settled back in his chair—"there are matters of greater importance to attend to..."

"Yes..." I looked down at the lushness of the grass, his feet, perfectly shaped, shell pink, networked by veins.

"To begin with... your name."

I looked up to see him smiling—and I laughed. I couldn't believe I hadn't told him yet.

"Nehemiah... but everyone calls me Nem."

"And I'm—"

"Nicholas. I know." It sounded much too bold. I added quickly, "I mean, I saw you... I attended your talk in college. It was very good, your talk."

"I'm glad you enjoyed it, Nehemiah." He glanced into the distance, his attention caught by something hidden to me. Over the time we spent together, this would happen often; a moment when he was suddenly, inexplicably elsewhere. An odd habit, annoying, endearing, that I learned to pay no heed to later, but for now, I wasn't sure whether to speak or stay silent. The gardener had disappeared, and the watchman also was nowhere in sight. It was only us in the garden.

This close to noon the day was beginning to grow too warm for comfort—I supposed we'd be moving inside soon. I would then have to leave.

From somewhere rose the cry of crows, and the muted honk of a passing car from the road. It was quiet here, quieter than I thought Delhi could ever be.

"Is this your first time?" I asked. "In India." Then, I regretted it, certain he was similarly queried by everyone he met.

"Why?" He asked with no trace of annoyance or impatience, only curiosity.

"Because... you're not from here. At least, I suppose so... ?"

In the shade, his eyes seemed darker, the color of evening mist.

"The places where I am I always feel I've been to before... isn't that why we're drawn to them? Else, why one city and not the other? Why the mountains? Or the sea? It's fathomable to long for home, the familiar... but why places you've never traveled to? Because somehow we've been there before, and they never leave us."

I looked at him with a quiet grief, remembering Lenny's map on the wall.

"Is that why," I asked quietly, "you bought a house here?"

He laughed, jostling his tea cup, "God no!" This was the family home of a friend. "Malini." He said her name softly, as though speaking it to himself. He'd studied with her in London. She was in Florence, working on her PhD, while her parents were away in the States, living with her bother, for a year.

"She asked if I'd like to be caretaker... while I'm here on fieldwork for my post doc." He glanced over the expanse of the lawn, the sudden, startling expanse of sky, the patient, overhanging trees. "I don't think I'll ever leave."

Malini. They were from her. The letters lying on the table. *I want you in me.*

Otherwise, no one would give up their homes to a stranger. Allowing them into their sacred space.

All my love, M.

I placed the tea cup on the table and said I should be leaving.

"To go where, Nehemiah?"

I told him, wondering if he could have forgotten already.

"Didn't you say it was term holidays?"

"It is."

"Will you not be the only one around?"

Technically, I explained, my roommate hadn't left for home either. "But—I went with him to a party... and he still hasn't returned."

"That's because he's someplace that offers greater delights than a student residence hall."

It wouldn't, I admitted, be too difficult.

He added, "As are you."

What did he mean?

He smiled, a rare, precious gesture brimming with untold kindness. *I was in his closest, most secret circle.*

"I think we always arrive at the places we are drawn to."

———

I will be honest.

My first few days at the bungalow weren't quite the ascent into paradise you might like to imagine. Rather, they were filled with bewilderment.

(And copious amounts of cheese. But I'll get to that in a moment.)

At first, it seemed utterly unbelievable that I was there. And I tried, most fervently, to decipher Nicholas' motives. Was he merely being considerate? Is this what it looked like—the plain, unadorned face of human kindness? No. For it was tinged also by solicitous intent. What Lévinas called *rapport de face à face*. I remembered Nicholas' hands, in the tower, reaching out in concern, hauling me through the forest, lifting me onto the bed. An encounter, made personal, face-to-face, that had installed within him a sense of responsibility for me.

He might have also been provoked by the simple desire for company. Yet his options were undeniably many. From the sophisticated to the fawning, the witty to the erudite. Why did he settle on—for he didn't quite select—me? Convenience perhaps, I was strewn on his path like some hurt, grieving creature. He'd had no choice.

Worse, he probably thought me somehow... unhinged. Emotionally unstable, capable of self harm. He hadn't yet asked why I'd ventured into the forest, the tower. That could only mean he'd come to his own conclusions. All this amounted to one verdict.

Pity.

That most wretched thing.

Well-meaning, misplaced, acerbic.

I tried to catch it in his eyes, when he was unwary, when they alighted secretly upon me, but I found his features cryptic—or maybe they held what I was least expecting, or hadn't imagined. Amusement. Yes, that was it. Perhaps I entertained him. Like a new toy or a disarming pet. Is that what I'd sometimes catch flickering on his face?

Although in my recollection now, I might be inordinately encumbering that time with questions. For there must be something said for youth, its easy, thoughtless flow, and joyous pliancy. He asked me to. And so I did.

I can think of nothing more thrilling.

I wouldn't be able to shape Nicholas' words, to wrench them out of his heart, but apart from all other things, the reason I stayed on at the bungalow was because, there, I never felt unremarkable.

———

One evening—perhaps the first?—after a shower in luxurious solitude, uncommon in a communal residence hall, I joined Nicholas in the veranda. He was seated on the divan, the lamp in the corner burning low, coaxing the areca palm to cast serrated shadows on the floor. The

air was summery yet cool, spiked with a fragrance I couldn't place—
something rich and pungent.

"Do you smoke?" He tossed something at me, a solid, dark green lump.

A friend of Malini's, passing through town a few days ago, had
left behind a tola of Manala hash. Regretfully. But he was flying to
Switzerland, and couldn't bank on their inefficiency. Or his ability to
stuff it... "You know where."

"You mean, his–?" I couldn't mask my alarm.

"His what?"

It was a word I'd only ever used in front of friends, people my own
age. Nicholas was at least a decade (or more) older than me. "His ass..."

"Perhaps. Although, usually, people take the ink cartridge out of a
pen and replace it with a joint."

In the dimly lit veranda I was thankful he couldn't see me flush.

I said I'd share the tola with my roommate Kalsang. If he ever
returned.

"And this..." he gestured to a parcel on the table, "you're welcome to
share with me."

It lay unwrapped and open, source of the mysteriously pervasive
odor in the room. Malini's friend had gifted Nicholas a selection of
cheeses. Hard, aged, and unbeaten by his travels from Europe. Piave,
Gouda, Sbrinz, Comté—names I could hardly get my tongue around.
Fat pale or straw-yellow slices, each reeking of the unfamiliar.

"Help yourself to your favorites," said Nicholas generously.

"I don't know," I faltered. "I've never tried any."

He seemed unperturbed. "Let's find out then..." and he sliced them
there with a pen knife, using *Time* magazine as a cheese board. (What,
I wondered, would Devi think?)

The golden Piave tingled, its sharpness filling my nostrils and mouth,
while the Sbrinz resisted, its hard surface crumbling easily into flakes.
"Oldest cheese in Europe," said Nicholas, and all at once I felt its age, spiced

and heavy, on my tongue. Pale and creamy Comté tasted lightly nutty and floral, like a spring pasture. Before he opened the rest, Nicholas halted, saying that this called for wine. He stepped out and returned shortly with glasses and a bottle. He'd brought it with him to India, and hadn't yet found occasion to open it. "Since tonight we simply must have red..." the cork slid out with a gentle pop; he held it to his nose. "Ah... perfect."

The wine was from a vineyard in Italy, in the north, a dark, ruby Nebbiolo. "The name," he said, swirling the liquid in his glass, "comes from the Italian word for fog... *nebbia*... In October, during harvest, an intense fog settles over the region... they say even the earth weeps, reluctant to give up these beautiful grapes..."

I took a sip and gasped.

"Or it could refer to your hangover the next day."

Even for someone accustomed to frequent doses of Binnie Scot, the Nebbiolo was immensely strong.

For a few days, though, with or without the wine, our meals were a feast. We paired the cheeses with anything we could find in the kitchen—chappatis, fresh mango, lychees, lime pickle—and lived, as Nicholas put it, gloriously lentil-free.

———

On another evening, we stepped outside.

It was exceptionally pleasant, clear, mild and almost full-mooned, and beside me—I could still hardly believe—Nicholas. Moving in his silent, delicate way.

The ground is all memoranda and signatures.

As the night deepened, the world lost its edges.

Around us, the trees were not trees. They were forms freed from their names, soaring into the sky in sudden freedom. Intricate, elaborate mysteries. That is what the darkness does—it removes the burden of having to appear as we usually are.

I could see better than I ever had in daylight.

Somewhere in the east, a pale orange glow throbbed over the horizon; the distant, unsleeping city. Here, though, we were removed, and the universe seemed heightened, offered up solely to us. We may have been its last two remaining inhabitants. That is how I felt, walking with him in the garden, the air shifting in the space between us. That it could only be now, it could only be here, it could only be with him.

This almost happiness.

When we sat, on wicker chairs damp with dew, he threw himself back, looking up at the moon, high in the sky now, veiled by a sheet of rib-bone clouds.

Nicholas. I said his name in silence, wondering when—whether some day I'd dare—say it out loud. *Ni. Cho. Las.*

I too leaned on my chair, tipping back, precariously balanced. A vision upturned, of silvery darkness and the fringes of trees. We'd drunk some wine earlier, and it had settled somewhere behind my eyes, humming in my ears. For now, all the caves that Lenny had hollowed within me were filled with smoke, and sadness—the kind I knew would never go away.

All we are not stares back at what we are.

I must have murmured out aloud, for Nicholas asked if I liked Auden.

"Not me. Lenny... Lenny liked his poetry..."

I don't know if his name brought a heaviness into the air, or into my heart.

"Who's Lenny?"

"He–was my friend... he died."

Nicholas stayed silent, watching from across the table.

There were some complications...

He waited until I'd finished, my trimmed, clinical version—Lenny was "unwell", a mix-up with the medication—then leaned over, placed his hand on my arm, warm, alive. "Cavafy says... *hetani sintomos o oraios bios*... Come," he added quietly, "Shall we go inside?"

He stood and I followed. The garden was wreathed in deepest shadow now, the lawn a dark pool, the moon shielded and lost. Before we reached the bungalow, I stopped and turned toward him.

"What did that mean?" My voice sank in the silence; I hardly dared to look at him.

He leaned closer—I could feel his breath on my face, all mist and seaweed, something sweet—and held me.

"The beautiful life is brief..."

⸺

Other nights, long and restless, saw me lying awake in the room with no clocks or calendars, staring into the darkness. It would creep back, the feeling that I'd splinter into a million pieces. That my breath was caught in my throat.

That's why I'd climbed the tower.

Because I thought from the top, I could breathe.

I'd sit up, listening for the sound of life. It was usually near dawn before I fell into a fitful, dreamless sleep. At times, when I'd wait for the shattering, it would not come. Yet it would still be there, a dull ache, running along my sides, in-between, changing its course when I shifted. I began to realize that was how it was always going to be. Death. Loss. They left their absences, filled with oddly shaped emotions that didn't quite fit, that pressed on this nerve and the other. Life chips away at flesh and bone.

Tell me where you came from. How you survived.

They looked at me with eyes like ancient raindrops, reflecting the sea and everything it carried within its waves.

Once, instead of turning into the guestroom, I continued to the back of the bungalow. Nicholas had left the door open. He was lying in bed, his clothes draped on a chair. Light streamed in through the window, falling on his skin, white as foam. I stood at the door, the threshold rising beneath my feet. He was awake, watching. He raised his hand and beckoned me in.

I crossed wordlessly, the floor cool under my bare feet. It wasn't cold, but I shivered, and my mouth was dry, as though I'd run for miles. He edged to the side; I climbed the bed and lay on the space he'd freed for me. Between us, an inch, no more, and yet it felt like the widest canyon—I couldn't reach across with my hand. Perhaps it wasn't expected of me. Better it stayed still. Unmoving. Until guided.

Until he turned slightly, his breath quick and close on my ear, my cheek.

"I'm thirsty," I blurted. I don't know why, my words formed of nervousness.

He reached to his bedside table, to the jug, tipped it to his lips, then moved his face over mine. When my mouth touched his, it was like kissing an ocean.

The air blue, flecked in dust, the sound only of our breathing.

"Wait," he hissed, "wait."

I had reached below, tugging away the sheet entangled around him. He placed his hand on my chest, spreading wide like a fan from rib to rib—I could feel my heart thump heavy against it as he pushed me back on the bed. He glanced down, laughing, "Although I can see why you're in a hurry..." I turned my face to the side, smiling but self-conscious.

"There's no need to be embarrassed..." He lowered himself, and pressed his hips into mine. I could feel him through the sheet. This time, no words, just a low moan escaped my lips. I could sense this pleased him.

He placed his face on my cheek—an unexpectedly tender gesture— and said, "Why don't you relax..."

I closed my eyes and breathed deeply. The smell of him, sweet and salty, the sharp tang of sweat.

Hesitantly, I raised my hands, this time, placing them gingerly on his waist. I dared not go any further. He was running his tongue over my lips—"Don't kiss me"—and I struggled to stay still, wanting, more than anything in the world, to disobey. It was endless, this dizzying circle, a burning, lilting loop. While in a daze, I realized he was loosening the knot of my shorts, but he didn't slide his hand in immediately, allowing it instead to linger, to smoothen, caress.

When he finally held me, it was a shattering, somewhere in my chest. A weeping.

Yet not in a way that he could tell.

If there were tears he could not see them.

And my gasps were taken for something else.

Only then was there a sense of something like liberation, an absence of the touch of guilt. My fingers dug into his waist. He moved over me like a wave, not needing to touch me for longer. I shivered, arching, everything around me falling away, until all that was left was his closeness with no particular weight, no particular shape.

After I washed, I returned to find him lying on his back, the sheet cast aside. He was slick and silver. I would not, could not, know how to proceed.

When I reached closer, he placed his palm on my shoulder.

I looked up at him, his eyes kindled like ash.

He took my hand and placed it on him, his inner thigh, and leaned over kissing me, tugging on my lower lip.

I was open, as ever, to instruction. To instinct. I felt it might never happen, that I could not make him reach where he made me journey. Too clumsy, I thought in small, rising panic, I am insufficient. I moved quicker, trying to find some secret momentum that I must learn and perfect. Until, finally, his fingers clasped at me, coiling into my hair.

His mouth fell open in a wordless gasp, his chest rising and falling in quick shallow breaths. A long while later, he opened his eyes, now soft and distant, pools of peaceful lead. He smiled and said my name, "Nehemiah."

———

Seahorses are strange creatures.

Upright, they glide, rather than swim, moving with the current. In lieu of scales, their skin stretches thinly over strong bony plates, intricately patterned in stripes, spots, swirls and speckles. Translucent yellow, electric green, liverish red, orange in love. They mate for long, if not for life.

Somewhere in China, they're dried, and powered, dipped into soup, and whisky, believed to bestow everlasting virility and youth.

They belong to that rarest of fish families marked by male pregnancy.

And, most marvellous of all, they dance.

A ritualistic courtship at dawn. They entwine their tails and float in unison, spinning gracefully through the water. They change color. They dip, and rise, coordinated ballet partners in a routine long and exhaustive.

On several occasions, Nicholas and I tried to catch a glimpse of this— especially if we'd been drinking late into the night.

"It's four in the morning... shall we stay up for our piscine lovers?"

Although, maybe they were shy, or, as I offered, not really in love, for we never saw them dance.

"It's a myth."

Perhaps they only danced in the sea.

I've often wondered what happened to the pair in Nicholas' aquarium. Whether he returned them to the resourceful shop owner in Chandni Chowk. If he gave them away to a fellow fish enthusiast in the city. And if he did, to whom? Whether they did or did not survive.

I could ask, I suppose, at the concert for which he'd sent me a ticket.

It was a fortnight away. And I still hadn't decided whether I would attend.

Instead, I drifted. Around me, the London autumn slid into the beginning of winter.

The trees stood bare-branched and barren. Theatrical against the sky, all arms and fingers, reaching out in grief of epic proportion—Elektra mourning Agamemnon, Medea for Jason, Hecuba for Polydorus. And always the wind, the tragic wind.

"It's the best we could do," said Santanu apologetically, when he showed me the room.

"But there's this..." I said, pointing to the window overlooking a small patch of garden, framed by a silver oak, leaves glistening in the rain. "Its perfect."

In there, I met students, revised their assignments, and offered, for what it was worth, handbook advice on craft.

The ones who dropped by brimmed with questions, their faces marked by intent judiciousness. I marveled at their devotion; I didn't remember being as driven or committed as a student. Had things changed so much so quickly?

No. I stand corrected. It had been *years* since I left university.

On the weekends, I'd often meet up with Santanu or Eva, accompanied, sometimes, by Tamsin. They took me to places they thought I might enjoy—an open air play in Regent's Park (rained out right after Olivia declared her unsought love for Cesario), a new tapas place in Islington (the prices as incendiary as the sangria), a walk through Highgate Cemetery (where, for the life of us, we couldn't find Marx), and several art exhibitions. To the Tate, where we were utterly unmoved by Rothko, and the National Gallery, where we stood captured by Caravaggio. His Ragazzo morso da un ramarro. A painting of a youth—voluptuously androgynous—starting back in alarm as a lizard concealed in succulent cherries sank its teeth into his finger. His red, full lips pouting in pain, in pleasure.

One Saturday afternoon, Eva and I were strolling down Whitechapel Road after we'd been to see a show at the Whitechapel gallery—artwork by an immigrant British-Indian artist. Heralded, in the catalogue as an "extraordinary contemporary illusionist", and we could see why. Smashed mirrors and perpetually spinning antique globes, a singing bowl, a rocking-horse unicorn, and tea cups in magically balanced towers.

"Oh," said Eva, "Tamsin would like this."

We were standing under a tree of faces.

Made of fiberglass, with branches ending in waxy molded heads of fantastical creature. Manticores, winged bird-women harpies, crown-headed basilisks, a multitude of dragons, Japanese kappa, and seven-headed naga snakes.

"And look," I pointed, "the Hindu bird-lion Sharabha... he looks ferocious..."

Eva giggled. "Also known as Santanu in a bad mood."

After coffee and cake in the gallery café, we stepped out, hoping to take advantage of a break in the incessant rain. When we reached a junction, curving around an isolated traffic island, I stopped abruptly—

"Is that a winged horse?"

A statue perched on a slender black plinth at the edge of the roundabout.

"That's a dragon..." said Eva.

The creature was painted silver, with details of its wings and tongue picked out in scarlet. Its clawed paws held up the cross and shield of Saint George.

"I think they're a dozen of these around London... they mark the old boundary of the city. Although..." she tilted her head, "it could be a horse... if it weren't for the scary tongue and teeth..."

Eva laughed, "Is this research for a story? My writer friends ask me the strangest things..."

Yes, I replied, it could be.

"Not that I know of... there's the Wellington Arch near Hyde Park Corner... you know, with the angel of peace descending on a chariot of war... but I don't think the horses are winged."

No, they weren't. I'd checked.

"What about the British Museum? Bound to be something there..."

I told her that was exactly where I was headed.

"I would've come along, but I'm meeting Tamsin for drinks... let me know if you find any." She wished me luck, and with a light hug, and a wave, she was gone.

A quick survey of the sky—overcast, overwhelming odds of more rain—and I abandoned my plan to walk to the BM; taking instead the Circle Line up to King's Cross. Even with the summer long ended, and the bulk of tourists long gone, the tube was crowded. This was a city that never emptied. The carriage was crowded with souls journeying underground, across the Thames, or the Styx. Perhaps they were the same river. I watched people staring blank-faced ahead, or peering resolutely into small shining screens, smiling to themselves, their fingers tapping, scrolling, flicking. The rush hour special to Hades. Stuffy, even while the temperature dropped outside. Which was why I preferred standing near the end of the carriage, next to the sign that politely requested passengers to "Keep the window open for ventilation."

Wedged in the corner to my left, a boy no older than twenty, with his hair clipped short along the sides and left to grow out, wavy and loose, on the top, like a musician from the '60s. I took secret sideway glances at his slender features moving in and out of traveling shadow. His mouth a Dionysian ruin, his hazel-green eyes fixed steadily on something unfathomable on the floor. Hard not to notice—the steep fall of his cheeks, the freckles lightly drizzled across his nose. Repeatedly, he settled his hair. Somewhere along the red line, a large group of passengers stepped off. Including him. Leaving the corner empty.

The carriage rocked back and forth, hurtling forward into the tunnel. Somewhere, a child wailed, shrill and merciless. A man stood by the door holding a bouquet of white lilies, a picture of hope. Further down, above the neatly bunned blonde head of a woman, a poem hovered delicately like breath—

You took away all the oceans and all the room.
You gave me my shoe-size in earth with bars around it.
Where did it get you? Nowhere.
You left me my lips, and they shape words, even in silence.

I took the note out of my pocket. Often, I held it in my hand, turned it over, to smooth creamy blankness, and back again. The ink remained as inscrutable as ever.

Winged Horses.

I'd done what anyone else would do. A Google search. Which had thrown up a number of scattering references. The mythical Pegasus, born from Medusa's head, after she was slain by Perseus, the humpbacked horse of a Russian fairy tale, a pub in Basildon, Essex, the definition of a Thestral on Harry Potter Wiki, a book of poems by a Bulgarian writer named Lyubomir Levchev. Compelling stuff, I'm sure, but leading nowhere.

Perhaps, that afternoon, something might be illuminated.

———

In Bloomsbury, I walked past the spectre of Senate House, its bold Art Deco lines towering against the grey clouds, and entered the museum via the back entrance, off Montague Place. Through the spacious Wellcome Trust room and into the Great Court with its high vaulted glass ceiling, soaring above me like a stupendous sky. The section I sought lay beyond the Egyptian and Middle East galleries. Room 14, or "Greek Vases", was wedged between "Athens and Lycia" and "Greece 1050–520 BC", smaller than the others, less crowded. Sparsely furnished apart from tall glass cabinets lining the walls.

I wandered around; uncertain now what I was doing there, or looking for. On the shelves, neatly arranged, edge to edge, were rows of urns, distinct in their black and golden-red colorings, astonishingly fresh and intact.

Impossible to imagine they were a few thousand years old.

There, on a deep, wide *krater*, a depiction of the return of Odysseus, slaying Penelope's suitors. On a glistening rotund amphora, whose handles were shaped as graceful snakes, a ribbon of carousing clay-red figures, holding horns and flowers. Another more slender pitcher with a cup holder at the tip of its neck, showed Poseidon pursuing Amymone. Both kept apart by long mended cracks running along the side. I couldn't remember the word for it... the art of repairing pottery... and understanding that the piece was more beautiful for having been broken.

Studiously, I inspected the vases, moving from one to another.

Yet even after I found it, I was still unsure.

No doubt, the urn was exquisite. A robed Helios perched on a carriage, rising across the curve, his head haloed by the sun, pulled by a quartet of winged horses. There was movement, and lively color, the figures and motifs glazed in a bright burnish against shiny black.

But it told me nothing.

I'd suspected Nicholas wasn't being literal in his note.

I had the strongest feeling he was giving me a clue. I simply wasn't sure what it was meant to lead to, or whether as in some bizarre treasure hunt, they were placed in a sequence. Something, I was certain, was missing. I was peering through a peephole, oblivious to a picture, vaster and more complete beyond me.

Yet wasn't that how it had always been?

With Nicholas. With anything to do with Nicholas.

I could lift moments from my life, hold them, study them closely like rare jewels, and then put them away still wracked with incomprehension.

It could be consumptive. I'd spend hours searching for his name on the Internet. Finding snippets. Fallen crumbs. He'd frequently been a visiting fellow in Turin, an assistant lecturer for a short stint in New York, a talk, a few years ago, at the Asian Institute in Venice. Conferences in Chicago, Brussels. Now that I was searching, I found traces of him everywhere. Currently, he was teaching at a university in a town by the sea. An hour away from London. It was easy, so utterly tantalisingly easy to reach.

A quick ticket, a step into the train. A short, swift journey.

He had never been closer.

———

One evening, Santanu, Yara, and I watched a play.

If that's what it could be called. For Beckett's *Acte sans paroles I* was just that—a mime. An act without words. We strayed far beyond our usual central London comfort zones. Yara, who preferred, as she said, life on the fringes of the city, knew of this theatre in the suburbs, in the far south-east, in a neighborhood below the deep bend of the Thames.

"Do we need a visa?" teased Santanu, as we rattled there, first on a train from King's Cross to London Bridge—swarming with commuters—and then changed to another bound for Deptford. She chose to reply by prodding him in the stomach.

They'd grown comfortable with each other since they'd met at Eva's, it was easy to tell. How she relaxed against his arm in the carriage, how he placed his hand lightly on hers as they alighted and disembarked. We'd discussed it, of course, Eva and I, but when we asked Santanu, he'd say cryptically that "things were proceeding as they were."

"He's infuriating," complained Eva, keen to sweep up credit for having made the introductions, and I agreed too, if only because it was quite flagrantly obvious. When Yara was around, he followed her—not literally, of course—with all the sense of her being there. Aware of her presence, I could see, as a cold traveler of a fire.

So when we stepped out into Deptford High Street, I was unsurprised to see them linking hands, their fingers intertwining in familiar nonchalance. The road was strewn with a hearty ethnic jumble—a Euro-Afro fusion kitchen, Chinese supermarket, Vietnamese restaurant, Halal butchers—and by the time we arrived, the theatre seemed anomalously brown-bricked and quiet. We had a quick drink at the bar, and then moved into the darkened confines of the auditorium.

The stage was bare.

There are few works that stay with me this long. Cavafy's *Ithaca*, Chopin's Nocturne in F major, Hariprasad Chaurasia performing at Music in the Park, Kieslowski's short film about love, Pessoa's *Book of Disquiet*. I suppose the greatest works of performance art become everyone's stories.

It was brief. Pithy. A mere forty minutes.

A person stuck on stage. With clearly no exit. Gifted things, a pair of scissors, a length of rope, cubes of varying sizes, a palm tree. And also things that were taken away. A carafe of water, suspended perpetually out of his reach.

When it ended, the actor stood on a bare stage looking at his hands.

Santanu and Yara discussed it on our way back on the train, quieter now at past eleven.

"It's a behaviourist experiment," he said. "Within a classical myth… you know, what was his name… Tantalus, who stood in a pool of water, which receded when he bent to drink it, and under a fruit tree, which raised its branches every time he reached for food."

"But Tantalus was punished for a reason," said Yara. "Didn't he steal the elixir of the gods, or something? Here, it's not certain the person is being punished for a crime... other than that of existing in the first place."

We'd almost reached London Bridge—from where I'd walk home, and they'd continue elsewhere, together. I thought it more appropriate to make an excuse not to join them.

"And what did you think?" she asked, turning to me.

I shrugged. "It could be a parable."

"Of?"

"Of resignation. One disappointment after another, but yet never learning to stop. Or... it could be, at the end, a small victory... a conscious decision to disobey. Ironically... the protagonist is most active when inert. That's when life acquires meaning."

And that, I decided, was the best way to deal with Nicholas. To do nothing.

———

Instead, I allowed myself to be courted by the city.

I was here for less than a year; it would serve me well to make the most of it. No one, I was adamant, not even Nicholas, could pilfer that from me. This would not be a repetition of Delhi, of that final year at university, when even a sighting of the Ridge from across the college lawn engendered despair. A loss made munificent, more wretched, by being in a place that reminded me, almost constantly, of him. They had once held his presence—the café and senior common room, the shade of the peepal tree, the corridors and forest pathways—and then they didn't. I'd venture often, all resolutions forsaken, past the bungalow on Rajpur Road but it stayed empty; Malini's parents, at least while I was there, did not return. How the pith of those months was a famished longing.

With a fervor, I stomped around, as Eva prefixed it, the "recently fashionable" East End. Not so much for the restaurants and bars in the area—transformed in the last few years from poverty-stricken to gritty, grimy chic—but its liveliness. What Yara said was true; the edges of the city didn't contain the sweet, despairing benignity of places like Bloomsbury and Hampstead, the ostentatious luxury of Kensington and Mayfair, the bourgeois smugness of Richmond. I'd walk from Bethnal Green to Aldgate, and pass seedy balti houses and Sylheti sweet shops, a crumbling mosque, and Huguenot silk stores. I sensed, in the air, the raggedness of Delhi. In the city I'd left behind, waves of history remained as fissures, between buildings and street names, foodstuff and clusters of communities. Here too were invisible fractures, somehow miraculously woven into a human lattice, what a poet called his "giant tempered cloth." People who moved as the birds, across seas and continents. Like the artist who created the fiberglass tree.

There was also adventure close to home.

Once, as I was leaving my front door, I heard the sound of bells.

On an impulse, I crossed the road, and turned into the yellow-stone gateway to the church, topped with a trio of grisly stone-carved skulls. It opened into a small, paved garden with a magnolia tree, drooping with blossoms, and tilting grey tombstones. At the back rested a three-tiered chapel, joined to a square stone and brick tower—"damaged by bombs during the Great War in 1941 and restored in the 1950s."

The church was open but empty, its medieval wooden ceiling rising in an intricate pattern of beams and cross-beams. Pews scattered with hymn books and liturgy, waited in silent, expectant rows. Ceramic saints perched on tall stands with pools of wax at their feet. Behind the altar, a large, ornate window carried a portrait of Christ, oddly similar to the picture hanging above the fireplace in my parents' drawing room—haloed head, pierced palms, and burning sacred heart. I walked around the edges, deciphering the stories on stained-glass windows—

the Annunciation and Last Supper, Jesus at various stages of condemnation and resurrection. On my way out, I almost missed it, hunkering heavily in the shadows, a confession booth of dark wood, elaborately carved around the top and across the plinth. More ornate than the one I was lead to as a child.

Thinking of it now, it was the stuff of nightmares.

I recall my fear in surprising clarity: the cavernous space of our town cathedral, incense-laced, sprinkled with the knuckled fury of praying faithful. That disembodied voice, a hidden priest, floating through the wooden panel. *Through the ministry of the Church, I grant you pardon and absolution for your sin.* And worst, as I grew older, the fact that I wasn't sure which "sins" I should confess. Often, I made them up—a fight, a rude reply, a lie to my History teacher—and embellished them with detail. The same sins, reshuffled and reimagined. Clutching secretly to the ones I didn't mention. My thoughts, my encounters. The things we did, my classmate and I, in nooks and crannies around school. The boy in math tuition. A girl, my sister's friend, who teased and tempted.

So when I was made to repent, to say prayers in succession, muttered quickly back at the pews, I'd always add an extra Hail Mary or Lord's Prayer. Just in case.

My pietical visits grew less frequent, stopping entirely when I moved to Delhi. Nicholas said he found my Catholic upbringing charming—I was destined to live a life joyfully burdened by guilt. Unless...

"Unless what?"

I could be converted to a new faith entirely.

And he'd add something ridiculous: "Come here... let me baptise you."

I smile still when I remember that.

Around me the church lay quiet and empty. No one there to see me creep inside the booth. It was smaller than I remembered, the dark and cloistered interior separated from the world by an intricate filigreed screen. And smelled of damp and faded incense, the sweet, bitter scent of reproach. *Forgive me father, for I have sinned.*

Sometimes, even if there was a listener, there could be no catharsis.

When I stepped outside the church, the bells had stopped ringing and the evening restored to stillness. At the foot of the tower, near the door, stood a young girl, with a sheet of golden hair, wearing a floral skirt and green cardigan.

"Hello." She smiled. She was pretty, younger than twenty, bringing with her all the freshness of the English countryside.

"Are you here for the bell ringers class?"

I shook my head. "I'm not, sorry."

"Alright then." With a wave she disappeared up the stairs, curving steep and narrow.

Often, late at night, instead of heading straight back to my flat, I'd walk across Goodman's Yard and along Mansell Street. Here, the roads were narrower, suddenly bustling, less scrubbed and polished. I'd stop at a late-night kebab shop, run by two Lebanese brothers—one as silent as the other vociferous—and sit at a plastic-topped table that wobbled with every touch. The light was white, falling unabashedly on snotty plastic ketchup bottles, grimy tiled walls, and finger-printed glass counters. But the kebabs were soft and warm, oozing creamy mayo with every bite. Several customers would walk in, pick up their orders at the counter, and stay on for a chat. The quiet brother worked at the back, slicing the meat off gently rolling skewers. He was taller and slighter than his sibling, who usually held court behind a line of wraps laid out in a row like phases of the moon.

Once, they lay forgotten as he told everyone about a whale.

"I'd just arrived in London... thinking, no reason for me to stay, eh? Grey skies, cold feet, no money... what they call the dark days. Ask my brother here?"

I thought I saw his brother nod, slightly, in acknowledgement.

"I was walking along the river... thinking, no reason for me to stay... and then what do I see?"

"What?" murmured his customers.

"Swimming along in the water... And I think, what is that? I'm seeing things. And do you know what it was?"

He placed his hands on the counter—"A whale."

There was a clamor of disbelief.

"I'm not kidding you... you think I'm kidding you? It was a fucking whale. And I think, if that whale is staying..." he gestured at himself, "I'm staying."

The tiny shop rippled with laughter. He waved his hand at them, and began doling out the fillings, quick and expert at his job. A dab of tomato and onion, a generous sprinkle of ribboned lettuce.

"What happened to the whale?" I asked. "Is it still there?"

He threw his hands up in the air, "The thing went and died. But... Al-h̩amdu lillāh ... I'm still here..."

I finished the sugary soft drink, the fizz dying in my throat.

"Ma'assalama," the owner called as I left.

Ma'assalama.

I held this close because it hinted at prophecy.

He, a modern-day Cassandra, and I, the only one in the world to believe him.

Isn't that what we all search for? A sign, a purported signal of things to come, a pointer, a marker of how life would unfurl before us.

Prophecies are the most scientific of supernatural phenomena, for they, like science, invest in a single outcome. The one truth.

And yet. And yet the universe is forever shifting, swelling with infinite possibilities and infinite outcomes. The power of prophecies lie in their self-fulfilment. They are the intentional narrowing of time, when the future, though wide and ever-altering, tapers into a door through which you walk, each moment constantly congealing into the present, forming a corridor, a line on a map, an indication of the hereafter. Prophecies can be snatched at will, and systematically contained by our own decisions, by our own beliefs that something will definitely, maybe come true.

The oddest encounter I might have had in London was when I once went seeking a pint.

"Drink?" I texted Santanu.

But he was with Yara. "Tomorrow?" he messaged back.

"Sure," I replied, but I was keen for something now.

I walked past the entrance to King's Cross underground station, the lime green shop front of Whistlestop, and decided to turn off the busy main road just before a crowded McDonalds. I was on York Way, running along the side of the bricked station building, its line of archways hidden behind scaffolding. London was a city of constant "improvements", a frenetic, relentless cycle of debilitation and renewal.

Everything within it, in turn, constantly updated. Everything apart from the light.

London was filled with old light.

Soon, I realized, that perhaps I hadn't wandered down the most suitable of directions.

It was a quiet road; I passed a Nando's and a Premier Inn, and to my left, a parked line of empty red double decker buses. A sudden, virulent intrusion of color. After a small B&B, I took a right, since the road straight ahead only threatened to turn wide and industrial. Running along the sidewalk, a fenced patch of land held the remains of a recently demolished building, while on the other side more airy scaffolding restricted the road. Even if there were any bars under all that tarpaulin, they couldn't be seen. Just where the scaffolding ended, though, at the edge of the row of buildings, stood what looked like a neighborhood pub—a signboard announced "Central Station." A line of miniature, faded Union Jacks fluttered over two round-arch windows, while above an unused door—"Entrance on the Other Side"—perched the back of an ancient air conditioner, the type I had seen only in India.

I rounded the corner; a set of wrought iron steps led to the entrance. A trio of men stood outside, smoking, holding pints. It was a pub, after all, one like so many others, with sticky tables, tatty printed carpet, cheap chandelier, and, most characteristically, the pervasive lingering smell of stale beer. I ordered a pale ale (nothing new or exciting for Santanu to add to his list), and sat on a high stool, prepared to finish it quietly and leave. The bartender, I noted, could easily double as a bouncer, with his gym-toned arms, heavily tattooed in Celtic patterns, and a chest designed for tight tee-shirts. He sported a clipped salt-and-pepper beard and neatly slicked Mohawk. Not someone, I thought, with whom I would pick a fight.

"Hello darling..." she called to the bartender. Her voice was deeper than a woman's, but not entirely unfeminine. He pushed a bunch of key across, which she picked up and jiggled in the air.

"Laters."

She headed back out, her heels clicking sharply against the floor. I nursed my pint, looking around surreptitiously, observing only now that among the people there, mostly middle-aged men, sat a few trans ladies, some more casually dressed than others.

I also noticed—and this I thought odd—the dull thud of techno, its musical beat muted yet filtering dully into the room.

"Is there a nightclub around here?" I asked the bartender, who was wiping the counter clean.

"Yeah mate, Sweet Saturdays' downstairs."

"It's open... now?" In my limited experience, most nightclubs were shut during the day.

"Yup... one to nine pm. Really rolling today." He winked, giving me a friendly smile.

The music beat steadily, a faraway, muffled heart. Outside, the street lay quiet and unobtrusive, bathed in tepid afternoon light; somehow an incongruous place for a club. Unless, and this would be understandable, they were intentionally seeking discretion.

When I finished my pint, I asked the bartender for directions.

"Out the front, door to your right."

It was a massive, sturdy door with the letters UNDERGROUND painted vertically on the side. I stood there wondering how to get in, when it sprung open, allowing a group of men out, music flooding over them in a wave. The stairs were steely silver, and rung curiously under my feet. At the end, the narrow foyer was painted electric blue, and a silky scarlet cloth dangled from the ceiling with "Sweet Saturdays' speled out in sparkly gold. One side led to the toilets, the other to a small cloak room, and a more spacious lounge area—velvet cushioned sofas littered with lounging figures, and a dimly-lit bar. The lady who'd picked up the keys upstairs was behind the counter.

Most people were in the space beyond a curtained doorway.

I stepped through into darkness.

The only light came from a large screen on a wall, showing a man sucking off another on a bed draped with white gauzy muslin.

Small bulbs along the ceiling seams cast a reddish-purple haze, more for concealment than illumination. Low tables were arranged in a line, and opposite, a row of black-clothed cubicles. Around me rose shouts and laughter, figures bumping against me as they stumbled past.

Someone whispered, "Pretty boy."

I looked around, at the cross dressers in lingerie and the trans women with their immaculate hair and make-up, boisterous, playful. The atmosphere was carnivalesque.

What struck me most, though, were the men.

Spilling through the rooms, standing against the walls like silent door guardians, holding their drinks and watching, a few sitting at the tables with the ladies. How they looked so ordinary, as though you could pass them on the street, or in a supermarket, share elevators or neighboring tables at a pub. In their Marks & Spencer suits and NEXT blazers, their Clarks shoes and Topshop t-shirts, the utter workaday, nondescriptness of things. Yet, as they avoided each other in this dark, airless dungeon, it felt as though most of them had things to hide. That embracing this place was something men did when hidden from others, outside of the track of acceptable conversation.

And the air was rich with it, a soup of sweat and stale beer, and strains of other things, embarrassment, excitement, fear, and a deep, sickly sweet odor of spent desire.

I'd read a news story once, about a man who built a secret network of passages under his house, discovered by his family only after his death. An unexplained intricate labyrinth, like "the workings of his mind" his daughter was quoted as saying, and this dungeon reminded me of that. It was carved into smaller sections—some with screens showing movies, or video cameras that clients could use to film themselves. In corners, people fondled and touched, others moved to a line of black-clothed cubicles whose curtains could be drawn shut, although many left them open, expecting, desiring to be watched.

A tall, black trans lady who seemed to be in charge, in a white chiffon top and skinny leather trousers, sashayed around, calling out to regulars, stopping to flirt, refilling people's drinks.

From where I was standing, I could see into several open-curtain cubicles—a trans lady in a corset and lace stockings gave somebody a lap dance, while an audience gathered and gazed. Next door, a man in his mid-twenties, probably the youngest there, wearing a sweatshirt and a yellow coppola, was being handled by an older trans woman in a flamboyant red dress. In a cubicle in the corner, the curtains were tantalizingly not completely drawn; I wasn't sure whether it was an invitation to spy, or whether, the occupants hadn't noticed the gap. I could see the profile of a man, probably in his sixties, looking down, watching, then lifting his head in rapture. He seemed engrossed, oblivious to the clamor around him. The other curtains were closely drawn.

"Can I get you anything, darling?" It was the hostess, her perfume strong and musky. Silver bracelets tinkled on her wrist.

"I'm alright, thank you."

She winked, "Okay, my beautiful."

———

"It's a convenient place," I told Santanu a week later, "if you fancy a spot of cross dressing."

He shrugged. "Plenty of those around London. There's one for feet fetishes, furry creature costumes... forniphilia clubs–"

"What's that?"

"The act of positioning a person as a piece of furniture... so you can combine sex with your love of interior design."

"I heard I didn't miss much at the art show." He was referring to the one in Whitechapel.

"Didn't Eva tell you what we saw?"

He nodded. "That's what I mean."

"You're a Bengali," I said. "For you, modern Indian art began and ended with Rabindranath Tagore."

"Yes."

In 1961, Italian artist Piero Manzoni sealed ninety cans containing his feces, thirty grams each, and calculated their value in accordance with the daily exchange rates for gold. Helpfully labeled "Conservata al naturale". Freshly preserved.

"The Tate has number 4," said Santanu, "the man's a genius."

"I'm afraid this nice young lady only made a fiberglass tree, with mythical beasts for leaves. And a rocking unicorn."

"No good," said Santanu. "Either you comprehend the specular self-sufficiency of the artist's body. Or you don't."

"In which case, everyone should be experimenting with farts or crap."

"You said it, my friend, I didn't."

The evening stirred to life as we passed the station, lit up by crowds and lights. A busker sang an Oasis song. *Back beat, the word is on the street that the fire in your heart is out...* A man with a bull terrier held out copies of the Big Issue. We kept our heads down, pushing through people, pressing our hands into our coats. The way to Camden was dotted with overflowing pubs and restaurants, and oddly quiet stretches where boys with beer cans gathered on the sidewalk, attracted to the dark like nocturnal animals.

We talked about a movie we'd watched together earlier that afternoon at the Prince Charles theatre. *Fish Tank.* About a girl who lived in a housing estate, a desperate dancer, trying to free a white horse from behind barbed wires. Our conversation drifted—a new Japanese shop near Green Park selling wagashi, delicate, rice-powder sweets in the shape of seasonal flowers. Plans for the holidays next month in December.

"Don't say I didn't warn you... but there's a work party you'll have to attend."

I said I didn't mind, that I hadn't made other plans anyway.

"You should travel out of the city if you get a chance," he said. "Do you have friends outside London?"

"No, not really."

"What about that guy from when we were in university?"

"Who?"

"The academic... wasn't he Brit? Didn't you know him well?"

A double-decker roared dully past us.

Nicholas and I only ever casually acknowledged each other if we met in college, and I'd walk away burning with the knowledge that I'd see him later, more privately, back in the bungalow. As far as I knew, we'd been careful, there'd been no "talk", not like with Adheer, who'd sought him out relentlessly, carelessly. Santanu's voice betrayed nothing more than casual interest, though, so perhaps—in my small panic—I was reading far too much into, what could be, an innocuous query.

"We lost touch."

"Pity."

I was silent, my breath misting in the cold air.

He continued, "Still, you should get out for a bit."

"I will," I said. "It's been good though... Eva always has something planned."

"That's because Stefan isn't around. Once he's back, she'll vanish like a bubble... for a month or two. Until, that is, he leaves again."

"He's never there... it can't be easy."

"Not as hard as it used to be..." While in college in Delhi, he said, he was seeing a girl in Calcutta. They'd write letters, speak to each other once a week. "I'd save up to call from a PCO. We managed that way until she also came to London the first year I was here."

"And then?"

"We broke up."

Camden High Street throbbed with life and music. Its early Victorian buildings, with open fronts, flat roofs, and boldly painted façades, taken over by tattoo parlours, vintage shops, and used records stores. Now, though, bars and clubs stayed open, their music thudding out onto litter-strewn sidewalks. We passed a number of seedy betting shops and cash points, a pub called At World's End and an extensive selection of cheap fast food joints.

"Where the hell is this place?" muttered Santanu, whipping out his phone. Following GPS instructions, we took a left into a tangle of narrow alleys, and crossed an empty yard, used during the day as an open-air market—skeletal stalls were piled along its sides. At the far end, I glimpsed the glimmering waters of Regent's canal. We walked toward a line of restaurants, quieter than the ones we'd passed on the high street. Youngsters smoked outside a place that called itself The Mexican; they all looked in their mid-twenties—a huddle of skinny jeans, fitted jackets and converse trainers. One girl, with cropped blonde hair, wearing a black floral dress and red buckle shoes, was holding up a phone, and taking photographs of her friends. Another, in a long patchwork skirt, was rolling a cigarette.

The Mexican was compact and crowded—a bar ran down the length of the room, ending just before an open space for tables and a small performance platform in front of a window that overlooked the canal. We ordered our drinks and joined Eva at a table she'd reserved. She was sitting alone.

"Where's Tamsin?" we asked.

"Oh... she couldn't make it. She... she's down with the flu."

"Are you feeling alright?" I slipped into the seat beside her. Her eyes were unusually red-rimmed and tired.

"Yes... yes..." She laughed, a little, I thought, nervously. "I might've picked up a bug too."

"Here," I said, pushing my drink toward her. "Nothing a Bloody Maria can't vanquish."

Soon, the crowd settled and quietened. Everyone's attention drawn to the musician. That evening, a dark-eyed girl from Portugal, wildly beautiful, with a face that reminded me of a seashell.

"Boa tarde, everybody." Her voice was surprisingly deep, rolling over us like a plume of smoke. "I'm Mariana... Thank you all for coming." She plucked at the guitar, her fingers slender and nimble. "I'll play a selection of my songs for you tonight... written over these past few years, and now to be compiled in an album. This first song... was written when I visited America... and it's about road trips."

She was a deft, soulful musician—lingering on the slow and dreamy, moving between Portuguese and English. Her voice molded the air, sweetly melodious, a sultry rasp lingering at the edges of her notes. Sometimes, she closed her eyes. Or gazed at the people sitting closest to her in the front. Toward the back. She played for almost an hour. When the show ended, there were cries for an encore.

She laughed and strummed her guitar casually. Easily like Lenny.

This next number was special, she said. Even though she hardly played it. It was called Dead Birds. "It's a song about leaving and moving on. Migration. Going forward. It's about leaving my family mainly... but also people and a country that were making me unhappy and holding me back. Leaving people who don't dream, don't take risks, don't try to live life fully and are scared of everything, and try to keep you in a cage too. Dead birds. It's about being forced to leave people who're making you unhappy, even if you love them. I guess it also carries a certain amount of guilt for not being able to save them, for turning my back on them. It's a very sad song. When I started writing it I couldn't even play it to myself..."

Amanhã
Não vai voltar
Amanhã
Não vai voltar
E se eu quiser lá chegar
Não vou voltar
Não vou voltar
Dead birds
Don't ever smile
Dead birds
So scared to fly
And that's why we left years ago
We had to grow
And off we go

It peeled away the skin around my heart.

When it ended, there was long, ardent applause. The musician stepped away gracefully, laughing, taking a bow. Then the murmur of conversation returned, people moved to the bar to refill their drinks, turned to talk to each other. I played with my glass, long empty. Eva, I noticed, was similarly muted. Santanu, on the other hand, had his phone out to write a text. When he was done, he said he was leaving.

"What? Why?"

To meet Yara in Brixton.

"Brixton?" said Eva.

"Yes, what's wrong with Brixton?"

"Nothing... only it's quite far."

"Which is why... sorry guys... I'm leaving now..." He gathered his coat draped on the chair, wound a woollen scarf around his neck, and headed outside.

"Five seconds," said Eva later, as we walked to the tube station. "That's how long it took for him to be out the door. He even left his pint unfinished." We were convinced. He must truly be in love.

It was half-past ten, and the streets of Camden were still buoyantly alive—youngsters shouted and play-fought across sidewalks. Despite the biting cold, people spilled out to smoke, clutching at their glasses and coats. At the station, oddly, the crowd lightened. Bright, white light reflecting off the corridor tiles made me feel as though I were in a hospital. A solitary black man busked on a saxophone, the sound echoing through the station in strange, rich echoes. *Dream a little dream of me.* Eva dropped a few coins into his hat as we passed by. He nodded in acknowledgement, not missing a beat. The Northern line carriage we stepped into was mostly empty, clattering in the darkness. A couple nearby, madly tattooed, sat in silence, punching the keypads on their phones. Further down, a group of inebriated youth, mostly male and white, loudly declared their allegiance to a football team. Names scattered past—Mornington Crescent, Euston, Warren Street, Goodge Street, Tottenham Court Road. I'd get off at Embankment, as I usually did, and walk home. Eva would change to the District Line.

When we got there, though, she seemed reluctant to part. "Do you... are you hungry?

I shrugged. "Sure." I didn't feel like going home either.

"Come, I know just the place."

Chinatown, around the corner from Leicester Square, lay waiting like a colorful golden-red surprise. With its elaborate gated archway, strings of paper lanterns criss-crossing the sky, and shops gaily lit up in yellow, orange and white. Its restaurants with rows of whole roasted duck, skewered and hung at display windows. Pasted on walls, posters for ingredients I hadn't come across before, bars hidden in shadowy crevices. We stopped at Café Hong Kong, a deftly functional yet disarming place, divided into compact cubicles with wooden benches and tables. It looked more like a canteen than a restaurant. Blue fairy lights, strung perfunctorily along the walls, illuminated unframed Chinese movie posters—*Tai Chi Hero, Moon Warriors, City Under Siege*. Our waiter, dressed in a red and black striped uniform, hovered nearby as we studied the menu. The list was helpfully accompanied by pictures—food, if it were to be believed, that looked uniformly glazed in something shiny, like clear melted plastic.

"Minced beef thick soup." For me.

"Luo Han Zai Beancurd." For Eva.

The waiter jotted it down.

"And a Tiger beer," I added.

"Make that two."

A few booths down sat a noisy, giggly trio—two Chinese boys and a girl—incongruously well-dressed for the venue, repeatedly holding out their iPhones to each other. In one corner, a couple—they could have been Indian—whispered, intertwining fingers across the table.

At another, a large mixed group of friends, what were called "young working professionals," had come to the end of their meal.

While we waited, Cantopop streamed over the speakers in synthesized sweetness. The singer belted out verse after heartfelt verse before the song dissolved in a drizzle of piano notes. Eva and I glanced at each other; despite the traces of sadness that had clung to us in Camden, we smiled.

"The first time I came here was with Stefan... I tell him that this music will now forever remind me of him."

The waiter deposited our beer on the table.

"To Stefan," I said, tapping the side of my bottle against hers.

She smiled, but didn't echo the toast.

"When's he next in town?" I asked casually.

"Oh, soon, I should think."

I'd read about a Garry Winogrand retrospective opening someplace soon; perhaps we could catch it together?

"Yes, of course, we could."

At times like these, I didn't know whether to enquire further, to ask about how it was between them, whether it took its toll, being apart. We talked freely about things easy to discuss—art, music, the weather— but little else more intimate, unless it was Santanu and Yara, or someone else at work embroiled in some stage of emotional engagement or error. Eva and I were friends, yes, but there was something in her deeply of this island. Reserved, closely guarded. A secret core wedged within an ancient coastal shelf.

The moment hung in awkward silence before it was saved by the waiter.

On my mat, he placed a wide, deep bowl brimming with meat topped with spring onions. And on Eva's, a plate of noodles with an assortment of vegetables and tofu. We ate briskly, and quietly. Eva spiked her noodles with the chopsticks, twisting and turning them with expert ease.

"I wonder..." she said suddenly, as though continuing a conversation she'd started in her head, "how inextricably bound some relationships are to particular places. Can we imagine ourselves with a person elsewhere? Under other circumstances. Would everything fall apart in another city? Another time in our lives?"

I coughed; my soup was strong and spicy, heavy with the saltiness of meat.

"I guess what's important is not the place, but how it changes you... or the other person.

"That's what I thought too... but now I feel it's the other way round... how a city is changed for you by someone else."

"As for the timing of fate..." I placed my chopsticks aside, "the measurement of serendipity...."

The latest offering over the speakers began with a melancholic pluck of piano keys.

Whatever else it may be, we decided, fate was not quite as predictable as Cantopop.

———

Later, our steps followed the streets of China Town as they wove their illicit way into Soho. Half a century ago, it might have been wholesomely disreputable, but the place was touched now by an unmistakeable orchestration. Girls at doorways in corsets and pantyhose, lurid signs at sex shop display windows and strip clubs—arranged as sets for a movie, or an extravagant performance for visitors. We walked faster, keen to get away, passing the Windmill Theatre with its red neon lights, scars in the surrounding darkness.

"I don't feel like going home yet... do you?" said Eva. "Shall we walk by the river?"

The Embankment was almost all ours; the chill of the evening had driven people indoors or away from the breezy banks of the Thames.

All along, lights glimmered on the water like fallen stars. Across the river, the London eye made a bright, angel-white circle against the sky.

"Did it make you sad?" she asked. "That last song..."

Something about the moment would have made it wrong to lie.

"Her voice did something similar," I said.

She stayed silent, her breath releasing as winter mist.

I felt my admission might prompt something similarly confidential from her, that she would begin to explain why the song was still on her mind. There was space for it, a gap in the air, waiting for her words.

Instead, she placed her gloved hand into the crook of my arm, and we strolled on.

We were near Tower Hill now, close to Trinity Square with its giant white memorials and garden. To our left, the tower complex hunkered in a silent splendour, its ramparts and turrets glowing under the gaze of strategically-placed lights.

"Would it be alright," Eva asked hesitantly, "if we could drop by your place?"

She'd like to use the loo, please, and request a taxi pick-up from there. It was too late now to take the tube.

We cut across through Seething Lane, past its odd jumble of steel-glass façades and graceful arched Victorian doorways. The church gateway was chained and locked; the garden beyond it lost in darkness. I let her into my building, flicked on the light, a little embarrassed by the place. I wished the carpet was newer, the walls more freshly painted, and the strange mushroom-damp odor be magically eliminated. "This," she said as she stepped into my tiny studio, "is charming."

She deposited her coat and bag on the chair; I pulled out another, unused, from the corner. I hadn't had guests over yet; it was always easier to meet elsewhere.

"Wine?" I offered, as she exited the bathroom.

"Why not?"

She picked up the concert ticket from the table and inspected it. "You're going to Lauderdale? I've been there once... it's a lovely place."

"Yes... I'm meeting an old friend."

"I haven't heard of this quartet... do you know who they are?"

I shook my head. She gestured to my computer—"May I?"—and typed quickly, without looking at the keyboard. "Here we are... no... I don't know them..." Gently, she shut the laptop. Next to it, stood the jade ox; she picked it up and placed it on her palm, stroking its curved horns, its smooth nose. "It's beautiful."

"I found it... many years ago. In a friend's house." *In a room with no clocks, no calendars.*

"The same friend?" she asked. "The one you went with for a walk in the forest."

The wine blazed down my throat, through my chest.

"No... he passed away."

"I'm sorry." She looked wounded that she'd asked the question.

"It was a long time ago..."

She placed her hand on my shoulder, lightly. A small gesture I'll always carry.

"I noticed you too were quiet after the song..." I ventured.

She swirled her glass, the wine sloshing to the top. For a while, she stayed silent, watching the blink of a helicopter move across the London sky, a pinprick of red-white light.

"Two years ago, when Stefan left for Beirut, people would ask me how I was doing, and I'd tell them this silly little Japanese folktale..."

"Which one?"

"The one about Tanabata. Have you heard of it? The story goes that Orihime, daughter of the Sky King, wove cloth by the bank of the Milky Way... the heavenly river. Then she met Hikoboshi, a cow herder, who lived on the other side, and they fell in love, and were married. But now she no longer wove for her father, so in anger, he separated the two lovers across the river... until, moved by his daughter's grief, he allowed them to meet on the seventh day of the seventh month. The first time, they couldn't cross because there was no bridge. Orihime cried so hard that a flock of magpies flew down and promised to build one with their wings. They say if it rains on Tanabata, the magpies cannot come and the two lovers must wait another year to meet. Then I'd smile and say, 'I'm waiting for the magpies.'" She sipped deeply from her glass. "Nauseating, isn't it?"

I was about to protest when she added, "Especially since I think there'll no longer be a need for magpies."

Avian or not, this was the closest she'd come to talking with me about her relationship with Stefan. Aided, perhaps, by the mingling of a multitude of beverages through the evening, but also something I hadn't noticed before. A quiet sadness. What, I asked cautiously, did she mean?

"It's hard to imagine sometimes, but it wasn't always this way... Stefan and I lived in London... we were happy." She said it simply, as though there was nothing else to add, that the word, by itself, contained every-thing. "Then he lost his job, and after ages found this one. A six-month contract to begin with... which seemed like nothing, really. Then, it was extended. And again. And yet again. He was meant to be back end of this year, but a few months ago, he called... and it was the same old story... He said he knew this wasn't what we wanted or planned, but with things being the way they are... and we're talking about jobs in journalism here... he felt he had little choice. Except it means he'll be away six more months. People wonder why I don't move to Beirut, but how can we plan such things when our lives move in half-yearly instal-ments like some sort of terrible repayment plan?"

"Would you like to move to Beirut?"

She shrugged. "I liked visiting the city... I don't know. My life is here."

"And his?" I asked.

"Here... or at least it used to be. Now... and it's understandable... I'm not so sure." The glass she held was empty, but she hadn't noticed. "Before he left the first time, he promised to send me a reminder each week, to mark the passing of time..."

I said I'd seen the lilies; they were beautiful.

"It was romantic, at first, even exhilarating... now they feel like a notch on a prison wall."

I struggled, and failed, to find appropriate words. Did this call for anger? Or commiseration? *I know what it feels like to be left behind.*

"I imagine," I said feebly, "it isn't easy."

"No," she said, staring hard at the floor. "But not for the reasons you imagine..."

In a moment, like a trick of light, her face had rearranged. Banished, that quiet sadness. Replaced by something more circumspect. She stood up briskly, as though that space, the chair, was tainted, and moved to the window. In her green dress, she looked like a slender leaf. She spoke softly, almost to herself.

"Not *only* for the reasons you imagine..."

"Is there something else?" I couldn't bring myself to say "someone."

I couldn't see her face, but her voice was small and tense. "I don't know..." Then she turned, suddenly vehement, "No, to think that is to demean it..."

She paced the length of my studio; she hadn't far to cover. "How hard I tried, Nem... I avoided them all, those casual meetings... you know, to invert a Japanese proverb, burn your house to rid it of mice... careful not to place myself in situations where... well... things *may* happen..." She stopped and laughed. "At one point, I even turned down drinks with Santanu."

In my mind, I tried to discern a face, who it was that she could have met, but it remained misted.

"I stayed home on weekends, on holidays when I couldn't travel to see

Stefan... I didn't meet friends... well, by the end I didn't have that many to meet. Who'd want to be around a moper? Talking incessantly about someone who wasn't even there. I ended up working hours overtime, just to keep myself busy, but fortunately that's when Tamsin joined us..."

She glanced at me, as though to gauge how I'd react to the mention of her name.

London can be the world's loneliest city.

Eva sat back down; her face pale with tiredness.

This time, I reached out, and placed my hand on her shoulder, lightly.

She turned to me, "Nem, I don't know if–"

"There's no need to explain..."

Her eyes held everything.

———

After she left, I sat at the table, in the sudden strange emptiness of the room.

All that remained was the faintest trace of her perfume. It was late, but sleep was more distant than dawn. I poured the rest of the wine into my glass, filling it uncouthly to the brim. Leaning back in my chair, I allowed the silence to quiet me.

She'd used the word close. *Close.* Suspended between us like a snow-flake, vapourising without further explanation. Now it lay in my hands, entirely pliable.

Tamsin would visit often, she'd said. Spend long evenings at her flat, where they'd grow sated on botched homemade sushi and sake and laughter. Sometimes, it would get too late for her to travel back to her shared apartment in Tuffnell Park. They'd watch movies, stay up late, and talk. "It just seemed," she said, "so... uncomplicated."

My imaginings were shaped by memory, a night long ago, a party when I was in university. Or had it been a dream? A lamp-lit room. A small window. Two figures on the bed. Fingers swirling over skin and clothes. Slow, delicate circles. Fiercely interlaced. A slight tilt of the head. A dip closer. The taste of menthol and longing.

There's no beginning and there is no end.

Perhaps it had also been that seamless for Tamsin and Eva.

Their touch, time after time, over weeks and months, turning shield and saviour against the world.

"Have you ever..."

"No," she'd flushed.

For both, she'd said quietly, it was something new.

"What about..."

"Stefan?" A prolonged silence. Sudden sharp resentment. That, didn't I see, if it wasn't for him, it wouldn't be... like this.

I know what it feels like to be left behind.

And as I walked her downstairs, to her waiting taxi, a last burst of incredulity. "It is impossible."

To truly map ourselves. To fully navigate the rooms we carve in our hearts.

I could now feel the press of tiredness mingled with a strange empty desire.

I thought of the Nepalese artist. His seashell skin. Weightless as a leaf. I wanted him to hold me as he did when he fell asleep.

Of Nicholas. His kiss like an ocean. The smell I could not name. I wanted to lie with someone beside me. Pluck them out of my memory, and arrange them here, whole. Why couldn't we do so when we carried everyone within ourselves? I looked around the studio; struck by its blankness. How could it be so physically bereft of its own past? I held the jade figurine, suddenly wishing to fling it against the wall, so it was marked or broken. Nicholas was wrong; things, even art, didn't carry laden histories. Only people did.

I placed my glass on the table, half-empty, and flipped the laptop open. Perhaps I'd write to the Nepalese artist... and see if he was willing to make plans to meet; I could travel, soon, to his flat in Hammersmith. Or I'd invite him here. The screen glowed; a page came up. The one Eva had opened earlier that evening. The Orpheus String Quartet. A list of its members. Andrew Drummond, Myra Templeton, Elaine Parker, Owen Lee. I glanced back, lassoed by a name.

Myra.

I opened a few new windows, clicked on several links.

It was her. Nicholas' step-sister. All this while, I'd focused solely on the note; I hadn't really given a thought to the ticket. The clue. It was here all along. I picked up the jade carving. It sat on my palm, its smooth surface reflecting light.

If nothing else all things are amulets.

The wedges that fill us where we are incomplete.

I turned the figurine over in my hand. It was cool against my skin, heavy as memory.

My-ra. Swift as the space of a heartbeat.

———

When my sister and I were children, my father would sometimes take us to an annual locality fair. Grand and exciting, I thought at the time, with stalls dispensing virulently pink candy floss, chilli-red hot chips, greasy chicken rolls, and dubious ice-cream soda floats, alongside an assortment of games—Lucky Dip, Ring the Bottle, Ball in the Basket. My sister was a sharper for these, while I mostly wandered away looking for Magic Box Man. So named for the stereoscope he planted in some corner of the fair. For the '60s his trade didn't seem at all vintage. I spent hours looking at Great Mammals, Great Cities, and my favorite, Wonders of the World. Bright, scratchy pictures moving in and out of my vision at the press of a button. Stonehenge, the Taj Mahal, the Colosseum, and, most wondrous of all, the Pyramids. Rising out of sand, filling the sky.

"Amazing," I'd exclaim.

And Magic Box Man, whose features have faded from my memory and reappeared as wrinkle-lined, grey-haired and stubby, would say, yes, but only because of the people.

"What people?" I'd squint.

The ones standing, walking at the foot, peripheral to the picture but in every way necessary. "Without them," he said, "the Pyramids could be a camel's droppings."

It was similar, remembering Myra, seeing her name. A shift, a rearrangement of perspective, a face, blurry and unclear, emerging from under the lens.

I hadn't thought much, or often, about her, until now.

Early December meant Delhi had cooled to a mellow, amber winter.

Tempers improved, gardens revived, and the city scrambled to new life, soothed and ameliorated by the weather. In many ways, it was spring.

And I suppose, Myra, the unexpected April shower.

By this time, I stayed mostly at the bungalow on Rajpur Road. Although I was careful not to be away from the residence hall for too long, in case people noticed, or Kalsang started asking questions. This was least likely—I'd snuck into our room after varying lengths of time away and my roommate, if he happened to be around, barely noticed.

Yet I'd been at the bungalow long enough to have fallen into a routine.

We creatures of habit, organising our days into tidy boxes.

The weeks had passed leisurely and uneventful. I'd attend classes and tutorials during the day, when Nicholas also worked. After lunch, I'd head over, accompany him to the pool, or venture into Connaught Place, to the British Council Library or The Bookworm, for a coffee at India House, or a cheap gin and tonic at Volga's. We didn't venture to the south of the city. He seemed little interested in what it had to offer, preferring to wander in Daryaganj or Chandni Chowk. Nipping in only as far as the National Museum in Barakhamba.

Sometimes, we'd sit in the study, with its vast, heavy table littered with pens and research material, and, in one corner, a small framed oil painting—of a woman looking into the mirror. Nicholas said it was a self-portrait by Malini. She'd gifted it to him before he left for India.

I want you in me. All my love, M.

He placed it there, I thought, to keep her close.

Yet she was far away enough for me to feel only a brief, tender jealousy.

In the evenings, he'd bring out the whisky. Or anything else that happened to be lying around, unopened or half-finished. But mostly, as he'd call it lovingly, the water of life. And when he could find it, a particular smoky brand that came, he explained, from the Isle of Islay, a remote, windswept island, southernmost of the Inner Hebrides.

"Here," he'd say, casting it under my nose, "you can smell it. The peat, and the Atlantic Ocean…"

And, even though, all that rose to meet me were acrid, pungent fumes, I'd agree.

"Some day," he'd say, settling back, glass in hand, "that's where I want to live…"

"In the… Hebrides?"

"No, my silly one. By the ocean."

Through the day, the gramophone would be left on, looping from the beginning of a record to its scratchy end. It was hooked to a number of speakers in the room, and he'd turn up the volume before a pre-dinner shower, and then leave it to billow through the bungalow late into the night. Playing, from what I could tell—rather, judging from the covers scattered on the floor—a host of classical-era symphonies. Haydn, in particular, seemed to be a favorite. ("The only place where I like order," Nicholas once declared, "is in music.") I didn't think about it then, but I can see now how it suited him—the clean lines of those compositions, their elegance and balance. Yet marked also by fluctuation, by changes in mood, and sudden emotional surges. Tightly controlled perhaps, but always hovering on the fringes of chaos.

Once, Nicholas asked what I would like to listen to.

I wished I could have given him an answer that might've intrigued and impressed him, something suitably obscure and rare, not merely a composer, or title of a piece, but the specifics of a recording, a date and venue, a particular conductor. But I hadn't listened to much— let's be honest, any—classical music then, and I told him so. He was unperturbed.

"Oh good. You're my blank slate."

He turned to the shelf—Malini's father's LP collection spanned the length of a wall—and flicked through the titles. "Let's see... something bright... fun..." He plucked out Franz Liszt, "and short."

He started with La Campanella. "By the magnificent Alicia..."

And in 4:23 minutes, the time it took from its brisk *allegretto* beginning to reach the crashing complexity of the end, I was held in rapture. Music, they say, can be transportive, sweeping the listener away, but with Liszt it was an anchoring, each note a peg that fastened me to my place, willing me not to move. Leaving me short of breath.

Nicholas laughed. "More?"

"Yes... yes... please."

Next, Schubert, a delicate string quintet in C, lilting through the air in waves. A gentle plucking. A slow burning. When Nicholas mentioned it had been written two months before the composer's death at thirty-one, it deepened, the sense of falling, the long, wistful contemplation, the sudden diving off a cliff into the sea.

On other evenings, I was silenced by Verdi—*Dies Irae* from *Messa de Requiem*. Nicholas turned up the volume further, and the voices echoed through the bungalow, dashing around corners, spilling through the rooms, the bass drums making the windows tremble. "This is magnificent," I shouted. It was the first time I'd felt music coursing through my veins.

Once, Stravinsky's *The Firebird Suite* had barely begun, its first few compelling notes, when Nicholas lifted the gramophone needle. "Impossible," he said, "for this to be heard and not seen..." He played Ravel's *Boléro* instead, and just when it was beginning to build up, underpinned by the lowly snare drum, running through it like a heartbeat, he switched it off. "I'd forgotten how much I hate this."

When he picked Tchaikovsky's Symphony No. 6, I sat on the sofa, almost afraid to take a breath, as though the smallest of disturbances would alter the perfection of the piece, the precarious balance of one note on top of the other, vastly soaring into the deep blue air, into nothing, nowhere. Endless.

We were in the study one afternoon; I was trying to finish an assignment while Nicholas sat at the desk, a book open on his lap. Neither of us was getting much work done. Plans to visit Connaught Place, or anywhere beyond the bungalow porch, had been discarded; it was a wretched blustery day, punctured by sharp, unpredictable bursts of rain.

"Shall I play something?"

He turned to gaze at me, but looked as though he hadn't really heard my question.

"Well... shall I?"

"Only if it's my favorite..." He was teasing now, a smile lingered at the corner of his mouth.

"Your favorite? Is it one of the pieces you played for me?"

He laughed. "Lord, no." He'd made me listen to the Romantics—"easy on the ears" he said—but he found most of their music greatly melody-driven, relying heavily on synthetic emotion. "I wouldn't," he added, "opt to take any with me to a desert island, no... apart from maybe..."

"What?" I asked, a little embarrassed, a little hurt. Did he think my ear that juvenile and untrained? He wasn't far from wrong, but I'd been listening carefully, paying great and undivided attention.

"Apart from this," he moved to the gramophone, picking up an LP that had been lost under the ones on the floor. Schumann's Dichterliebe. He slipped out the black disc, blew on it gently, and placed it on the turntable, sliding the needle into place.

The room filled with the plucking of a piano, and a voice. A man singing in German.

Nicholas sat on the sofa, and leaned back, not saying a word, closing his eyes, the light and music arranging itself around him.

I couldn't follow the words, but they were rich and voluptuous. Tinged with incredible beauty, and sorrow.

When Nicholas spoke, his voice was barely audible; I had to abandon my place on the floor and move nearer, bringing my face close to his. "This song cycle moves in circles... composed to float, always, in a state of uncertainty. The pieces dither, hesitate... the idea of a neat, rounded ending becomes, in principle, impossible. Schumann's songs start with a gesture... and that's where they stay..."

I placed my hand on his chest, casually, as though I could claim him anytime I wanted. "So nothing by the Red Hot Chili Peppers then?" In my room back in college, their latest album, in cassette form, was lodged in Kalsang's Walkman. I'd listened to it on my most recent foray back.

"Who? Listen... *ich liebe alleine die kleine, die feine, die reine...* this is when he says now I love only the little, the fine, the pure: you yourself are the source of them all."

Apart from Lenny, I'd never met anyone else who lived so much out of time.

On non-musical nights, Nicholas and I would head to the lawn, armed with mosquito repellent coils, perched on little tinplate stands, and our drinks. We'd settle ourselves on the wicker chairs, pleased to be out in the cool, November air that carried the faintest twinge of winter. As the night wore on, our words would flow easier, unclasped by alcohol and the darkness. Time was marked by the refilling of glasses, the growing line of ash that fell in a spiral below the coil. I told him about my father, a doctor, and how he started out in a humble government hospital in town, and stayed until it transformed into one of the biggest in the state. By then, he was head of the intensive care unit.

All my life, I said, I felt he didn't tender me much attention because I wasn't suffering a life-threatening disease. How could it compare? A cough and cold. A bit of homework. A grazed thumb. A teacher's chiding. A football match. The only times he "intervened" was to inflict frequent childhood punishment for a rude talking-back or an unimpressive exam result, with his bare hand, or a rolled up newspaper, sometimes—and this hurt worst of all—a wooden ruler.

"Then," I laughed, small and—I'm ashamed to say—bitter, "even that stopped."

For the longest time, especially after I befriended Lenny, or rather he befriended me, I'd view my family, not with aversion or intolerance, but a bafflement, deep and profound: how was I part of this?

"In my family too," Nicholas told me, "I was *barroco...* a misshapen pearl."

His parents were Cypriot Greeks (Titania's friend was right; I remembered the conversation I'd eavesdropped one distant afternoon outside the college café), and their families moved to England after the Second World War. In London, after they married, they lived in a flat close to the British Museum.

"Every time a fight broke out in the house, I'd walk across, and stay there until it shut in the evening."

His father taught Classical Studies at King's College, while his mother was Keeper of Special Collections at the Senate House Library. ("I've always been jealous of her job description," he added, smiling.)

Yet it was at the British Museum, that Nicholas, all of fifteen or sixteen, wandered upstairs to the northwest wing—China, South Asia and Southeast Asia.

"At the time, it made little sense... I think my first afternoon there, I was even a little frightened... perhaps a bit like Adela in the Marabar caves... this astounding visual unfamiliarity. But I was fascinated, it was unlike anything I'd seen in any museum my parents had taken me to, in Florence, Rome, Athens, Vienna. My father couldn't begin to comprehend... why study anything else apart from painted Greek pottery? Or the glory of Hellenistic sculpture."

Nobody, apart from Lenny, understood why I drifted toward Literature.

"Nicky, stop wasting your time on Eastern monstrosities." Impossible, of course, to explain to him the invalidity of applying Western classical norms for appreciating *all* art. So I went ahead and enrolled at the Courtauld, making vague mutterings about Byzantine symbolism... or some other such thing he'd approve of..."

"And?"

"And emerged with a PhD in Eastern monstrosities."

His thesis, he explained, had explored the cultural biography of a set of third-century bodhisattva statues.

"What does that mean?"

He laughed, saying I should know better than to invite an academic to talk about his work. With a large, quick sip, he finished his whisky, and looked around, seeking something. "Let's see... no, give me a minute..."

He walked into the bungalow and returned, before long, carrying a figurine. A miniature oxen carved in mottled jade. He placed it on the table.

"Have you seen this before?"

Admittedly, it looked familiar.

"It was in the study?" I offered.

I was wrong.

"Malini's parents are keen collectors," he said, "so I'm certain this is of some value. Let's assume it dates back to the early Ch'ing dynasty, the late 1600s, and somehow it found its way here, to this veranda, before us. It may have been carved as a trinket, a child's toy, a decorative piece for an altar... its changed hands a thousand times, from home to shop to museum."

"It was in the guest room," I interrupted. Placed on the table alongside other miniature carved creatures.

He picked up the figurine, holding it in the palm of his hand as though weighing it, running his fingers over its smooth lines.

"That is how I looked at sculpture, as fundamentally social beings whose identities are not fixed once and for all at the moment of fabrication, but are repeatedly made and remade through interactions with humans. Often, religious historians and art historians privilege the moment of an object's creation as the essential meaning of the object... but some of us hold that subsequent reinterpretations are equally important and equally worthy of enquiry. Would a person's biography be confined to an account of his or her birth? No. Objects come to be animated with new significances... their lives are just as filled with change, disjuncture, and readjustment as those of humans."

He placed it back carefully on the table. The oxen faced us, a third party to this conversation.

"Do you see? This evening too..."—and Nicholas looked around as though to acknowledge the quiet, silvery darkness, the overhanging trees, the night sky, me—"is forever intertwined in its biography."

"Is it similar to that? What you're working on now?"

"You're spoiling me... showing all this interest... I might have to take you away with me when I leave..." He leaned closer and traced a finger down my cheek.

Even that slightest touch would make me feel that my next breath depended on what he would do after—whether his hand would travel around the curve of my ear, down my neck, linger at my collar, the line of buttons, the hollow of my chest.

Then swiftly return to his glass.

Or whether he'd continue further, lower, over the plane of my stomach, the top edges of my jeans. A zipper pulled, a button unclasped.

Sometimes, just our palms and fingers.

Or the bed and I catching every push, the sheets marked like a map by our movements, the pillows disarranged.

In time, I learned the things that pleased him. To discern the shape of, as my own, his desire. This, most intimate act of togetherness, was tied intricately with a craving for dis-union. To long even in that miniscule moment of parting, to meet. And when meeting, to part. Like music, to wait for the next note, to be incomplete without the silences.

We'd sleep in the hush of midnight, or distant blush of dawn. Morning after morning, I'd awake with the taste of him on my tongue.

———

Myra dropped into this.

A stone casting unwelcome ripples.

One afternoon, after class, I headed to the bungalow, hurrying down the forest path to the main road. All of a sudden, the Ridge was behind me, and I was in the midst of a bustling city. A roadside barber, shaving a man seated on a stool, holding up a small mirror. A row of makeshift cigarette stalls. Hawkers selling bhel puri and spicy channa.

Soon, I turned off into Rajpur Road, wider, quieter; its sidewalks empty apart from a lady under a tarpaulin tent swiftly ironing clothes. I nodded at the guard by the gate—our acquaintance hardly evolved beyond this—and entered the lawn. The gardener was cleaning a flowerbed, digging the soil between a glorious line of many-colored phlox.

The wicker chairs were empty, but on the table, I noticed a tray with two empty teacups. Who would have visited so early on a Saturday?

The bungalow stood in mid-afternoon silence. Cold now in the winter, and almost every room had a small electric heater, lit in the evenings. Nicholas wasn't in the study, so I wandered into the drawing room, and peered into the veranda. The aquarium hummed quietly, a clear, bright bubble.

Chairs, table, potted plant, everything in its place.

Except that someone lay on the divan.

On her back, sleeve fallen off her bare shoulder, her hair bright and cropped against the cotton spread. She was covered by a woollen shawl, her feet curled under. From here, I couldn't see her face, she'd turned away. I could only trace the outline of her neck, her jaw, the sharp curve up to her ear.

It was Malini, I was certain, back home from working on her PhD in Italy, here to be with Nicholas. The girl he'd studied with at the Courtauld. Whose house he so casually inhabited. The one who wrote him those letters. Whose painting took pride of place on his desk.

I want you in me.

I refrained from edging closer afraid I might wake her. Instead, I backtracked to the corridor, past the empty guest rooms, to the main bedroom. Nicholas had just emerged from a shower. His hair, wet and wavy, clung limply to the edges of his face and neck, dripping down his bare back and chest. He'd wrapped a towel around his waist, tucked precariously on the side. Without his glasses, he looked younger, his eyes deep flints of blue-grey.

"I was wondering when you'd show up." He stood by the window and light glinted off his skin. One summer in Delhi had darkened him.

I sat at the edge of the bed, uncertain.

"How was class?"

"Alright." I didn't elaborate as I usually did.

"Anything exciting?"

"The usual... Eliot's Gerontion."

"Our favorite ultra-conservative anti-Semite..." He smiled. His lips soft and rounded, the water had rejuvenated him, filled him out.

Some other day I might have playfully attempted to defend the poet, but not that afternoon. "There's someone... in the veranda."

He whipped off his towel, using it to dry his hair. "I see, so you've met..." His words were lost in a muffle of cloth and hands.

"Who? Who is she?"

Nicholas looked amused by the urgency in my voice. "My sister."

He threw on a shirt the color of sand, it floated over him, sliding down his arms, over his head. "Well, my step-sister... after my parents' divorce, my mother married another man and had a daughter."

"I'm sorry. About—the separation." I was disoriented. As though I'd uncovered an unread chapter in a book, a painting hidden behind another. Why hadn't Nicholas told me?

"That's kind... thank you." He laughed. "But it was only a divorce... they didn't die."

The mirror on the cupboard reflected us and the mirror hanging behind us on the wall, creating an endless tunnel of images.

Would it be rude to ask how long she'd be staying? Perhaps.

But I could enquire about when she'd arrived.

"This morning..." He reached for his glasses on the dresser. "I think she's sleeping... terribly jet lagged, I'm sure."

"What does she do?"

"Myra's a musician. Don't worry," said Nicholas, playfully throwing the towel at me, "you'll love her."

"What does she play?"

He reached out and touched my arm. "I'd prefer it that way." His eyes had changed color, behind glass they were light, a shade of grey feathers.

"Of course," I said. "I understand... except..."

"Except?"

"Should I stay... or leave? At night, I mean..."

Nicholas stood and smoothed down his shirt. "Come stay over the weekends..."

"Tonight?"

He paused, working out the calendar in his mind. It was a Saturday. "From next weekend... that way it seems like it's a break for you from university. Rather than... you know... a regular thing."

I wasn't quite certain whether to be pleased or affronted.

———

I didn't see Myra until well after lunch.

She emerged from the bungalow, early evening, as the trees braided long shadows across the grass, and the air was filled with the scent of damp earth. The gardener had just finished watering the flower-beds. Nicholas had headed indoors, saying he needed to work, and I was reading, dozing, working on article ideas for Santanu. She walked out barefoot; her hair, cropped into short waves, was the color of autumn leaves glistening wet. Her long smoke-grey dress fit close and loose all at once. It was easy, I noticed, to trace her contours through the material—slight, but with the hidden energy of an athlete.

She gave me a sleepy smile, shading her eyes against the sun.

"I'm Nehemiah."

"Ah," she said. "Nicholas told me about you."

My heart swelled with pride.

"Myra." Her eyes were blue, and edged with slate. "His sister... well, half-sister."

Her voice sounded low and liquid, perhaps because she'd just awoken.

She sank into a chair and turned her face to the sun. "Gorgeous. Such a change from our despicable British winter." Her words dropped like polished marbles, smooth and round.

"When did you arrive?"

"This morning... I gave Nicholas such a surprise." She smiled to herself, indulging in a secret.

That explained it all then. He couldn't have told me if he himself hadn't known.

"I think I'm hungry for breakfast but it might be suppertime."

"You're in time for tea."

"Marvellous." She raised her arms, chiseled like ivory; on her fingers, thin and long, she wore numerous silver rings.

"Nicholas said you're a musician..."

She laughed. "Studying to be... not quite the same thing."

"What do you play?"

"The viola."

"Is that... similar to the violin?" I wished I hadn't asked—it suddenly seemed a silly, childish question.

She ran her fingers through her hair; her neck was pale and translucent, untouched by the sun. If she spent a summer here, she would be as tanned as Nicholas.

"Bigger," she said. "And more mellow. It has a deeper pitch than the violin, which I prefer."

"Will we see you play?" I thought it polite to ask.

"Oh, be careful what you wish for... I brought my viola... can't go too many days without practice."

How many, I wondered, would that be?

As instructed, I stayed away from Rajpur Road.

Around the college campus, there was a quickening end-of-term excitement, a flurry of concerts, a small book fair organised by the Literary Society, and the general unraveling of classes and tutorials. Soon, I'd be traveling home for Christmas.

It was hard not to think about Lenny, the only reason I wouldn't have minded making the long journey back.

In the residence hall, things moved along as they usually did—the drifters wandering from room to room in the evenings for a chat, a smoke, a drink, diligently avoiding the serious science scholars, or the third-year students preparing for their CAT or civil service exams. Slowly, people would fall away, retiring to sleep, while some stayed up late, their rooms hazy with smoke, reeking with the fumes of cheap whisky, mingled with the strains of Floyd or Grateful Dead. I usually kept to myself before, but now I felt even more estranged. Watching it all from a distance. Back for long stretches in my room, sparse, bare, and suddenly... small. Everything downsized, and somehow so provincial. The latest rumors and petty rivalries. The silly victories. The same, stale mockeries.

When people remarked that they hadn't seen me around in a while, I'd say, casually, "Yeah, I was at my local guardian's place."

And that was an unexciting enough reply for them to lose interest.

"Hey," said Kalsang when I met him, "Whassup?"

"Not much. You?"

"Not much."

If he was intrigued about my sporadic absences, he didn't show it. I noticed he now spent time with a group of boys from Darjeeling. Loafing around, sharing spliffs and stories. Our late night talks had come to an end.

———

When I visited the bungalow over the weekend, I found Nicholas and Myra just back from a swim. Somehow, I was certain she was a good swimmer, that she could probably race Nicholas across the pool, and do complicated maneuvers like the butterfly stroke.

"It was *so* cold," he complained.

"Nonsense," said his sister. "It was refreshing. You're a wimp."

Their banter would continue—a constant volley of testing and teasing. At those times, I assumed the role of an onlooker. I thought Nicholas would prefer it that way, that his sister should have his attention, that our plans be molded around her whim—the places she wanted to visit, the things she wanted to eat, the demands she made on his attentions. I moved through the bungalow like a ghost.

On the few occasions I stayed over, it felt strange to return to the room with no clocks, no calendars. Nicholas, a few doors away. Myra in the second guest room next to mine. I'd hear her moving about, drawing back the curtains and finally, she would settle, for there'd be sudden silence. Once, I awoke after midnight, dry-mouthed—the fan heater in the room had been on for hours—and found the jug on my bedside table empty. I stepped out for some water, still in a sleep-heavy daze. On my way back, I noticed that the door to Myra's room was slightly open. Moonlight streamed through the window falling on an empty bed.

Most of the time, I was unsure how to behave around her—rather, I was never certain how she'd behave toward me. One day, while Nicholas was away at the National Museum, we spent an entire afternoon in the veranda in silence. A solid chunk of hours where she ignored my presence. She sat with notebook in hand, wearing one of her brother's white shirts, staring out dully, while I fidgeted around, read a magazine, and repeatedly, for amusement, fed the fish.

"You'll kill them," said Myra. And that was the only thing she uttered.

On another occasion, I'd barely walked into the bungalow when she accosted me, linked her arm through mine as though we were old friends, and ushered me into the kitchen.

"What is it?"

"It's my kheer..." She pronounced it *ke-er.* "I asked Devi to teach me how to make it."

"Oh, well done." I pushed a spoon into the mess.

"Taste it first..." Her face lit up with expectancy.

The dessert was blindingly sweet, the rice still a little raw, but I ate the bowlful, saying it was delicious.

"Oh, you're precious," she declared and planted a kiss on my cheek.

What distressed me was how I rarely found myself alone with Nicholas.

The one evening I did, Myra was in the veranda, practicing on her viola. The notes rose through the bungalow, a wild wind, suddenly swelling and falling. It was a piece by Brahms, said Nicholas. "Some sonata or the other..."

The notes stopped abruptly. In a moment, they started again, from the beginning of the composition.

"She's a terror, isn't she? I finally asked her, though... she'll be gone after Christmas."

We were in the study, images scattered across the table. Nicholas had spent hours at the National Museum photographing, as he called them, "Buddha's brothers". Exquisite sculpted faces stared up at us, enigmatic, some smiling benevolently.

We were drinking, after ages, his favorite whisky.

I warmed the glass with my palms, swilling slowly. As I'd been taught. Holding it up, breathing it in, my mouth slightly open. Every sip stung my throat, and leapt to my head.

I moved closer to him. I missed his smell. Wood and musk and something else I couldn't name. "I'll be going home soon."

"And you'll be back soon?"

I shrugged. I wanted to draw this out a little, make it last.

"After New Year, I suppose."

"Perhaps you could return... sooner." He placed his hand on my waist. Pulling me closer.

"I-I don't know." I could feel myself faltering. If I could, I wouldn't leave at all. But it had been almost six months since I'd seen my parents; my mother was sentimental about these things.

I could feel Nicholas against me, our fingers entwined, my hand guided to the knot around his waist.

In the distance, the notes continued in unfailing diligence.

Somewhere in the distance, the music stopped. A door opened, and then another. The slap of footfall, growing louder.

By this time, I'd straightened up and moved to the other side of the table; Nicholas sat down and adjusted his clothes.

"Darling!" Myra fumbled with the door handle, and then rushed inside the study. "I did it. I managed the allegro appassionato..." She sank into the sofa, viola in one hand, bow in the other. "It took me long enough."

"Splendid," said her brother. "Can't bear Brahms though... go play some Haydn..."

She made a face. Then turned to me, standing there, quietly cradling my glass.

"What have you both been up to?"

"Nothing," we said, too quickly, too loud.

———

By the time I returned to Delhi, a little after New Year, she'd left and there were no traces of her in the bungalow. As though it had been a vaguely remembered dream.

Apart from those three weeks, she might not have existed.

But she was real.

I could see her in my mind now, as clear as the image glimmering on my computer screen. It was her. Nicholas' step-sister. Performing in a fortnight.

Is that what he wanted then? For us to attend her concert. To meet again, that strange, unlikely trio.

Surely I was owed more than this? More than a rendezvous at a formal social event at which we could play-pretend to be perfunctorily polite and civil, drink a glass of wine, and return home.

Yet what was it I hoped for?

What else did I expect?

In the garden, I stopped next to a lady in a Victorian dress and wide-brimmed hat.

She looked at me either in disdain or despair, it was hard to tell. I leaned against the stone base on which she'd been standing for two hundred years, gradually marked and mildewed in the wind and rain. Behind her, the lawn trailed away like a green veil, hemmed by a high stone wall. In the middle sank a rectangular pond topped by a non-functioning fountain. There weren't many people around—a man threw a ball for his dachshund, a couple of young girls smoked on a nearby bench, a woman and her toddler played with a white balloon. I watched them, constantly expecting the balloon to burst as the little girl gripped it tight against herself.

The far edge of the garden was once a burial ground, although the eighteenth-century tombstones were now all propped in a line against the wall. I examined them in some amusement—*Thomas Gibson MD In God's Keeping, Elizabeth Marley She Sleepeth with those She Loved, Henry L Lawson Until the Day Break and the Shadows Flee*—and then wandered away, down a paved avenue, lined by oak trees. I'd read that oak trees lived for almost half a century. These ones had seen many funerals, I imagined—their trunks wider than myself many times over, their branches flickering with the color of firelight. Perhaps the wisest and most ancient had watched poor Thomas Gibson MD being laid to rest, over two hundred years ago. Nabokov said that trees were always journeying somewhere; those looked as though they'd reached their place of pilgrimage.

I grasped the ticket in my pocket and felt that, somehow, I too had reached mine.

Lauderdale House stood behind a row of graceful hedges and neat flowerbeds brimming with snapdragons, late-blooming carnations and purple dahlias. It was a large white structure that reminded me of the homes I'd seen in movies about America's old South. With classically inclined pillars, well-spaced windows and an airy veranda. How odd, that this should be where we'd next meet, Nicholas and me.

What would I ask him first?

About the seahorses.

Questions unfurled endlessly.

The last time I saw Nicholas, he was lying asleep, bare except for the white sheet entwined around his legs.

Time had done it again. Turned into itself, inverted, and dropped away all the years in between.

What would I ask him first?

At ten past seven, twenty minutes before the concert, I decided to head inside.

It was cool and quiet, the large central space leading off into galleries and offices—hard to imagine this had once been a family home. Landscape paintings hung on creamy walls, smooth as the interior of an egg. Far above arched a modest octagonal dome, edged with a rococo molding of flowers and leaves.

"In the lower chamber," said the lady at reception, smiling and pointing toward the stairs.

The usher at the door checked my ticket and waved me inside—a long carriage-shaped room, with rows of velvety red-backed seats. I wondered where Nicholas would be sitting. For now, the chairs on either side of mine were empty. Some people were already seated, talking, checking their phones. Gradually, more wandered in. The auditorium was small; it probably couldn't seat more than sixty. I played with the programme. A page. Reading it over again, the words simply sitting there, lost in the space between the paper and my eyes.

A Selection of Schönberg... String Quartet No. 1 in D minor, Op. 7, String Quartet No. 2 in F sharp minor... Andrew Drummond, Myra Templeton, Elaine Parker, Owen Lee. I'd searched for them on Google. Andrew, like Myra and Elaine, was a graduate of the Royal College of Music. He played the cello. Owen had studied at St. Andrews. Violin two. Which left Elaine with violin one. *The Guardian* had called them "a substantial achievement" while *The Independent* said Orpheus were "consistently inventive." They'd been performing together for five years now—at concert festivals around the country, even a few times at the BBC Proms. I'd also done an image search and seen what each member looked like. A generously proportioned man with a friendly face and a bow tie, another who was taller, more melancholic, with a head of dark curly hair, a slim, wispy lady, her blonde hair falling on either side of her face like curtains. Myra seemed as beautiful, her hair the color of autumn.

To my left now sat a middle-aged lady in a soft floral dress, while the seat on my right remained empty. Beyond that, the row had filled up. I glanced at the door, waiting for a face I'd recognize, but everyone who walked through were strangers. On the stage, carefully adjusted lights shone on an arrangement of chairs, microphones and music stands. A piano gleamed in the corner. It was half-past seven, but perhaps they were waiting a few extra minutes.

Finally, a lady in a navy skirt and blazer, walked up to the podium. "Good evening, ladies and gentlemen... welcome to the third of our Accomplished Concert series..."

The musicians streamed on stage and took their places. For a moment, I forgot about the empty seat on my side. Myra. Wearing a simple black dress, scalloped around the neck, falling demurely to her knees. I didn't remember her being this petite. Her hair now long, but pulled neatly away from her face by a silver headband that caught the light as she leaned over to the music stand.

The lady introduced them; they bowed in turn, acknowledging the applause.

Perhaps it'd be occupied at the interval. Nicholas hadn't made it on time for the first half.

The first piece, explained the programme, was unusual for being composed in a single movement. It plunged immediately into urgency, the instruments braiding in breathless agitation. The notes lifted— dramatic, but refrained from resolution, weaving into one another, continuing as an endless spool of thread. Or persistent, unanswered questions. I watched Myra, her movements suddenly familiar, bringing back memories of evenings in the bungalow. The same intent absorption on her face, though something was missing. The passion for the piece. Perhaps she didn't love Schönberg as much as Brahms.

Halfway through, I closed my eyes; I could see why they were taking a break after this performance—it was exhausting. It reminded me of a dream, of being followed in a dream. Schönberg had made certain there was no escape from the composition. It was contained, hemmed in by the notes, spilling here and there but never managing to flee.

When it was over, I opened my eyes to loud applause and the quartet standing and smiling. I thought for a moment that Myra had seen me, that miraculously I'd caught her eye, but she swiftly looked away.

"Thank you... we'll be back in fifteen minutes," said Elaine, tucking her hair behind her ear. Her silver-green dress looked translucent in the light.

I stood up to have a wander, use the restroom; when I returned, I was certain, Nicholas would be there.

I took my time, strolling upstairs to the toilets on the first floor, lingering by the refreshments counter with a coffee. Walking back slowly, down the stairs, the carpeted corridor, into the chamber that smelled of wood and musty velvet. The seat was still empty.

Then, at the door, I stopped and turned—Myra walked on stage, followed by the others.

My-ra.

I made my way back to the seat.

The next piece was written when Schönberg learned of his wife's betrayal; she was having an affair with their friend and neighbor, a young painter. It was marked by painful clashes and sudden, plummeting drops, dark notes hovering around the edges. Sometimes, it was rhythmic, like a heartbeat. I listened numbly; I didn't understand the purpose behind this evening.

Why had Nicholas sent me here only to betray me again?

A puppet. That's what I'd always been. I wished I hadn't danced attendance this time, that I hadn't showed up.

Yet, at the end of it all, I could still meet Myra. Somehow, I must speak with her. I'd wait, until the concert was over, and seek her out.

The music finally ended. The room filled with clattering applause, extended in appreciation. The quarter stood, and bowed, smiling, and bowed again. Then they glided off stage, in a line.

I waited, until the crowd shuffled out, the murmur of conversation falling and fading. Slowly, the chamber emptied. Myra would probably be backstage—I slipped away to the side, and no one stopped me. The quartet were packing up, putting away their instruments. A bottle of wine stood open on a table, half-filled glasses. There were other people there, acquaintances, mingling, having a word with the musicians. I waited until Myra was alone, gathering sheets of music.

"Hello."

She looked at me with vacant eyes, blue as an April morning.

"It's me... Nem... Nehemiah..."

"Oh." The word stayed in her mouth, round and perfectly formed.

Up close, I could tell the years had changed her, in small, surreptitious ways. Her face was thinner, as though time had washed away her softness. There was something about her that had hardened. Broken, and hardened, as though she'd melted and been recast.

Now, though, I could see it seeping through her skin, her lips, her eyes. A sudden vulnerability.

"Oh," she repeated. She looked down at the sheets in her hand, as though she didn't know what they were, that they'd explain why I was standing before her.

"It was very good... the concert."

"Thank you." She'd adjusted her face, a mask of composure. "This is a surprise..."

"A pleasant one, I hope."

She lifted the corner of her mouth into a brief smile. "How did you... you know... happen to be here?" Her fingers fiddled with a silver bracelet on her wrist; she still wore rings, but they were discreet and more elegant.

"Your brother..." I decided to make it sound light, airy.

"What?"

"He sent me a ticket for this evening... I presumed he'd be here, cheering you on... but the seat next to mine stayed empty..."

"S-sorry... I don't understand." Her face had collapsed again into confusion. She glanced around the room—people still mingled around, paying us no heed.

"Could we speak elsewhere? Shall we go upstairs?"

She gathered her things quickly, the viola case, her handbag, a smart winter coat.

At the bar, I ordered a whisky and, for her, a sparkling lime.

When I finished, she stayed silent for a long while. There were fewer people around now, the bartender was on the far side, talking on his phone. A couple were hovering over their glasses of wine. According to the sign—"Opening Times"—the place would be closing soon.

"So, where is he?"

Myra finished her drink. The slice of lime dropped back into the bottom of the glass, amid the cubes of melting ice.

"I don't know."

I knew she'd take his side, they were siblings after all, and blood, even half-blood, ran thicker than loose decade-old connections.

"Alright," I said. "I'm sorry to have intruded on your time. And your brother's... I thought..."

Myra laughed—a deep and wholly uninhibited sound. The bartender paused his conversation, the couple glanced over, disapproval flickering on their faces.

I felt a familiar spark of anger. Her joke, whatever it was, came at a cost—mine. I finished the whisky—the alcohol flaming in my throat—longing for another, but last orders were done.

"I'm sorry..." she said, touching my arm. Even through my shirt I could feel the cold of her fingers. "It's just that... well... I can't believe... it's just..."

"What is it?"

Her eyes were inky graphite, pinpoints of blue lead. "He's not my brother."

I smiled, politely, saying yes, I too often expressed similar exasperations about my elder sister.

Something softened, the lines around her mouth. She reached out, her hand on mine, like something brought in from a winter's night. "No. He isn't, *at all*."

If I hadn't believed her earlier, I believed her now.

From behind her, at the top of the stairs, emerged a figure in silver-green. "Myra," she called. "I'm headed back..."

Myra started gathering her things, pulling on her coat.

"Wait," I said. "Y-you're leaving?"

"I'm afraid so."

"But... I have... there are..."

She started to say something, but her words didn't reach me. Elaine was waiting.

"Wait... can we meet?"

For a moment, Myra looked undecided.

"Please..."

"Alright... tomorrow. Eleven o'clock. At Costa in Paddington Station."

She picked up her viola, and joined Elaine. As they walked down the stairs, she turned, as though she'd remembered something, and then carried on.

———

If we grow into our past, more than we grow out of it, we live lives that are, in substance, acts of fiction. For memory, as it fades, must be embellished, made real by fabrication. Which is why it becomes impossible to discern borders, their lines of separation. Although the question is, would we want to?

Strip away the narratives of our lives. These small, valiant acts of rebellion. It would leave us bereft, diminished, clasping only our meagrely cold, hard nuggets of truth.

Did that really happen?

Does it matter?

One morning, at dawn, light filled the veranda, coming from nowhere, and everywhere.

A distant secret source, a sun that couldn't yet be seen.

We watched and waited, sitting still and silent. In the aquarium, that entire universe, the fish glided, pecking at invisible specks, chasing each other around the rocks. It might have been a little after sunrise, when the seahorses started dancing—the veranda now blazing with slanting light, new and radiant. We sat close to the aquarium, where the water trilled blue and clear. We watched the seahorses. Perched

close together, their tails entwining, moving in a slow, spiral dance.
They stopped, faced each other, one bowed, and then the other, swimming in a circle, moving through air.

It's a dream.

I was on the divan, amid the cushions, when he swooped down in a
single elegant movement and placed a finger on my mouth. His touch
was cool, as though he'd just emerged from a shower, or the sea. As
always, at that moment I couldn't breathe.

I was right; he must have been immersed in water, for the taste and
texture of his skin was different. Damp, and woody, an underwater
cave.

"Why me?" I asked.

He ran a finger down my cheek, my neck, my shoulder, the sliver of a
scar. "The Japanese have a word for it... *kintsukuroi.* The art of repairing
pottery and understanding that the piece is more beautiful for having
been broken."

From somewhere, like a long-forgotten song, a cool breeze swept
through the veranda. Bringing with it a faint scent of lilies. It seemed
the only sound in the world was our breathing.

This was our aquarium.

"What we saw this morning... the seahorses... they were moving...
was that their dance?"

"It's what they do... a ritual... courting each other at dawn. They are
strange... and beautiful."

Like us, I thought. Like us.

III

ON A MORNING LIKE THIS, London could be the world's greyest city. A big-bellied sky pressed against the tops of buildings, their roofs and chimneys, while pale, pallid light clung to walls and windows, settling dully on the ground. The parks, unused and abandoned, cradled lakes of grey water, and the trees seemed extinguished, their leaves defeated by damp. It was raining—an odd drizzle that made people undecided about opening their umbrellas. Instead, they buried themselves into their coats, willing to be warm, to shield their faces from the pallor of a lifeless sky. The city had awoken to monochrome, bereft of all color, except the splash of a telephone-box, a bus, the sudden silvery glimmer of passing cars. A city in long mourning for summer.

Inside the skeleton of Paddington Station, encased in ribs of steel, the aspect, perhaps given its containment, was more lively. Passengers scurried around, stepping off, and into trains, or headed underground, standing on escalators that traveled into darkness. A busker played her violin, the bow clasped in her frayed mitten-clad hands, and the sound rose through the air like a bird trapped inside the belly of an enormous beast.

Above that came the flatline call of automated announcements—the 10:45 First Great Western service train to Cardiff leaving from platform 5; the 10:57 to Reading delayed by twenty minutes, *We apologise for the inconvenience*; the 11:06 to Oxford departing from platform three. The 11:15 to Bristol...

I'd ordered a coffee, and now another.

How long could I make it last? I sipped slowly, cradling it in my hands. The trouble was, in this weather, it cooled rapidly; soon, the liquid swirled weak and insipid in my mouth. I was at a small table outside the entrance to Costa, along a row of shops lining one side of the station. Above the grand doorway to my left, a three-faced Victorian clock counted the minutes between announcements.

She would come, I told myself.

She asked me to be there. She must show up. I didn't want to reflect on it now, but if she didn't we had no way to be in touch. We hadn't exchanged addresses, or phone numbers. We didn't have the time— rather it hadn't struck me to, in the midst of all her pronouncements.

He's not my brother.

I could still hear her voice, calm as a windless sea.

If I hadn't attended the concert, and stayed behind, I may never have known. No, the points at which to pick a moment of fated ruse lay further back—multiple and many. This venue was, if nothing else, appropriate. Stations, airports, and docks are sites of infinite departure, reservoirs of potential journeys, of possible events, the slippery and fleeting, worlds aborted and almost born.

I looked at the train tracks, joining and parting, reflecting light.

How difficult was it to comprehend this web of connections?

This complicated intersection of lines.

At some point, we feel compelled to account for every decision, every circumstance that places us in a particular moment.

We paint a surface and leave no free spaces.

Horror vacui. The fear of the empty.

In the end, we are all cartographers—looking back at a map of our lives. Marking out the uneven course of our existence, hoping there'll be no disappearances, of ourselves and the people we love.

"Are you done?" said a bright, young voice to my right. A blonde pony-tailed waitress in a neat red apron stood at my shoulder. Her gaze fell on my unfinished coffee. "Oh, I'm sorry…"

In the background, I could hear a call for the midday train to Oxford.

"No, I'm done, thank you." I gestured that she could clear up.

"Would you like anything else?"

I hesitated. The three-faced clock made a mockery of my expectations.

"No, that'll be all."

I pulled on my coat, buttoning it up tight, and wove a woollen scarf around my neck. As I walked away, headed down the platform toward the escalators, I heard someone call, "Excuse me... sorry... excuse me..."

When I glanced back it was the waitress, approaching, holding a bit of paper in her hand. "I almost forgot... were you by any chance waiting for someone named"—she glanced at it—"Myra?"

"Yes... I was."

"Are you"—she scanned the paper again—"Nehemiah?"

"Yes, I am."

She smiled, pleased and relieved, holding it out. "A lady dropped by this morning, and requested one of us to give you this. She said she had to leave earlier than expected..."

"Thank you."

"You're welcome... I almost forgot... but no one else sat here as long as you... I should have asked you earlier... I forgot..." She was young, barely out of school, and I can only imagine the kind of adventures this encounter had conjured in her heart.

I said she'd been most kind, most helpful.

"Not at all." She wished me a good day before hurrying back.

The paper had been torn from a notebook, the edges raggedly uneven. It carried a hasty scribble, an email address. "Write me."

———

One evening at the bungalow, I remember, Myra was filled with a fiery energy. Her spirits soaring, driven by something unfathomable. Everything, she declared, would be transformed. The drawing room into a stage. The heaters lit and radiating warmth. The bar opened and displayed. The curtains drawn to withhold a secret.

In the center, her space. A stool and a music stand.

Everyone, she pronounced, must wear a suit for her soirée.

"A suit?"

"Beg or borrow, darling."

"But—"

"Find one. Steal."

Nicholas, sitting aside quietly, said he'd dig out something suitable for me. He rummaged through his cupboard, throwing options on the bed. A pair of trousers, too long but they'd do. An exquisitely tailored ivory shirt. "Are you sure—" I began. He waved the rest of my words away.

Finally, I was fittingly attired.

The get-up may have been bulky, but the bow tie, he remarked, was perfect.

Later, Myra joined us in the drawing room, where we were waiting with our drinks.

She sat beside me on the sofa, trailing her fingers on my arm, watching me with cool, clear eyes. She leaned closer when I spoke, her neckline low and flimsy. Her perfume heady, sweet like lilies.

What would he think?

I saw her glance across at Nicholas, sitting separate from us, on an armchair, but I couldn't decipher the look on their faces.

Did she want to rouse him to anger?

"Why don't you commence your performance?" Isn't that why we're here." His voice was as smooth as the whisky we were drinking.

"When I'm ready, I will." She turned to me. "Will you be my cupbearer, my precious? And fetch me more wine?"

I refilled her glass, and my own.

The room, ablaze with heaters, had warmed up; we were uncomfortable in our suits.

She wouldn't permit us to loosen our ties, take off our blazers.

When it was well past nine, she prepared for her recital. For that evening, she announced, she'd picked something by Brahms...

"Naturally," murmured Nicholas. "Can't we have something else?"

She was stirring him like the wind whipped the sea.

"I'll play what's on the programme," she said, "Brahms Sonata in F minor, Op 120., Number 1... Vivace."

A lively, crescendo piece, that wavered between moments of long strung melancholy and fits of vivacious energy. Almost schizophrenic in their ability to exist alongside each other on the same page of music.

Like Myra herself.

She was with me, my arms around her waist, the dip of her hips—while he was watching. Her breasts pressed against me as she leaned back and laughed. Then, it was all three of us, falling over each other, the alcohol flaming in our heads, clinging to someone's arm or shoulder. Soon, the night scattered, like snowflakes, into patches that fell out of our memories.

What I do remember was returning to the guest room, where I sprawled on the bed, the alcohol burning away all life. It was sometime before dawn, before light had flooded the sky, when a figure moved swiftly toward me, reaching for my shirt, my trousers. Undoing them with fumbling fingers. In the air, her perfume lingered, strong and heady, sweet as lilies. I said her name when the person leaned in.

"It's me..." He hushed into my ear.

"Myra," I said, "you smell of Myra."

———

It was difficult to push those memories away while chastely typing— *Dear Myra... I hope this message finds you well... Will you be in London anytime soon?* In honesty, it hardly was that seamless. How should I begin? And end? "Love, Nem," or "best wishes." I spent an entire afternoon reworking the middle. Eventually, I kept it polite, and brief. After all, this was meant only to put us in touch.

A few days later, she replied, with a line of apologies, pleasantries, and affirmation. Yes, she was in London, but for a string of pre-Christmas concerts; it was a busy time. Perhaps it might be better if we worked out something else—how long would I be around?

At first, I toyed with the idea of suggesting a visit, I could travel to the countryside. I remembered Santanu saying I should get out of the city, for a break. Eventually I didn't. Somehow, I had the feeling I needed to be careful, in case I pushed her away with a gesture, a word. So I was restrained, giving her my dates, ending my message lightly—"Whatever, for you, is most convenient." The edges of our emails pulsed with things unsaid, and unanswered questions; I suppose it was silently understood that we'd talk when we met.

But despite my caution, she didn't write back.

Everyday, I left my laptop on, waiting for the ping of a new email. Rushing to check when that did happen, only to find PR announcements for art exhibitions, or messages from Nithi—something related to work, an article due soon, a piece that needed editing. And when I was out, I obsessively checked my phone. What if I didn't hear from Myra again? What if she'd decided otherwise.

The screen ridiculed me with its emptiness, with its reiteration of her silence.

A week passed; it seemed endless.

It didn't help that all the while we were assailed by dismally wet weather.

And Christmas.

Both of which began long before the 25th of December.

Carols spilled out of shops, reminding everyone to be good, that Christ was born, and we must, in joyful unison, dream of snow. Oxford Street was lined by cheer mostly manufactured in China, and the city heaved under the relentless stamp of shoppers.

A bit like Diwali back in Delhi, I told Santanu.

We were elbowing our way through Covent Garden. Above us, gigantic silvery-red baubles dangled from the arched ceiling, wreathed by pythons of green tinsel.

"I think I prefer this place in the eighteenth-century. You know," I said, "when it was a notorious bohemian red light district."

"What?" said Santanu. "Oh, yes."

This wasn't the first time I noticed he was distracted; lately, he seemed unusually preoccupied.

"And this weather," I continued, "apparently the wettest December on record for a century."

"They always say that," he muttered vaguely. "In this country, every month sets a new bad weather record."

"Is Yara coming?"

"No."

"I thought you said–"

"Earlier she said she would... then today, she texted saying she couldn't make it..."

"Why?"

He shrugged. "I don't know."

We trudged past shoppers and loungers, digging our gloved hands deep into our pockets. The cold stung our faces like invisible airy nettles.

Yes, I replied, long ago, with my sister and other children from our neighborhood.

Instead of explaining why he'd brought it up, he said, "I wish we didn't have to go to this thing."

We were on our way to the Institute's annual Christmas party. "Join us for some holiday cheer!" the email invite exclaimed, and it didn't seem like Santanu was in the mood for any this season.

When we passed the old Faber & Faber building, he stopped.

"Nem," he said, "do you feel up for a quick drink?"

I was about to remind him we wouldn't be left wanting a bar at the party, but something about him—the look on his face, his gestures—made me acquiesce.

Our nameless bar was surprisingly busy that evening, invaded by students intent on end-of-term revelry. The management had made a not wholly uninspired effort at festive décor, and Santanu and I squeezed in at the end of the bar counter with an assortment of plastic candy canes and fat Santas dangling above our heads. All around us, the tables were crowded twice over, the air vivid with snippets of laughter and conversation.

We ordered our drinks—two pints of St Peter's, a dark, sweetly smooth stout—and I waited for him to speak. I'd hardly, if ever, seen Santanu at a loss for words. For as long as I'd known him, he was articulate and eloquent, at times happily loquacious. Now, he gazed at his glass, at the wooden counter, the beer taps, as though these things might offer him some inspiration.

"Is everything alright..." I offered, thinking it might make it easier for him to begin. "I mean, with Yara..."

"That's the problem, I'm not sure..." He sipped his ale. "I suppose it all started at the Queen's Head..."

I couldn't tell where this was heading.

We'd spent a few evening there. It was nicer than this bar, more atmospheric, complete with roaring fire, standing piano, and an excellent beer and whisky list. But it was also further away. Hidden in a row of bleak sky-grey buildings down Acton Street near King's Cross.

"Remember that evening... ? You, me and Yara..."

Not long after they first met. They invited me for an aperitif, and I found, when I arrived, that it was a special occasion—the publication of her poetry chapbook. I ended up walking home well past midnight.

"We were talking about the dedication..."

"What dedication?"

"In her book…"

My memories of the evening were dim. She'd pressed a copy into my hand, navy, with an illustrated cover. Santanu was rifling through his. "For Maher and Liana… your mom and dad?"

Yara sipped her wine; her cheeks the same color as her dusty pink sweater. "No, my boyfriend and his wife."

"Ex-boyfriend I should hope?" said Santanu. "Or else his wife might be upset."

"Perhaps," she tapped him playfully on the cheek, "he and his wife have different arrangements to the ones people think of as *normal*…"

"Like an open relationship…"

"If you want to call it that…"

"I'm not really aware of other terms."

She smiled, wide and carefree. "There are many others, habibi… look them up."

We clasped our pints in silence. The student crowd around us burgeoning; a group nearby had ordered multiple rounds of tequila, and I could hear enthusiastic cheers.

"A few weeks ago," continued Santanu, "I met her in Brixton… remember?"

After we'd walked to Camden to join Eva at The Mexican.

He swilled the stout in the glass, a dark miniature whirlpool. "We talked for a long while… and at the end of the evening, she gave me this…" From his pocket, he pulled out a paper napkin. On it, in pencil, a sketch.

"An... infinite heart?"

"It's meant to be a symbol of polyamory..."

Between my fingers, the paper lay thin and soft, insubstantial tissue.

She told him she wanted to be honest. *She was of many loves.*

Maher lived with his wife in Hackney. Liana too loved a man there.

There was no need for secrets. No subtraction of affection, only an infinite multiplication.

"She said they didn't condone these hierarchical terms, but it made it simpler to explain the relationships to me... Maher and Liana are a "primary" while she and him share a "secondary"... so does Liana and the other guy... are you following?"

I nodded.

"But you?" I asked. "Are you okay with it?"

"What would you prefer?"

He lifted his gaze, to the Santas with their big-bellied grins and the cheap, cheerful candy canes. "I don't know, Nem. I just don't want to seem... uncool."

When we arrived, the Christmas party was well underway—Michael Bublé on the stereo, and chatter and laughter spilling generously into the air. It wasn't as extravagant as I'd expected. (I suppose, everything else appears subdued when you step away from the glittering streets of Central London.) The gathering had convened in a courtyard on the ground floor; one corner taken up by a decked tree sprinkled with tinsel and star-shaped lights. A buffet table, spruced-up with wreathed holly, was laden with wine, mulled and otherwise, and an assortment of seasonal foods. I hadn't imagined there'd be such a crowd—I came into contact with so few; mostly only with the faculty from the literature department.

Eva and Tamsin were there already. Conversing with the dean, a small balding, bespectacled man with fascinating elfin ears. I watched them carefully; even in public there were hints of their closeness. Or perhaps every gesture—Tamsin's hand briefly on Eva's back, their touching shoulders—was now laden with new meaning. I remembered the evening in my room, Eva's quiet sadness. Today, she was wearing a high-necked red silk dress that wrapped her entirely to the knees. Like a cocoon, an exquisite plaster to hold her in place, to make her invulnerable. When she turned, though, her dress was gashed at the back, opening in a pointed oval. An elegant Achilles heel.

Eva smiled. "Well, you'll soon find out."

They were heading to Japan for a fortnight, she explained. An impulsive, last-minute decision. When Tamsin turned to greet someone else, Eva added quietly, "I didn't feel like spending Christmas in Beirut."

"You can't spend it alone."

I assured her I wouldn't.

"But what will you do?"

I said something suitably vague—see some friends, get some work done. "Also Santanu's around…"

She looked doubtful. "He'll be busy with the poet."

And Maher, I wanted to add, but held my silence.

Later, I stood aside, watching the party unfold; Bublé, on loop, was singing about a winter wonderland for the third time now, someone had brushed against the tree and it stood woefully lopsided, and the buffet table had lightened, as had the bar. I checked my phone surreptitiously, but it stared back grim and blank. Only once, a hopeful blip.

An email from my sister. A chain letter, containing a novena started by Mother Teresa in 1952. Not sharing it placed me in immediate danger of, among other catastrophes, dying, losing my job, losing my family.

I hit delete.

It had been many Decembers since I'd headed back to my hometown for Christmas.

My father, retired now from his job at the hospital. My mother said he spent most of his time in the garden, growing masses of purple hydrangeas, lines of pale roses, and an assorted variety of orchids. Gardening, I thought, was as solitary an undertaking as healing people. Initially, my mother would ask often about my plans to visit, but I think she'd grown resigned now; I could hear it in her voice. Rather in the silences that had replaced the questions.

My sister, long married, with her young children, working as a nurse at the same hospital where my father had retired from.

How close, and how distant, the threads of our journeys.

———

One evening, after what seemed a century of waiting, it was there.

A new unread message. Bright and shining.

Myra didn't begin with an apology—perhaps, for her, it hadn't been long at all—and asked instead if I had plans for the December holidays. I held my breath, swiftly scanning the lines. *Would you like to come up to where I live in the country?*

She understood, of course, if I had made other plans, and if so, we could work out something else... maybe early in the new year. I would have liked to hit reply immediately—*I'll come I'll come I'll come*—instead I paced my room, to walk off a sudden sharp burst of energy. I still had a choice to turn away and let things be. Like the man at the end of *Acte sans paroles*. To do nothing. But I'd already thrown the pebble in the pond, and this was one of its inescapable ripples. Somewhere, in the distance, I could hear the tolling of church bells. From nowhere came the image of a girl at the bottom of a stone tower, her hair the color of golden corn, fresh as the English countryside. Suddenly Myra, in a grey dress, walking sleepily across a sun-lit lawn. And Nicholas, always Nicholas.

I sent her a reply late that night. Saying I looked forward to taking a break from the city. If she could send me her address, suggest suitable accommodation...

The next morning, already, I had a reply.

I could stay, she suggested, at a bed & breakfast in the village closest to her house—"The Mildmay Arms is small but, to my knowledge,
exceedingly comfortable"—for three days—"So we may, depending on
the weather, perhaps drive to the moors... which are well worth a visit."
I pre-booked it all online, my room and tickets, and waited.

A week after the Christmas party, I traveled out of London.

The journey felt momentous.

The carriage was soggy with the smell of damp clothes and lost hope
that they'd ever dry. A man in a billowing black coat read *The Times*,
a woman fed a toddler in a buggy, two teenage girls giggled into each
other's ears sharing secret after secret, a gangly young man with a guitar case stepped in, glanced around, and stepped off.

Leaving London by train was like pulling out of the innards of the city,
still caked with the industrial grime of the Victorian age. The tracks
were vast exposed veins, cutting and crossing, flanked by buildings
with rattling rooms shaded by dirty curtains. Some were higher, floor
upon floor of boxy windows, through which I could see people watching
television. A vision of some forgotten dystopia. Sometimes, the screens
were left on in empty rooms with images dancing like mad ghosts.

Or the tracks were backed by warehouses with empty car parks
hedged by tall wire fences. On some, ballooned colorful graffiti—"Hang
the bankers."

This was a city visited by a whale, and the creature had died.

Slowly, like long drawn breath, the buildings fell away, and we came
upon quick glimmerings of wilderness—a hedged station, a cluster of
bare oaks, the hint of open space, until it unfurled and opened and
stretched into all the horizon. In summer, this must look different, the
grounds brimming with radiance—although even now, it surprised me,
the muted beauty of the earth. Rinsed and rained upon until only the
resilient colors remained. As the afternoon drew on, a light mist rose
above the fields, the earth's silvery aura.

It pleased me, my reflection on the glass. The quiet suspended stillness of this space.

We stopped at increasingly desolate stations. At one point, we were
shuttled off into a bus for a stretch where the railway lines were sub-
merged. The weather reports, I overheard someone say, predicted continuing storms. At times, I dozed, lulled by the motion of the bus, the
low roar of the engine.

At a small, barren station, I waited on the platform, the winter light
already fading around me. I was almost there—this was the shortest leg
of the journey. A thin rain trickled down, timid and indecisive. Myra
had offered to pick me up—"there may not be any taxis waiting"—but
I assured her I'd manage. We'd meet the next day in the village for an
early lunch.

Back on a carriage the world rapidly fell behind. Time, I've often
thought, could easily be captured inside a moving train. When the
natural light outside has faded until it is even with the artificial light
inside. And a passenger, looking at the window, sees two images at
once. The dim landscape rushing past and the interior of the carriage,
reflected with its motionless occupants.

Moving and still. All at once.

Moving and still.

———

When I arrived, the late afternoon was already wrapped in darkness.
The carriage door parted with a gasp and a handful of people stepped
off. I gave way to an elderly lady with a shopping trolley. Apart from
the open gates, everything else about the tiny station looked shut
and empty, sealed within itself. I'd stepped into a strange, diminutive world, in every way contrary to London. A shiver ran through
me—the cold, and a fleeting rush of panic. I had never felt more alone.

Myra was right; there weren't any taxis waiting. The other passen-

gers settled into their cars and drove off, or walked off into the surrounding darkness. I followed. Armed with a map in case I failed to
remember directions—*left from the station, down South Street, first right
into Long Street, another right into Mill Lane.* An empty taxi passed by,
and I wondered, for a mad moment, how much it would cost to drive
back to London. A loud, uncontrolled laugh almost bubbled from my
mouth. A quietness hung in the air like I'd never experienced before,
in my hometown, in Delhi, London. The chilly, wintry silence of a
cold country. A car sped up the road and turned, toward my direction, blinding me with stark all-encompassing headlights. It swerved
off and, all of a sudden, it was just me, the slick wet road and the rain,
suspended in the yellow glow of lamplights. The heft of old houses,
leaning over the sidewalk. A Tudor building incongruous among stone
façades, a lit pub, a line of closed shops. My coat wasn't keeping out the
chill; I longed for a hearty dinner, a warm bath, and a bed with white
bedsheets. In that precise order.

The B&B stood along a line of gated houses with their own gardens.
Walking up to the door, I could see, in the dim light, a strange assortment of items on the lawn. Mostly rugs, in heaped abandon, bits of
oddly-shaped wood, tin trunks, and standing tall and anomalous—a
shiny full-length mirror.

Perhaps, they'd set up a flea market. Or an outdoor art installation.
I rang the bell.

"Oh," said the lady who opened the door. She might have been in her
late fifties, with curling peppery hair, and a thin, wide mouth.

"Oh dear," she reiterated after I'd given her my name, "we've been
trying to call you."

I'd lost steady mobile phone reception hours ago, and when it
returned, it didn't hold for long.

They'd been flooded, she said, breathlessly. Never happened before, or
at least not since the '40s, but they'd had the fire engines in for three hours

the day before, and four today, pumping out water. "Coming in faster than we could get it out." She was terribly sorry but the B&B was closed.

Couldn't I have a room upstairs? Just for tonight.

The council, she said, wouldn't be happy with that. She was truly sorry...

"We've been trying to call you," she added unhelpfully.

Was there anywhere else I could stay? In my head, the hearty meal, warm bath and bed receded. I was left with an aching tiredness.

"Let me call the Stag for you." She moved to the telephone on the counter. The floor was damp, and in places, still puddled. In the corner, the sofa huddled, a heavy, soggy mass.

"Oh, I see... thank you," I could hear her say. It didn't sound promising.

They were full up, she informed me, and not with ordinary customers. "Flood victims... from villages on the Somerset Levels... using the place for temporary accommodation."

Was there, I asked on impulse, a train back to London?

Yes—she glanced at the clock on the wall—in an hour. Although, with all the disruptions, it would probably get in very late. If at all, I thought ominously.

She began to apologize again... if I wanted I could take the train to the next village... although there wasn't a guarantee of any vacancies there either.

"Do you have a phone book?"

"Yes, we do. Somewhere here..."

She scurried behind the counter, and brought out a bulky tome marked by the dusty air of disuse. I flipped to "T", and glanced through the pages. Stopping at a name. I had no idea if it was the right listing; but it was the only Templeton in town.

I thanked her, and walked back out into the night.

My phone had a single feeble signal bar. I'd try the number while walking to the station.

I dialed. It rang three times. "Hello," said an unmistakeably male voice. For a second, I had a wild thought—could it be Nicholas? But his voice was deeper, older, too different, it wasn't him.

"Hello... is this the Templeton residence?"

"Yes." The word was clipped and curt.

"May I speak to Myra, please." I waited to be told that no one by that name lived there...

Instead, "Who is this?"

"I'm Nehemiah... a friend." I added quickly, "From London."

I couldn't decipher the silence on the other end. Was he waiting for me to elaborate?

"Just a moment."

Perhaps not.

"Thank you..." I began, but could tell he'd already placed the receiver down.

I could hear muffled voices, footsteps.

Finally, Myra came to the phone.

"Nem? How did you get this number?"

"From a directory."

"A what?"

"The telephone directory... but, Myra, listen..."

"Are you here? Have you arrived?"

"Yes, but..."

"Good, then I'll see you tomorrow for lunch, yes?"

"Myra, I'm here but I might have to leave now... for London."

"What? Why?"

The signal, faint as it was, dropped.

I called back.

"Nem, what happened?"

After I explained—that there wasn't a place for me to stay—our conversation hung around a pause.

"I'm so sorry Nem..."

I said I was sorry too.

"This wretched weather..."

I was almost at the station now, the cold had deepened, the rain strong and steady.

Rather than the weather, I was discomfited by a thought—why didn't she ask me to stay over, at least for the night?

The signal dropped again. This time I didn't call back.

On an impulse, I ducked into The King Arthur, the pub I'd passed earlier. I could feel the stares as I walked in—a scattering of men mostly, white, middle-aged or elderly—but I was concerned with little else apart from the expedient task of acquiring a drink.

"Glenfiddich please... large."

The man behind the counter was suitably swift and surly. Soon enough, whisky blazed down my throat, inspiring a lucid, familiar warmth.

I was tempted by the coal fire, blazing at the other end of the room, but I had little time—and space. A group of locals occupied the table closest to the hearth, and perhaps it wouldn't be wise to challenge their territorial authority.

Where, I wondered, would I find some dinner?

I mulled over the last few sips, not wishing to step back outside.

Suddenly, a beep from my pocket. A phone call.

A private, undisclosed number.

"Hello?"

"Are you on the train?" It was Myra.

"No, it's at..."

"You can't go back. You must come home."

I hesitated. "Are you sure?"

"Yes, of course... where are you?"

"In a pub at the moment..."

In half an hour, she said, she'd pick me up from the station.

———

At that time of the evening, it was an abandoned movie set. The ticket counter closed, the gates indiscriminately open. I waited by the entrance, trying to steal some shelter from the rain. Behind me, on the other side, the platform stretched long and empty.

Soon enough, a car turned in from the road.

"Nem!" I heard my name but was bathed in the glare of headlights and blinded. The engine turned off. I blinked, still sightless. A door slammed. Quickened footsteps.

"I'm so sorry..."

Myra looked red-cheeked and flustered, her tweed coat unbuttoned, her beret askew.

"It's alright... I haven't been waiting long."

"Oh, but you have... and walking around in this rain."

Before I could offer or protest, she picked up my suitcase, walked to the car, and threw it into the back seat. It was an old Austin, dark blue, with shiny silver bumpers and hub caps. I squeezed into the front; it smelled of leather, mud and dust. Myra slipped into the driver's seat, placed gloved hands on the wheels. "Right... we won't be long..."

"Thank you," I said.

She looked across, her face outlined in shadow. "Don't be absurd."

A twenty-minute drive took us through winding country lanes, flanked by tall hedges, dipping and rising. Sometimes so narrow that, at one point, she had to stop at a lay-by to give way to an oncoming car. With the rush of darkness on either side, the world had ceased to exist. I wondered how she managed, a life so remote, and why, what kept her there.

I didn't ask.

We spoke about the train journey, the weather—there would be time later to speak of other things.

Soon, the lane opened out into a road, the night stretching on all sides apart from the patch of yellow headlights.

"Not far now... the house is just beyond the hollow."

The road sloped low and deep, cutting through a forested hill, an ancient path carved out by centuries. And then we rose, and turned left, through a gate, and down a gravelly drive leading to a double story house, with white stucco walls and Georgian windows. Instead of opening the door, Myra stared out at the building as though she could barely recognize it. She started to say something then stopped. Hesitated. Then she turned to me, "Just a word about my father... he isn't the easiest person to be around."

I wasn't certain how to react. What should I say? Polite thanks for the warning, or request for elaboration. I opted for neither.

Was he the one who'd answered my phone call?

She nodded.

I tried to make light of it, saying not to worry, she'd never met mine.

"No, you don't understand..." she fiddled with the car keys. "Just... he can be a bit difficult."

"I hope it's alright... me staying over..." I couldn't believe it hadn't struck me until now to say this.

"Of course." She was suddenly vehement. "We couldn't possibly have let you spend the night in a station..."

"I was going to find a manger."

She laughed and we stepped out. The countryside silence was interrupted by the strains of a piano. A rhythmic repetition of chords, deployed, admittedly, not with the greatest skill. Perhaps her father liked to entertain visitors with recitals.

"This way." Instead of heading toward the house, Myra walked down a paved path leading to what looked like the garage. I followed, the stroller suitcase bumping behind me on the gravel. Like magic, a motion-sensor bulb switched on, flooding us in golden light. The ground floor was fitted with a wide green garage, and a flight of steps on the side, overgrown with climbing plants, led up to a wooden door.

"You're staying in the loft," explained Myra.

The top floor had been converted into a studio, with space enough for a modest circular dining table, a large wrought iron bed, a cupboard, and fitted in the corner, a fridge and sink. The low roof sloped over us, with skylights cut into it like rectangles of darkness. A painting took up the space of an entire wall, drawing all attention towards it. An explosion of fruit, insects, and flowers scattered across a canvas of unwavering Mediterranean blue. A Dutch still life broken free of stylistic constraints.

"My mother painted that," she said, "a few years before she died."

It contained, I wanted to tell her, all life.

We stood, for a moment, in silence, before Myra moved to the door. "I'll leave you to freshen up... supper is at a half seven. Come downstairs before?"

It was unusual, her precise delineation of time. Perhaps her father was particular about these things.

"Who was playing the piano?" I asked.

She smiled—"You'll meet him"—and was gone.

With twenty minutes to spare, I unpacked my suitcase. A gift-wrapped box of Neuhaus chocolates for Myra from Harrods—they'd cost me a week's rent. I realized then I hadn't brought anything for her father. But it couldn't be helped since, originally, I wasn't meant to meet him. I placed a pair of trousers, shirts, socks into the cupboard; they filled little of the cavernous space. Finally, from my coat pocket, the jade ox figurine, which I carried with me everywhere. I placed it on the table, next to a bowl of potpourri.

From the window, I could see the formless shapes of trees, and hedges, and length of wall, shadow layered upon shadow.

By the bed, a narrow bookshelf overflowed with old classics—Dickens, the Brontës, Hardy, Keats, Shelley, Wordsworth. Going by the collection, modernism and everything after had never taken place. The fridge stocked a lonely bottle of milk, a loaf of bread. In the corner, an unobtrusive door opened to a tiny airplane-style bathroom, fitted with a toilet and shower. I washed at the sink, flinching in turn from icy water flowing from one tap, and scalding heat from the other.

Finally, I walked out. One step down and the flood light blazed on. It felt as though I was alone on a stage, and didn't quite know which part I was meant to be playing.

I walked across to the house, my breath forming spirits before my face. Should I go to the back door? No, I was a guest. Not a family friend.

I pressed the doorbell, and waited. The piano player had stopped. Above the wooden mailbox hung a nameplate carved in dark grey stone—Wintervale.

I expected Myra to come to the door, or her father, but it was opened by a boy, no older than nine or ten, breathless, clutching what looked like a decapitated toy penguin. We stared at each other—thick dark hair curled messily around his ears, his cheeks flushed.

"Hello," I said.

He had bright, wide eyes with no hint of wariness or fear. They were green or grey, it was difficult to tell.

"Is that for me?" His gaze had fallen on the gift under my arm.

"Elliot." It was Myra, coming down the stairs at the end of the foyer. "You mustn't keep people waiting." She looked at me. "I do apologize."

We entered the drawing room, spacious and surprisingly modern, with an ivory sofa set in the centre, arranged around a fireplace draped with holly. At one end, wide shelves and an elegant chaise longue, more for style than convenience, and at the other a deep bay window. The ceiling rose pristinely white, while the walls were papered by pale floral damask, tinged in leaf-green. In a corner, a Christmas tree gleamed and flickered, decorated in silver and gold.

For a moment, everything seemed touched by something unreal.

"This is Elliot..." Myra paused before adding, "my son."

I tried to sound casual while greeting him, hoping the surprise didn't show through.

"Elliot," she continued, "this is an old friend... you can call him Nem."

The boy, still holding on to the headless seabird, gave me a long scrutinizing stare. "Mummy told me you're from India... is that true?"

"Yes, I am."

"Do you have an elephant? I saw on TV... a man from India who had a pet elephant."

"No... but I know a man who can speak to birds."

The boy's eyes widened.

"You can ask him all about it tomorrow," said Myra. "Now, go find Flapper's head, and put all your toys away."

You didn't tell me you had a son...

Except, of course, she had no reason to. We'd shared no more than a fleeting encounter, years ago, in a bungalow in the old city on the other side of the world. Nothing in common but Nicholas. Then and now. Running through us like a fault line. But it was enough to have drawn us here together so we could untangle the past.

"This is for you..." I handed her the chocolates.

"Thank you, Nem... you shouldn't have..." She walked over to the tree, and placed it alongside a pile of other gift-wrapped boxes.

"What's in it?" Elliot stood at the door, Flapper dangling inelegantly by his side.

"It's a surprise, darling," said Myra. "Now, let's get you ready for bed. Come along..."

She said she'd be down soon and ushered him upstairs.

I stood by the fireplace and put my hands to the flames. It made me nervous, this scrupulous pristineness. What if my shoes had dragged in dirt? I checked, quickly. They hadn't, but I wished I'd worn a smarter pair. (Thank heavens I'd splurged on the chocolates.) The overmantle mirror calmly reflected the door and walls, a large impasto painting of white tulips, a floor lamp, me. A framed certificate hung left of the fire-place, a blue insignia with a declaration of an appointment to the Order of the British Empire. I stepped closer: for services to education. More intriguing, though, was the cabinet below that held an assortment of alcoholic beverages, as well as a decorative glass dome covering a pair of taxidermy birds. Mud brown apart from a gash of scarlet on their heads, they looked eerily, disconcertingly alive.

On the mantelpiece, stood slender candle holders on one end, and on the other, two tilting black and white photographs. Of Myra's mother—clear skin and fine bones, her eyes, I imagined, in shades of cloudy sky—and a man in uniform, glancing into the camera, rippling with youth. A heavy mustache, a strong chin. I leaned in, drawn to the shape of his mouth, the curve of his jaw.

"When did you arrive?"

I whipped around.

"Half-past five," Sir. I almost added.

"Just off the boat then?"

He held out his hand. "Philip." It was firm, cold to the touch.

"I'm Nehemiah... Myra's friend."

"So she told me. From London, did you say?" His eyes were pale blue, shadows in the snow.

"Yes, I mean, that's where I am now... for a few more months. I'm from India."

"India." He said the word with affected grandeur. "Brought the mon-soons here, have you?"

I smiled. "Seems like it."

He gestured to an armchair—I sat down—and he moved to the table with the bottles and birds.

"Would you like a drink?"

My polite refusal was met with boisterous disapproval. "Come now, nothing to warm you up? Whisky? How about a gin and tonic? Or a nice dry sherry? Yes?"

"I was offered a job once in India…" He mentioned a public school in the north of the country. "You might have heard of it…"

I said I had. Did he take it up?

"Oh no… I didn't." He didn't offer a reason why.

Since the conversation seemed to have halted, I asked the most perfunctory of questions—whether he'd ever visited the Indian subcontinent.

"I'm afraid not," he said. "The closest I got… was Australia… no, Jakarta, for some conference or the other."

The glow from the fire spilled into the room; above the spit and crackle of the wood, I could hear the low drum of rain. Discreetly, I studied Philip's profile—an outline of bold strokes, a long, sturdy nose, a rugged expanse of forehead and cheek, and oddly delicate, feminine lips. A portrait by Francis Bacon, completed by someone else.

His face seemed strangely familiar.

Where could I have possible seen him? Perhaps it was a trick of light. Or alcohol. My G&T, I could tell, was more generously supplied with gin than tonic.

"So how do you know Myra?"

The safest answer was we'd met through a common friend.

"Over in London?"

I hesitated. No, years ago in India.

Surprise glimmered on his face for a moment, and then it was gone, replaced by mild curiosity.

"Oh, I don't recall when she went…"

I could tell him. To the day.

He laughed. "But then, one can't be privy to everything in our children's lives, can we?"

"No." It was Myra, at the door. "One can't be privy to everything in anyone's life."

Supper, she went on to announce, was ready.

———————

The dining room across the foyer was a smaller space painted egg-shell blue, with a series of still life paintings—fruit, fish and game—on the wall. We sat on slender, high-backed chairs; Philip at the head and Myra and I on either side. Her dress matched the hydrangeas arranged at the centre of the table, a deep royal purple. Strung around her neck, a discreet line of pearls.

As with every meal shared, this too began with a ritual—the flurry of napkins, the polite passing around of food. A dance of hands and cutlery. We started with a creamy mushroom soup, and moved on to long-simmered coq au vin. On the side, glistening Brussels sprouts, potato mash, and rolls of crusty, rosemary-infused bread.

Myra served herself small, tidy portions. Philip poured the wine, a rich Burgundy Bouchard Aîné Fils, elegantly woody and spiced. I was ravenous but ate slowly, taking care to compliment the food—"Did you make this, Myra?"

She laughed. "No, I'm afraid my culinary skills are mostly non-existent. We have a lady coming in to help around the house... Mrs. Hammond... you'll meet her tomorrow."

Of course, I should have known, and not asked what now seemed a silly question. Given where they lived, it was hardly likely Myra managed the household. Somehow, the exchange dampened my hunger, compressing it into a tight, leaden ball at the bottom of my stomach.

"What are you doing in London?" asked Philip. "Do you play a musical instrument too?"

No, I didn't...

"Ah, you play cricket then, I'm sure."

"Not everyone in India plays cricket," interrupted Myra.

"Daddy..."

"I'm only joking." He looked at me. "You know I'm joking, don't you?"

I nodded.

"Besides," he said, "I prefer tennis. Do you play tennis, Nehemiah?"

No, I was afraid not.

"Swim?"

Not much.

He went on to say that was a pity; else we might've used the pool or courts at Kingsley, a school nearby where he used to be headmaster.

"They're indoors," clarified Myra. "What are your plans for the holidays?" she added, perhaps in a bid to change the subject. She sounded like Eva.

"Let me guess," said Philip, looking at me over the rim of his wine glass, "you don't ski either?"

"I do."

"*Do* you?"

"No... I was joking."

Philip laughed, a hearty, wholesome laugh—with me, or at me, I wasn't sure.

We'd just started dessert—apple crumble and warm custard—when Philip said he'd met Geoff, while taking the horses out that afternoon. "Geoffrey Ritchie... he lives down the road from us," he added for my benefit. "Poor chap... still having problems with his neighbors."

"You mean the young couple?" asked Myra.

Allegedly, they'd driven a fence a few meters into his property, and after a number of rows, each more escalated than the last, he was taking them to court.

"Oh, dad, he's a crotchety old man."

Her father chuckled, sipping his wine.

"I think it's silly, to fight over a bit of mud..." said Myra.

"I suppose he feels, well, three meters today... four tomorrow... and soon he'll be feeding them supper too."

"What horses do you have?" I asked.

Philip leaned back, appraising me, my question. "Only ever kept Irish Hunters."

"May I come round to see them? If that's alright..."

"Do you ride, Nem?" Myra seemed surprised.

She didn't remember.

"Yes... although it's been a while."

The dessert sat tart and ripe on my tongue. I could feel the tiredness now, seeping into my limbs.

"Come see the horses tomorrow," said Philip. "General and Lady. Fine animals. Unless you have other plans..."

"I thought I'd take Nem for a walk... down Triscombe Way." Myra sketched out our plans for the next three days—perhaps a drive to the moors, a visit to the village. "All depending on the weather..."

"I'm in London on Saturday," said Philip. "You can do what you like, but don't take the horses out. Not if I'm not around."

"We won't." She turned to me, "Dad goes up for monthly meetings at the Whiley Club."

"What sort of club is it?" I asked.

"Like the Bullingdon," he replied, "only the members are fifty years older." He pushed himself away from the table, "Now, how about a whisky? I've got a lovely twelve-year Lochnagar... they say it's the Queen's favorite."

———

Later, Philip retired to his study, while Myra and I sat by the fire; the flames now burning low. I still cradled the whisky; denser than I was accustomed to, though with a pleasant dryness around the edges.

"I know it's absurd but I feel like I've seen your father before... some where..."

"It *is* absurd! Dad doesn't leave the house. Apart from going riding or hunting."

"And London."

"Yes. To mooch around with a bunch of stuffy old men."

I hesitated. "I hope I haven't offended him in any way..."

"Good grief, no. He's—I told you, he can be a bit... forthright."

"I wouldn't like to be here if—"

"It isn't a bother, Nem... I invited you. It was only fair. We couldn't possibly have you travel back to London or god knows where in the middle of the night. Besides, it's quite a victory he relented. One of few."

"How did you convince him?"

"I told him you were an Indian prince."

We laughed into our drinks, and I said, "It would've been a waste, to come all this way and then leave without seeing you..."

She nodded. "Yes, I think we both need... help."

I'd expected her to say *to talk*.

She glanced at her watch. "I must check on Elliot... and look through some music. You must be tired... would you like to go to bed? Shall we talk tomorrow?"

I couldn't wait any longer. Suddenly, I didn't think I could ever sleep.

"What about tonight? Later..."

She hesitated. "I'll come across if I can."

Back in the loft, I lay on the bed and stared out the skylights into pitch darkness. Waiting for footfall, for a soft knock at the door, but no one visited apart from the wind, stronger and louder here, away from the enclosures of the city. A fluttering came from the roof, the movement of small creatures, birds or bats. My eyes burned, but I couldn't sleep. Perhaps it was the silence. In London, always the stirrings of the night, the wail of police sirens, or ambulances, the distinct whir of helicopters.

When the creatures stopped moving, the quiet lay deep and unyielding. The strangeness of being here kept me awake. The utterly unexpected turn of events. The awkwardness of being a guest in a household where I was little more than a stranger.

I stood up for a glass of water. Maybe I could read something from the bookshelf. Or, if I was truly enthusiastic, work on my article for Nithi. That would send me right off to sleep. Yet I suppose what truly provoked my sleeplessness was that I was here, and still hadn't had a chance to speak with Myra. I'd waited a century already. And who knew how much our stories would tally, how many of our memories were similar, how far they'd diverge.

Do you ride, Nem?

What other things had she forgotten?

And what of all the things I couldn't remember?

When I moved to the window and looked out, I saw a lit window in the main house. What a strange, unrestful place. If Myra was still up, why didn't she come across?

A figure moved into view; it was Philip. Standing between the gap in the curtains, looking down, at something in his hand. He lifted his head and glanced outside, the darkness held his stare briefly before he moved away.

———

One afternoon, when I visited the bungalow on Rajpur Road, Nicholas and Myra were talking about horses. The previous night, they'd visited the Delhi Gymkhana Club, and one of the members offered them, on his invitation, to ride at the Army Polo and Riding Club. Myra was thrilled.

"She attended some horribly posh school where they learnt useless skills like that," said Nicholas. A shower of cushions flew at him across the veranda.

"While you played rugby at your all-male, all-gay boarding school."

"I won't deny it. I was star scrum half."

Myra was nursing a gin and tonic on the divan; she'd declared it much too warm for tea that day, even in the dead of Delhi winter. "Won't you come with us?"

"Who? Me?"

She laughed. "Of course, who else do you see here?"

It was hard to believe, since, so far, she'd hardly taken the trouble to include me in any of their plans. Nicholas was sitting at the table, watching me. I wished he'd offer an indication of what my answer should be.

"Well," I replied. "I don't know how to ride a horse." That was an understatement. I'd never been near one in my life.

This time, Nicholas spoke up. "Don't worry, all you need to know is which way is front."

The next afternoon, I found myself wishing it really was that simple.

We were at the riding club, nestled in the leafy environs of central west Delhi, carved out from the Ridge,

What petrified me was their height.

I hadn't imagined horses could be so tall. That far off the ground.

And I looked ridiculous in the gear, the shiny boots, the fitted pants, the nut-shaped helmet. Hastily sourced from Nicholas' wardrobe and the alleyways of Connaught Place.

At the dressage arena outside the club house, Myra adjusted her riding boots, while Nicholas spoke with one of the instructors.

"Two advanced," I could hear him say, "and one absolute beginner."

When our horses were led out, I was relieved to see I'd been allotted the smallest of the trio—a black mare with patient eyes and a sweetly curved mouth. We were encouraged to acquaint ourselves with the animals, speak to them softly, stroke their long noses. Soon, Myra had mounted her horse, laughing in delight. It was easy to see she was a skillful rider, light and confident. She'd been doing this all her life. Beyond the arena lay acres of forested ground, with winding trails crossed by jackals and peacocks; that's where, she said, she'd like to head. Nicholas too, mounted, and moved about in a gentle trot.

"Have you been on a horse before?" asked the instructor. He was a petite man, with an elfin face and large, toughened lands.

Did you not hear him say 'absolute beginner'?

"No, I haven't..."

"Okay, no need to be afraid." He smiled, and I tried to feel a little more encouraged. Rather than allowing me to mount straight away, he first explained the equipment—the halter and the bridle, the reins and the stirrups. By the time I stepped on the mounting block, Nicholas and Myra were nowhere to be seen. He led me circuitously around the arena, at a slow, steady pace, all the while calling out instructions. *Keep your elbows tucked in... sit square in the middle of the saddle... keep your hands level when holding the reins... push your heels down and point your toes up to the sky...*

After an hour, he allowed me, for a short instance, to move on my own. It was frightening, and thrilling. I liked that it depended on small gestures, moving gently on the saddle in sync with the horse's rhythm. It was easier than swimming; somehow, less alien, less unfamiliar.

"Good... good," said the instructor as I passed him. I could see Nicholas approaching, with Myra a short distance behind, their horses cantering swiftly. Nicholas slowed down, and dismounted by the arena; he leaned on the railing, watching, smiling. "Well done," he called. "You're a natural."

I swelled with joy and pride.

Slow down by briefly squeezing your thighs against the horse...

The instructor helped me dismount. I slipped off my helmet, turning around to Nicholas. I looked past him at Myra; I should thank her for inviting me, but I stopped short—she was frowning at the sight of us, her face twisted into something raw and enraged.

Perhaps, that's why I was there. Because she hoped I'd make a fool of myself.

Yet, in an instant, it was gone. I could have imagined it. She waved, laughing. Like a cloud moving across the sun, or a bird's shadow rippling on water.

———

That first morning at Wintervale, I breakfasted in the loft.

Myra had said I was welcome to join them, but they ate early, at half past seven.

Maybe I'd prefer to lie in?

Wastrel, I was certain Philip would say.

Which is why I had every intention of waking up on time and proving him wrong.

But it was almost dawn before I finally fell asleep. I'd watched the sky lighten, gradually like a slow miracle. When I opened my eyes, the clock showed past nine.

If there'd been a chance to impress Philip with my rigorous self-discipline, it was irrefutably lost.

I took my toast and tea outside, to the wooden stairs. It was a cold but patchily sunny winter day. Beyond the stone wall around the edges of the garden, the Hawthorne hedges along the road, farmland dipped and swelled, marked by the straight tallness of poplars, the rounded sprawl of oak. Wintervale had no immediate neighbors, surrounded instead by windswept fields. What struck me was not the unfamiliar quiet, the unfamiliar sounds—the persistent mooing of cows in the distance, the whir of machinery—but the smell of the countryside. How the air was laden with richness. Each shift of wind carried earth and grass, or the deep, piquant odor of dung and wet leaves.

It was, strangely enough, un-repulsive.

At that time, the house lay stonily quiet, and I thought I was the only one out, but in the yard, Elliot was riding a bicycle. In regular untiring circles. I hadn't yet had a chance to observe him well until now.

I watched the boy, his curly dark hair, the shape of his nose, the slant of cheek.

In daylight, all could be revealed.

Soon, Myra emerged from the back of the house and strolled over to him, her boots crunching heavily on the gravel. In the pale sunlight, her ochre-blue jumper, asymmetrical and oversized, looked like a piece torn out of the sky. She stroked Elliot's head, and glanced up towards the loft.

"Good morning," she called.

"Sorry I wasn't up for breakfast..."

"That's alright; Dad thinks you're a wastrel."

I said I wasn't surprised.

"I'm joking... did you sleep alright?"

"I think the bats kept me up all night."

"Oh, I was going to warn you about that... I'm afraid we can't touch them... we're part of some bats conservation trust. Volunteers drop by to check on them... we'd have you to blame if anything happened."

"I'll make sure I sing them a lullaby tonight."

She laughed, squinting up at me. The sun was in her eyes. "Would you like to go for a walk? You can see the horses after..."

I sipped my tea. "Alright."

Swiftly, I washed up and changed, and twenty minutes later, walked past Elliot's abandoned cycle. Outside the kitchen door, I found Myra surveying a pile of muddy, military green wellington boots.

"I wasn't sure of your size."

None fit perfectly, so I wore double socks and pulled on ones a size too large. She'd changed into a black pair.

"Is Elliot coming along?"

She shook her head. "Mrs Hammond will keep an eye on him."

I hesitated. "And your father?"

"Out with the horses."

I silently hoped we wouldn't run into him on our trail.

We set out and walked along the main road for a short while before turning off into a dirt track flanked by thick blackthorn hedge, too late now for their sloe berries that would have ripened in October. Fields unfurled behind us, pockmarked by frost, the soil hard and bitter-brown, scattered with sycamore trees molded into strange shapes by the wind. They were barren now, and their branches looked like a vast network of veins against the sky. The short tough grass crunched beneath our boots.

"How old is Elliot?"

"Ten... almost eleven..."

"He's Nicholas', isn't he?"

Her silence was affirmative.

We walked without speaking; somewhere I could hear the sound of running water. Soon the blackthorn that flanked us dipped and disappeared; the path swerved to the right alongside a swift, clear stream.

"Nem," she began, "I called you here—"

"You said we needed help? What did you mean?"

To my surprise, she laughed.

We were approaching a cluster of weeping willows, their branches so low and heavy they formed a long canopy, a bare, brown cage. She twisted through, and I followed.

"Don't you see?" Her eyes were the color of morning frost.

"I'm not sure what you mean..."

She tugged on a branch, it dipped easily.

"When I met you at the concert... and you told me you were there because of Nicholas... you had that look on your face... such hope. That he'd be there. You hoped he'd be there, didn't you?"

I didn't reply.

"How many years has it been?"

"Since?"

"Since you lived with him in Delhi... for... oh, I don't know... six months..."

"Eleven," I corrected.

Myra fished out a cigarette and lighter from her pocket. I'd never seen her smoke before.

In the wind, the branches curled around us, drawing closer.

"I was exactly like you... Nicholas was... was like breath. I met him in London, at a concert. He told me he watched only my fingers while I played... and my mouth." She exhaled a thin stream of smoke. "I was twenty-one and thought I'd met a god. Someone so impeccably perfect... I found it hard to believe he was real. We didn't seem to do what other people... other couples did... with him I felt I was watching the world from afar... that it was all out there, everything I ever wanted, and I could reach out and touch it. It was that simple. And so it continued... until one day, he told me he was leaving for India, that he was going away on fieldwork..."

She lifted her head, gazing at something ahead that I couldn't spy.

"Have you ever counted time? I mean, really, counted the minutes, the days, like your mind is some kind of giant hourglass. I wrote him letters everyday—some I just tore up and threw away, scared they might overwhelm him... some I posted..."

"You wrote him letters?"

"Endlessly..."

I want you in me.

Always,

M.

Even though it was midday, the sky had grown overcast, the sun swiftly hidden behind low, quilted clouds. The day glowed with a hidden light, lit from within.

"At some point," she continued, "I planned this elaborate surprise to travel to India to see him... I was full of him, and only him, and being apart felt like a million needles tearing at me..."

I thought of that afternoon on the lawn, when Myra walked out in her grey dress, still sleepy. "And then you landed up..."

She nodded. "That December... yes, he was so angry. I'd never seen him... anyone... so ... angry." Her voice was soft, almost as though she was speaking to herself. I could only imagine his fury; he'd never directed his wrath at me, but I'd had hints of it, an abrupt stormy sullenness, a swift impatience.

She tugged at a branch again, and let it swing back. "I'd built up this vision of happiness... and he was enraged by my appearance. I couldn't understand it. But there was nothing to be done... I was there, and I couldn't leave... at least he didn't make me leave. I remember that morning, he went away... I don't know where... for a while, and when he returned, he was calmer, saying we could work something out. That I must say I was his cousin or step-sister... that people in India were conservative, and they would talk, and it wouldn't be acceptable for us to be in the same house if we weren't related somehow."

"And you believed him?"

"I would've believed anything to calm him down... and put him in a better mood."

She stubbed the cigarette, and walked through the canopy, finding her way out.

Our boots squelched through endless mud, the smell of dung rising thickly ripe and sweet. The hills in the distance seemed painted, hazy behind a light, gauzy mist.

"At first I didn't know what to make of you. When I asked Nicholas... he told me you were delicate... disturbed, in fact... that he'd saved you after you tried to harm yourself..." Myra stopped, and turned to me. "Is that true?"

"It wasn't quite like that..."

She didn't move.

"No. I didn't."

She continued walking. "He said you'd developed a deep and intense gratitude, this psychological dependence on him... and he was afraid to upset the balance and tip you over again... so I was to treat you well..." She smiled. "He called you his pet."

My blank slate.

"I felt sorry for you, of course... but sometimes, I was jealous, I hated your proximity to him... something just didn't seem to fit... but I couldn't place it." The wind blew her hair across her face. "Now, I know. It's true, isn't it... you and him?"

"And Elliot?" I asked softly.

She leaned over the gate, the bar pressing into her stomach. As though she was reaching out for something she couldn't grasp.

"When Nicholas returned from India, we were together for a while in London. I was finishing music school, and things were fine for a few months, or so I thought. And then, suddenly, like it so often happens... they weren't. He'd be annoyed at me... for—I don't know—forgetting to wash my teacup. Silly things that turned into everything. We'd argue, he'd leave... I'd leave... it was terrifying just for how long we could go on... this endless, relentless battle. Like Elliot and his little toy soldiers and forts... destroying and rebuilding. Then, one day he left. He disappeared and didn't return."

I said it had been that way too, in Delhi. When I returned, one July morning, and Nicholas was gone.

"At least you didn't find out two weeks later you were pregnant." She laughed, thin and hollow; it reminded me of Eva.

"You didn't tell him, did you?"

The silence was broken by the distant rumble of a vehicle. The roar of its engine echoed in the quiet country air.

"In my eighth month... in sheer desperation... I crawled back here..." she gestured grandly around her, "where I've been trying to get away from my whole life."

"And your father... ?"

She lit another cigarette. Then, absentmindedly, or perhaps she changed her mind, she flicked it away. "My father took me in... disgusted as he was by his daughter. I had no money, no savings, no job... I was a musician, for Christ's sake. All the while I thought I'd get rid of it, and I put it off... again and again, until it was too late... but he took care of everything, my father... Elliot had a nanny, he's being given music lessons... he's going to boarding school soon... no expense spared, really..."

"It's good of him, to look after you like that."

"Me? He's not doing it for me. It's for Elliot... my father has an immaculate sense of fair play... it's not my son's fault and therefore, he won't be made to suffer."

"And you?"

Her eyes were a long-lost evening blue. "I offer him... my obedience."

"Myra..."

"Yes?"

"Don't you think you ought to..."

"Tell Nicholas?"

She climbed over the gate, and started making her way across the field. Here, the scent lingered of freshly turned earth, something light, and mildly flowery. The mist was thickening, rising over the ground like smoke; the light that had throbbed through the day earlier was beginning to drain away.

I caught up with her.

"He abandoned me..."

He abandoned everybody.

"I have no wish to see him again." From the look on her face I could see it was true. "And so it should be with you."

We crossed the field, and walked down the narrow country trail that joined the main road. The air echoed with the clopping of hooves. It was Philip on a mare with a glistening chestnut coat, her mane, tail and lower legs edged in lighter hazel, and a streak of white running down her nose.

He stopped beside us. "I'm heading back... she's tired this morning." He patted the horse's neck.

"We're going home too," said Myra. "We walked by Coram's Way. I was showing Nem around—"

A small, speeding car suddenly rounded the corner and zipped past. The mare shifted nervously, flicking her ears—I reached out and touched the side of her head and stroked her. She nuzzled my hand.

Philip edged her away from us. "I'm taking her home... before we meet more idiots on the road."

When he was out of earshot, I said I wasn't certain he meant only the driver.

Myra laughed. "He likes you, Nem... although the horses are the only creatures he truly loves. We used to have three, but when Charlie was put down, Dad vowed these would be the last ones he'd keep."

"We went riding in Delhi... when you were there."

"Did we?"

It was hard to imagine how something so embossed in my mind, could be equally absent from hers.

"Yes... you and Nicholas would go swimming..."

"I remember that... to a pool at this big white hotel."

"Then you met someone who was a member at a riding club... I don't know why you invited me along. You probably wanted me to fall off and break my neck. Or worse, make a fool of myself."

"Probably... I wanted to show off."

We were at the dip of the Hollow, and above us, oak trees domed across shutting out the leaf-tangled sky. For a while, we were in shadow, and then we emerged, at the crest of the slope, into sunlight.

Later that afternoon I headed to the stables.

It stood on the other side of a field at the back of the house, hidden from view by tall, rambling hedgerow that hemmed its borders. In the spring, Myra told me, the field was flecked gold with buttercups, and along the shady edges, replete with bluebells. Now, bereft of flowers, it rolled out in shades of dull brown and listless yellow. I even came upon a dead sparrow, a small, upturned tragedy, its eyes ever watchful as I passed.

The stables were a surprisingly modern structure of light wooden planks and a neat tin roof. Inside, clean and warm, cheerful with the sunny smell of straw and sawdust. Someone from the village came in to help everyday.

"But I like doing this myself," said Philip. He was brushing Lady down with a soft brush. "I can lament the fate of the world, and she just listens. Myra would come in here quite often... not so much anymore."

I was in the neighboring cubicle, stroking General. He was a larger, more muscled animal, with a deep charcoal coat, white stocking marks and a star on his forehead.

"They're both beautiful..." I said.

"General's a good-looking fellow. We could take them out tomorrow, if you like... how long are you here?"

Two days more. Leaving Sunday, on the afternoon train.

"What did you say you did in London?"

I told him.

"A what—?"

I tried to explain what it entailed, a fellowship from the Royal Literary Fund, but I couldn't help feel he wasn't all that captivated.

"And back in India?"

"I write on art."

He brushed down Lady's forelegs, his arms stretching, straining. I could see why he still looked the way he did, physically spry and spirited.

"Wonderful," he said, straightening up. Either as a response to the admission of my profession, or the competent execution of his task.

On my part, it was affirmation.

Of the worlds we choose to inhabit. And the ones we exclude. In school, I enjoyed Venn diagrams not for their mathematical functions—of which I have a hazy recollection—but their aesthetic intricacies. The infinite possibilities of patterns, intersections, unions, complements, symmetries and overlaps. You could say Philip and I inhabited circles that didn't, would never, touch.

For him, I might have been of less interest than the horses.

———

If prophecies carve a design for the future, premonitions weave patterns into our past.

They're tricky things, unattributed until an event has already happened. Coincidences magnified in our mind, given the weight of instinctual foresight.

At Wintervale, I often dreamed of Lenny.

Was it a sign, I still wonder? Could dreams presage death? Tragedy? Look how many words we've invented to speak of knowing the future. Omen, portent, forewarning, augury. All these signals we should somehow recognize.

I dreamed I visited Lenny's grave. Wandering lost, searching for it among weathered tombstones. Finding it on a hillock, under the shade of a sal tree. A quiet spot, away from the rest. His grave blanketed with wilting flowers, with candles burnt down to uneven stumps.

I'm sorry I didn't visit sooner.

On the wooden cross, a name, a date of birth, and death.

I'd forgotten to bring a token, to show I'd been there to pay my respects.

Empty-handed.

I'm sorry.

Sitting beside the grave, on short, prickly grass, above me the leaves whispering in their own tongues, gesturing in the breeze. Everything around me carrying traces of him. Then they too falling, wilting and dropping to the ground. My friend was part of something larger and more secret than I would ever know for now.

———

The morning I went riding with Philip I was greeted with a well-aimed jibe. "You're up," he said, "well done."

He had reason to provoke, I suppose.

The previous evening, after my visit to the stables, I fell asleep and almost missed dinner.

I was woken by a soft yet persistent knocking at the door.

It was Mrs Hammond.

"Sorry... but I'm afraid everyone's waiting."

I rushed over, and found them seated at the dining table, their plates empty.

"I'm sorry... I was tired... and took a nap."

Graciously, Myra said it was alright.

Philip remarked that he was glad I was having a truly relaxed holiday.

"I head out early with the horses... think you'll be able to hustle out of bed by seven?"

I flushed. Yes, of course.

Which was why I was standing outside the stables, shivering in my riding gear. Philip had brought the horses out, all saddled and bridled. Since I didn't have boots, I was attempting this in wellingtons.

"I'd be careful with those," Philip pointed out. "If you fall off, there's a risk your foot could get caught... they don't have smooth soles..."

"*If* I fall off," I muttered.

I found myself wishing I hadn't ever asked about the horses. Least of all, agreed to go riding in the dead of winter. After the alarm sounded that morning, I'd lain in bed wondering if I could escape this somehow, come up with an excuse—and I hadn't.

"General's tougher to control sometimes... so you can ride Lady," said Philip.

I was relieved; she was smaller too, and less intimidating. Before I mounted, I wondered whether it was worth reiterating to my host that I hadn't ridden in a while. I stroked Lady's neck, trying to recall it in order—I could picture my instructor's face, all those years ago, his elfin features. His voice. I wished there was a mounting block. I stood on the left and faced the saddle.

"Adjust your reins," said Philip. "Shorten the one inside."

I lifted my left leg into the stirrup, reached for the pommel, and slowly pulled myself up, sinking gently onto Lady's back.

"You haven't ridden in a while, have you?" asked Philip.

"No."

"Don't worry." He sounded cheerful, if not reassuring. "We'll take the easy track today, show you a bit of this part of the country."

Now, I slowly eased into the rise and fall, remembering why, for me, this had always been a source of delight. For the moment, the day was overcast yet dry, the clouds a light and smoky grey. My mood, like the morning, lifted. Perhaps this hadn't been such a terrible idea after all.

Off the main road, Philip led us along a desolate farm track. Apart from the clop of hooves, the air hung cold and quiet. Here, the smell of dung grew fainter. Instead, a mix of wet leaves and old mulch lifted up to us, sweet and decadent. Soon, we crossed a maple wood that edged, he told me, an abandoned limestone quarry. At the end of the farm, we came to a ford—normally easy to cross, but the recent rains had swelled it to a fast-flowing stream.

"This way," shouted Philip, and we diverted, taking a longer route that led us over a stone bridge.

"You're alright riding uphill?"

I hesitated. I'd never done it before. The grounds in Delhi were routinely plain and flat.

Couldn't we, I suggested, stick to something similar?

"Stunning views from up Middle Hill..." said Philip, as though he hadn't heard me, "come along..."

It became apparent that he would outline exactly what I was required to do on our ascent. He seemed pleased about playing tutor; I wonder if he mistook me for one of his school boys. We made our way up slowly. Philip rode behind, calling out instructions—lean forward slightly over the saddle, stay centred, balance carefully, inch your feet back. Finally, when we made it to the top, we found most of the valley cloaked in low rumbling clouds. It gave me a strange pleasure to see our efforts thwarted, as though to prove this ridiculous idea was his alone. Nevertheless, I was treated to a description of what we might have viewed—on an especially clear day, it was possible to see as far as the River Parrett delta where it joined the Bristol Channel.

To be polite, I said I was certain it would've been beautiful. That this was atmospheric in its own way, despite the world being hidden away. Eventually, what made us leave was the wind, swift and icy, unfailing in its energy.

The skirmish happened on our way down.

We'd descended about halfway, carefully picking our path, when Lady stumbled on some loose rubble. It would have been alright if I hadn't lost my balance and swayed back, spurring her forward, fast, and then faster, at a canter. Despite the flash of blinding panic, I managed to stay centred, and somehow retain my balance until we reached level ground, and I drew her to a stop. I turned around, laughing in relief, ready to receive some sort of commendation. But Philip's face was marked by a look I'd once seen on Myra's, long ago, at the riding club. Before he even caught up, I could sense his displeasure.

"What was all that about?" His tone betrayed little. Perhaps a stain of displeasure.

"She slipped, I think..."

By this time he'd dismounted. "She has a weak knee," he said, inspecting her. She could've been hurt, badly. It wasn't the correct thing to do, go galloping down a hill.

"I'm sorry—" I stuttered, unsure why I was apologizing, but it was my first and instinctive reaction. To placate.

On the way back, we rode mostly in silence.

Often, he glanced at Lady. I could've told him she was alright, moving as normal, but he didn't ask, so I said nothing. When we reached the stables, I offered to help unsaddle the horses and rub them down. I allowed Philip to show me how to do this methodically—starting with the curry brush in gentle circles at the jaw, down the neck to the shoulders, the entire body, and finally to the inner and outer parts of the legs. And then a quick damp towel rub. Their hooves, he said, he'd clean himself; I could go freshen up.

"Good job," he threw at me when I was at the door.

And since I didn't know how else to respond, I said thank you.

———

The next day, I couldn't move.

I'd had a warning of this when I went to bed inflicted by soreness, but I was unprepared for the onslaught of pain in the morning. It was an effort, to stand and dress, to walk down the loft stairs.

Somehow, I made it for breakfast. At half-past seven, I rang the doorbell at the main house. When no one answered, I let myself in, and headed to the dining room.

The table was laid but empty.

I peered into the drawing room, the Christmas tree, still flickering, looked comical in daylight, and then the kitchen, but not even Mrs Hammond seemed to be around. During the day, the rooms, softened with natural light, lost some of their formality.

I decided to head back to the loft for breakfast. Maybe even catch a nap. Either the family had already eaten, or they'd all headed out without me.

It was Myra, tousle-haired and sleep-heavy.

"Oh, it's you." She wore a silk robe, silvery grey, with long kimono sleeves. "Tea?"

"Yes, although I'd prefer something stronger..."

"This early? Well, why not..."

It was, I explained, for the pain.

"Are you sore from riding?"

That might be a slight understatement.

"Come." She gestured for me to follow her to the kitchen.

"Where's Mrs Hammond?"

"You forget I live in India."

"Ah, yes, of course, I remember. Didn't Nicholas have a battalion of household help?"

She filled the electric kettle, and plucked two cups off a shelf.

"No milk, no sugar, please."

She pulled a face. "Disgusting. Have you not developed a taste for English builder's tea? Strong, full-bodied, milky."

"No."

The kettle rumbled behind her.

"What happened to breakfast?" I gestured to the dining room.

"Dad drove to London early this morning."

I'd forgotten.

"I love these Saturdays," she continued. "They only happen once or twice a month, but they're such a luxury. I sleep in... Elliot sleeps in... you should've too." She tapped me lightly on the shoulder.

"Except I thought I'd make the effort to show up on time... for break-fast."

Myra laughed, pouring water into the cups. The tea leaves unfurled, turn-ing rusty. "You did well. In vain, but I appreciate your good intentions."

"When is he back? By lunch tomorrow? I'll be gone by then..."

"Don't think your father would agree... he'll be happy to see me leave..." The tea was sharp and strong, almost bitter. "Did you say he was a schoolteacher?"

"He was headmaster... at a string of public schools... here, Canada, Cape Town, Australia..."

"That explains why I feel like I should snap to attention whenever he's around."

She smiled. "But today, he's not."

I added more hot water into my cup, lightening the color. "Where's Elliot?"

"Upstairs," she said. "My little monster's watching TV."

Later that morning, the weather cleared just enough to inspire Myra to set out on a picnic.

"But Mummy, it's winter," protested Elliot.

"I might have to agree with him on that," I added.

"Hush now. We'll take our sandwiches to the river. Let's go... so we don't lose the light."

According to her, the more I exercised, the less it would hurt. (I'm certain, I muttered, that's what they said in the army.)

We strolled down the main road, and then turned off into the dirt track flanked by blackthorn hedges. It was hard to believe the world could be so quiet, sunk to the sound of our voices, the grasp of stone, mud, and grass. On the way, we met an elderly couple walking their black Labrador. I marveled that even in this weather their clothing was so light—the gentleman in a dark green bomber jacket, and the lady in a violet fleece jumper. They looked the picture of resilience, their skin reddened by the winter air, their strides even and purposeful. The man nodded curtly at us, while his wife was more vociferous—"Lovely to see you dear... how big your son has grown... and how is your father?"

Myra introduced me to them—Geoff and Elizabeth—as her friend from London.

"Where are you from?" asked Geoff.

"From—"

"London," interrupted Myra. "Born and brought up in the city."

I couldn't catch her eye, so I smiled on, pretending I wasn't surprised, or puzzled.

The lady did better than her husband at hiding her incredulity.

After a few minutes of small talk, during which time Elliot and I petted the dog, we parted.

"That's Geoff Ritchie," whispered Myra, "Remember? My dad was telling us he's filing a court case for his land..." She cast a glance back at the couple. "If I was their neighbor, I'd ram a fence into *them*."

"They might not feel it. Did you see how little winter clothing they were wearing?"

"I'm sorry I lied about your origins."

"Yes, why did you?"

She pulled a face, mischievous, like a child's. "I don't know... to shake them up a little... baffle them... I have a feeling they subscribe to things like "England for the English"."

"They probably think I'm Elliot's father."

"He's much too good looking to be your child."

When we reached the end of the lane, where the blackthorn ended at the stream, we took a left. A right would have led us to the weeping willows. Elliot wasn't permitted to splash at the edge of the water. It was cold, said his mother, and, also, since the stream was swift and swollen, unsafe.

Elliot looked massively disappointed.

"How about a story..." I offered.

"About the man who could speak to birds?"

I laughed, amazed at his recollection. "Alright..."

He looked up, his eyes wide and shiny as marbles.

Myra slipped her arm through mine.

"Once, a man was walking through a forest..."

"What was his name?"

"His name was... Stefan. So, Stefan was walking through a forest, when suddenly a storm broke... the winds rose, clouds gathered, and lightning flashed... he ran to take shelter under a tree..."

"But grandpa says we mustn't stand under a tree if there's lightning..."

Myra laughed into a gloved hand.

"And your grandpa is right. He was running past a tree, to get to a cave, but before that... what did he see in the branches? A bird's nest..."

"What kind of bird?"

And so it continued, until we reached a clearing where Myra wanted to stop. "More, please, more," pestered Elliot. Eventually, we reached a compromise; I promised to read him a story later, before bedtime.

We sat on a bench—dedicated to "Arthur, who so loved this place"—and unpacked our basket. Chunky roast beef sandwiches, mince pies, Victoria sponge, and hot chocolate in a squat flask. Across the churlish water, the countryside swept away from us, patches of field hemmed by neat hedges, distant low-lying hills, and clusters of poplars like fine pencil drawings etched into the sky.

It was a rare sort of happiness. An inkling, a rush, a feeling that somehow this, and only this, was where we were meant to be. Nowhere else in the world would come close.

After our picnic, I showed Elliot how to skim stones on water—one, two, sometimes three quick skips. He had to hunch low, balance on the balls of his feet, and fling—"Fling," he said joyfully, enraptured by the word, by its carefreeness. "Fling! Fling!"

Before the light faded, we headed back. It was much too cold to stay out any longer; the wind whipped about us, tugging at our coats, stinging our faces.

The next time I visit, said Myra, we'd drive to the moors. "You should ask Mrs Hammond for moor stories... giant black hounds and ghostly lights, and a rock that's supposed to be a man turned to stone by a witch..."

Moors, like forests, were mystical places.

When we were almost home, it started raining, cold, sharp pebbles falling hard on the ground. I hitched up Elliot for a piggyback ride, running through the gate, and across the gravel. He screamed with laughter.

That evening, we lit a fire in a room at back of the house, a smaller, less formal place, and cheerful, with butter-yellow walls and floral curtains. Originally, explained Myra, it had been used as a "lady's letter-writing room"—"Can you imagine? The things these walls must know."

For supper, we warmed a pot of leek-potato soup, buttered some rolls, and ate sitting on the floor, the firelight flickering on our faces.

"Do you do this every time Philip's away?"

Myra nodded, happily.

And in the spirit of celebratory excess, even though we were all sated, she dug out leftover apple crumble from the fridge, and served it drenched in custard. The other night I'd been too tired to enjoy this; it was delicious, tart and sweet, creamy and crumbly. A few card games, and a round of snakes and ladders later, Elliot was asleep on a cushion, his thumb in his mouth. I carried him upstairs, light in my arms as a bird, dressed him in his pajamas, and tucked the covers around him.

His curly dark hair, the shape of his nose.

In the low glow of the night lamp, all could be revealed.

When I came back downstairs, I found Myra opening a bottle of wine. "Daddy's finest." An opulent cabernet sauvignon from Château Saint Pierre, St Julien.

"Tell me about your time in London," said Myra. "Your work, your friends... everything..."

And so I did, slow and halting at first... unused to talking about myself in this manner... the journal I joined on Nithi's persuasion... its almost closure... my bid to get away for a year from Delhi... its seren-dipitous fruition. "All because of Santanu, of course..."

"And Santanu, what does he do?"

I told her.

"What's he like?"

I laughed. "A bit of an old soul, in love with a poet."

"Aren't we all?"

I didn't reveal what he'd disclosed before I left London. When we stopped at the bar on our way to the Christmas party. Yara and the infinite heart. Bold, beautiful Yara with dark eyes stained by silver light. I suppose Myra could say he hadn't known her long, that if he were to lose her, it wouldn't be all that difficult. But time and love have little to do with the other. On occasion, love is a burst of light, and the inten-sity of a week, a month, a year could scarcely be replicated in a lifetime. Brevity should not be scorned, for it bears no indication of the absence of depth. Else, dismiss the sunrise, the arietta, the haiku.

In life, everything, including love, is fleeting.

I hadn't spoken to Santanu again before leaving London.

Perhaps Eva would prove a more helpful companion, but by now she would be across the world, with Tamsin in Japan.

Then I told Myra about Eva.

Her silken peacock dresses. Her immaculate hair. Her great and gap-ing emptiness.

I told her about Stefan. "He sends her flowers to mark time."

Love came in the shape of lilies.

Myra sighed. "How can I say she's foolish? I have no right."

And neither did I.

We burned log after log to keep the fire going. I told her how, when we were children, my sister and I would dry orange peel in the sun, and then toss it into the fireplace. They'd splutter in the flames, a mini fireworks display that thrilled us each time. Oranges were the smell of my childhood.

"Paint," she said. "Mine is paint." Sitting close to her mother, for hours playing with old tubes and brushes. "She'd call me her little helper." Myra laughed, tipping the glass to her lips. Then she looked at me, her eyes the color of a summer evening, a deep, endless blue. Her hair glowing liquid bronze. Like the trees in London in autumn. My lost season. For an instant, I wanted to reach out and touch her, the slope of her cheek where light slanted off, the plane of her hand lit by firelight.

"What do you think it is?" she asked. "The memory of happiness that has passed, is it happy or sad?"

The wine swirled full and viscous on my tongue.

Neither, I said. And both.

Memory only gives us back what we had on condition we know it has been lost.

To remake the world, we need first to understand it has ended.

Later, filled with a low tuneful humming, I climbed the stairs to the loft, slip-sliding on the wet wooden surface. The room lay in unbroken darkness; here the rain sounded louder, closer, drumming on the skylights. *Let me in.*

As I drifted to sleep, lulled by wine and the wind, I thought I heard the door open, the soft pad of footfall, the hush of breath. I dreamed a warm, rain-splattered body slipped into bed beside me.

It was Nicholas.

It was someone smaller, lighter, with longer hair, and a softer mouth. A silky gown that slipped off easily. Someone with skin smooth as a seashore pebble, a neck that arched, a pool of deep, endless wetness. In the dark, she was above me, her lips parted like petals, light under my touch, on her, so clumsy. A small mole on the nape of her neck, a beacon I returned to again and again. She was wine and fire. A furious rising. Tonight, the creatures above us were silent. We were watched only by rain and darkness, somewhere behind that, the stars. At the end, I buried my face into her shoulder, and she gasped and held me with fingers that felt like butterflies.

⎯⎯⎯

Once, on my wanderings around London, lost somewhere near Green Park, I chanced upon an art gallery open late in the evening. From the outside, it glowed white and glassy, and I walked in because there didn't seem to be any works on display. Apart from mirrors. I was intrigued.

"The past behind… and the future before us."

A sum of all we are, and all we are becoming.

"Or," she added, "in the case of the Aymara people in the Andes, the past lies ahead."

For it can be seen. This is who you are—the entirety of everything that has come before—and it stands there, a steady yet fragile reflection. The future stays behind, unknown, unseen, unfathomable.

Standing there, glimpsing myself in those strange paintings, I thought of how they inhabit the same, and different worlds entirely, one perpetually in the state of becoming the other. Yet there is a moment, in the split second when you lift a finger to the mirror when they touch, and are inexplicably identical.

It felt that way in Wintervale.

⎯⎯⎯

"It's another country."

I shouted, to make myself heard above the wind, lashing across the moors.

"I brought Nicholas here once," said Myra. "He hated it. For him, only the frenetic madness of the city."

She stood beside me in her tweed coat and woollen beret, smoking, her gloved fingers speckled with ash. I could still taste her smoke-wine tongue. In the early hours of that morning, I'd awakened, amazed by the length of her by my side. Her bare back turned towards me, pebble-smooth, angular, dipped between her shoulder blades, her skin marked by pale freckles. I wanted to run my fingers along her outline, to trace her and place her like a leaf between my hands. She left soon after, saying she wouldn't like Elliot to awake and not find her home, but even now, after breakfast and an hour's drive to the moors, I was still replete with her. I wanted to stand behind her, beside her, in front, all at once, so wherever the wind would blow, it would carry her fragrance.

How infinitely modest are the steps that change our lives.

How unassumingly bereft of all fanfare and flourish.

At that precise time, if it hadn't been for the storm, I would have been on a train bound for London.

Philip, who returned that morning, earlier than we anticipated, came bearing news that fallen trees had disrupted rail services to the city. They'd closed the line, and since it was Sunday, it possibly wouldn't reopen until the next day.

"Oh, so you can't possibly leave now..." said Myra.

I said I was sure they'd arranged a rail replacement service; it might take me an extra few hours but I'd get back to the city eventually...

"Those coaches are beastly... do stay... and we can drive to the moors... they'll have it all cleared up soon, I'm sure... Isn't your ticket valid for the rest of the week?"

It was.

Philip sat aside, stirring his tea, watching us in silence.

"They're one of the oldest breeds in the world... can you imagine?" said Myra. "To have been around unchanged for twelve thousand years."

Like seahorses.

"It makes one feel so... fleeting."

I placed my arm around her waist; at the moment, I didn't want to hear talk of ephemerality. I'd dreamed again of Lenny, and if it hadn't been for her, lying beside me when I awoke, I would have been filled with an old sadness. But it had dissipated when she smiled sleepily, and reached out to stroke my cheek.

Before us, the moors sloped and rose endlessly, while behind, they were as flat as the sea. It hadn't snowed yet this winter, but sprinklings of frost glistened in the afternoon light. The longer I stood there, the more I felt steeped in beautiful desolation.

We walked back toward the road, stepping carefully on the sedge, keeping a lookout for patches of boggy marsh. Myra said she'd take the longer way home, and drive by the coast, so I could see the highest sea cliffs in the country. A twenty-one-mile route, along which we could stop at a pub for a meal.

"And tomorrow," she added, "we can visit Exeter... glorious twelfth-century cathedral..."

In the car, the radio crackled, disappeared, returning only in patchy stretches. Elliot sat in the back, playing with his toy soldiers, who were now riding imaginary moorland ponies.

"I've been thinking," said Myra, "why don't you stay on for Christmas?" It was, she added, merely a few days away.

I hesitated.

"It'll be fun... Mrs Hammond's magnificent roast turkey... crackers at the table... eggnog... and I promise I'll buy you a present."

I said I wasn't sure about her father, what he'd have to say. Only for him would I prefer to leave as scheduled.

She kept her eyes on the road, unwavering.

"Have you had... friends... staying over before?" I asked. When she didn't answer, I wondered wildly whether I had been intrusive. Here existed such firm, delicate lines of etiquette. "What I meant was... has he been alright... in the past?"

Her features were set, firm, defiant. "He has no right to say no."

When we met him later, at supper, she'd tell him, that I would stay on a little longer.

"Won't I see you in London? For concerts..."

Not anytime soon. There was a reason why January was called the dead month.

The narrow road winding through the park hit the coast and—just as a million others whose eyes unexpectedly glimpsed the sea, its sudden vastness—we fell silent. In the distance, the coastline curved, a ribbon of rock, edged by feathery white water.

"Mummy," shouted Elliot, "we're at the edge."

"Yes," said Myra, "the very end of land."

———

That evening, when we sat down to supper, Philip seemed, to my relief, quite affable. Loosened by his time away in London. It mustn't be easy, I supposed, having to care for his daughter and grandson on his own. Perhaps the strange net he cast around them sprang from a need to keep them protected and close.

He asked about our day.

We told him where we'd been. "It was quite incredible." I still hadn't lost the urge to end my sentences with *sir*.

"I'd go riding there on Charlie," he said. "Poor boy loved it... we'd do part of Coleridge Way, from Stowey to Monksilver... can't take General, though, he's terrified of ditches... had an accident when he was a foal... never quite got over it, poor chap. I remember once when I was out with

Charlie, we were caught in a storm, snow in May... and then suddenly blazing sunshine... crazy weather out there on the moors..."

"Yes," said Myra, "who said only cities were mad."

"We saw horses!"

"Ponies, Elliot," corrected his grandfather. "Exmoor ponies. They almost became extinct during the war... fifty left... fortunately they survived. They're rounded up every year at Winsford Hill and counted. Took the boys for a school trip once..."

The conversation lapsed into appreciative dining silence. Mrs Hammond had slow roasted a leg of lamb, sprinkled with fresh herbs, alongside crisp new potatoes and charred parsnips. We were drinking a deep, majestic red, Côtes du Rhône it said across the label.

"How was London?" asked Myra.

"The usual... frenetic as ever."

He gestured at the wine; she passed the bottle to him.

"We're planning a drive to Exeter tomorrow... to see the priory and the cathedral. I even managed to convince Nem to stay on... for Christmas."

If she was nervous, it didn't show. I balanced the sliced meat and vegetables carefully on my fork. I kept my eyes on my plate.

There was brief, concentrated silence, and then Philip said, "I see."

Mrs Hammond walked in to ask if anyone would like an extra serving of roast. She'd been keeping it warm in the oven.

"Oh, yes, please," said Myra. "It's divine. I'm starving... must be all that fresh moor air."

For the rest of the meal, we said nothing more of my staying or leaving—conversation veered far and away—yet I could feel, sometimes, the flick of Philip's glance, on me, on Myra. I drank my wine slowly. Keeping mostly silent. I'm uncertain how to describe it plainly—it felt similar to the fear I knew in the forest, in the Ridge, something dark and elusive, tainting me with its wings. After our meal, I didn't linger by the fire as usual, but headed to the loft, leaving Elliot to watch his

Sunday special television show and Myra to usher him to bed.

She walked me to the door—"I'll see you later"—and, after a quick glance around, kissed me. Her lips tasted of dessert—sweet, tangy rhubarb.

The loft felt more enclosed than ever. Pacing the room, I could count it out, fifteen steps across, ten the other way. In London, my studio was smaller. I wished I could open the skylights, freshen the place with some cold night air. If there was a radio, I would've turned it on, the murmur of voices to keep away the silence.

At about half past ten, Myra crept in through the door.

I was trying to read through my article, although mostly it lay face up on my lap.

"Do you think..." I began, but she'd already crossed the room, and lifted herself on the bed, on me. The papers fell to the floor, scattering.

"Maybe it's better... I leave tomorrow..."

I cupped her face, her hair tangled in my fingers. In this light, her eyes were inky, like the horizon of the sea.

"But... why?"

"Your father... I don't think..."

"I don't care," she said. "I can't not... don't you see..."

For a moment we held our stares in silence, then I pulled her closer, and we kissed. I ran my hands over her ankles, her calves, her thighs. She had nothing on under her knitted dress—it was woolly and grey as though she'd draped on a cloud or a plume of smoke. I slipped it off; she shivered, under my fingers, at the touch of air, the nip of coolness.

They are different, the skin of men and women.

And Myra's softer than I ever could imagine. Tonight, brushed by the smell of the moors, its secrets and wildness. She sat up and pinned me back, her hands quick and cold against my chest, as she pulled off my jumper, unbuttoned my shirt, reached for my belt.

It is always like this, the shrinking of the world to touch.

The sudden discovery of wetness, a gathering on the tongue of everything felt and swallowed. Saltiness like sea water. The heaving of waves, of arched backs. A sound forced from between our meeting skins, loud, incongruous. Like a fart. Our quick laughter.

The bracing heaviness of limbs.

"Wait," she said and stopped me. She stepped off the bed and opened the cupboard door, aligning the mirror so it caught our reflection, glowing ferociously in the light of the small, low lamp. It watched us, moving, Myra facing herself, the curve of her shoulders, and me further away, behind her, my arms outstretched on her back, along the length of her spine. We watched ourselves. Until the knot tightened, in the pit of us, and suddenly it was everywhere.

After, she switched off the lamp, and lit a cigarette, a glowing pinprick in the darkness. For some reason, I remembered Kalsang. His long, tree-twig limbs.

She was looking at the ceiling, and didn't turn to me when she asked, "Why did you love Nicholas?"

There was only one answer. Which I'd searched for as long as I could remember.

"To you, he was breath... for me, he was like a beautiful word that you learn to say... and your tongue is forever changed because you can pronounce it."

For a long while we didn't speak, the silence interrupted by the soft flutter of wings coming from the rafters above us, and her voice: "The sex was good too, wasn't it?"

"Yes."

We looked at each other and laughed.

She rested her head on my shoulder, on my scar, a line of white. "Why did he say he saved you?"

"Because... in a way, he did." I told her about the friend I'd lost.

"What was his name?"

"Lenny."

Buried in a cemetery in my hometown, which I hadn't visited in many years. I found it—difficult to go back.

She looked up at the painting, reaching out as though to touch it. "She was an art teacher at the school where my father was headmaster... nobody could understand why they were together, least of all why they got married, had a child. They were so different..."

They hadn't been close, she and her father. Although circumstances had created prolonged proximity. Sometimes, that was even more difficult to discard.

When her mother died, Myra was nineteen. She studied music, because she couldn't paint.

I traced her outline slowly on the sheet, making a cut-out to carry with me always.

"Did he ever say anything... about me?"

"Who?" She asked even though she knew.

"Nicholas... about why he left Delhi."

She sat up against a pillow, balancing the cigarette so the ash wouldn't tip over on the sheets. "Not about you, no... I mean, not that I asked him either," she added quickly. "But he did say, once, that if he'd stayed, it would have killed him..."

"The city? Or the summer? Or me?"

"The summer," she said earnestly, "I'm sure he meant the summer."

I laughed out loud.

"What?" asked Myra. "What is it?"

Instead of answering, I drew her forehead to my lips.

She stubbed the cigarette on the bedside table. "I spoke to dad again... about you staying... it's fine, honestly. He doesn't mind at all."

Somehow, I found that hard to believe.

"Anyway, wouldn't you miss me?" She pressed closer, her legs entangling mine, guiding my hands over her, and I conceded.

Myra was on her side, asleep, her hair smoothed like fire over the pillow. I stood at the window; Philip, it seemed, slept very little. A light burned in a room in the house; I could see him through the gap in the curtain. He was up, the glow of the computer screen falling on his face. I stared at his profile a long while, before he stood up and shifted out of sight.

———

By morning, Myra was gone.

And the world was white. It had snowed a few inches during the night, although it didn't seem like it would stick for long. Most of it was already melting into muddy slush.

I walked outside and picked up a handful. It wasn't the first time I'd seen snow—my parents took us to Tawang once in January, a town in the hills of Arunachal Pradesh—but it had been decades. It stung my fingers, dissolving against the warmth of my skin.

At breakfast, the radio was left on, tuned into the local channel. The weather forecast predicted more bad weather, especially to the south-west where we'd planned on a drive.

"Best if we stayed in," said Myra. "I hate driving with ice on the road. We could take a walk later, if you like... there's a ruined castle not far from here."

That, I said, sounded a better alternative; I was all too aware of Philip, at the head of the table, buttering his toast, watching us.

"Why don't you come for a ride?" he asked. "I was hoping to take both the horses out today. They're a bit restless cooped up over the weekend."

Myra said that sounded like a good plan. I'd like that, wouldn't I? "Although you were quite sore after that first day..." she added.

"Still a bit painful," I began, "I'm not sure I'll manage..."

"Well," said Philip, "the more you ride, the easier it'll get."

Later, after I changed into my riding clothes, strapped on a helmet and wellies, I met Philip at the stables. Today, as before, I'd be riding Lady—"Try not to injure her this time."

I could never tell if Philip was joking. His jibes divided by a fine line from his jests.

Again, gripped by sullenness, I wondered why I'd agreed to come out riding. Oh, but I hadn't. I'd been pushed into this. And I was too polite to adamantly decline. Methodically, and meticulously, Philip saddled the horses; we mounted and made our way out the gate.

I began to relax, my posture loosening. This is why I'd agreed. I enjoyed it greatly. Out in the open, the air stinging my face. A sense of delicate balance, poised carefully at the top. The sudden, uplifting freedom.

"Careful," said Philip. "Move your calves closer to Lady's side."

"Yes... sorry..."

In the daylight, Philip's features were less complex, flattened, bereft of shadows. I was wrong when I'd called him an elderly Hercules that first evening. He was wholly, utterly, human. Not a sculptural force carved with the vigour and resplendence of a god. But something pettier, more paltry, more real.

I glanced at him—the strong nose, the oddly delicate mouth.

In winter, the birds are silent.

Finally the path broadened and we could ride side by side.

"So, Myra says you're staying on... for Christmas."

I tightened my grip on the reins, wondering which direction this would take. "She's been very kind... and asked if I'd like to stay on..."

Philip laughed; it didn't sound as though he was amused.

"Of course, if you'd prefer—" I began.

"There are many other things I'd prefer, but it's not always the way life pans out, is it?"

"I don't know what you think may happen... what this great wave of generosity may bring to you... but it will not be my daughter."

"I'm afraid—"

"That it's none of my business? She made it my business when she showed up eight months pregnant at my door like a common...." *Slut.* He didn't need to say the word.

Lady was moving faster, as though she'd sensed it, the frisson running along my back.

"My grandson has a father she can't even name."

She hadn't told him. Nicholas.

"I've put her back on her feet... do you know how long that takes? To put a person back together?"

I glanced down, the ground seemed liquid and far away.

Into a mold that should not contain her... perhaps that's why people break apart in the first place. That's why they found places that were dungeons of secrets.

"And now you come waltzing in here," Philip was speaking in a steely, steady tone. "thinking you can fuck her to happiness."

The word hung in the air, crystallized like a snowflake.

I don't think I imagined it, the trace of disgust in his voice. I struggled to stay calm, but it seeped into my throat, a seething anger—"It isn't as though Myra has no agency, no will of her own. She—"

"I don't think—"

"I don't think you understand me. You've had your little holiday, your trip to the moors, your bit of pre-Christmas snow, your fun with my daughter, and now... it's very simple really... it *ends.* Let me ask you again... are you staying on for Christmas?"

The track had taken us to the other side of the field, where instead of the wall ran a length of barbed wire fencing, and beyond that a road.

If I looked down, I knew I would fall. Lady had broken into a canter. General had no trouble keeping up.

I tried to steady my hands, but they burned, like the rest of me, with a strange heat.

"Perhaps you should tell Myra."

For a moment, Philip seemed confused, but it was swiftly replaced by annoyance. "What do you mean?"

"Perhaps you should tell her what makes you this way. So... *wretched*."

My host was silent, out of confusion or anger or surprise, I couldn't tell. I continued, "The day I arrived, I stood by the fireplace in the drawing room... and looked at your photograph... and then you walked in, we talked and had a drink. And over and over again, I was thinking, I've seen him somewhere before... When I told Myra this, she dismissed it, saying you hardly left this house, except to go riding... or to London."

"I don't have time for this nonsense. I asked you—"

"Sweet Saturdays... I saw you there."

The mud and stone crunched, brittle under the horses' hooves.

Philip's voice was scornful. "I haven't the faintest idea what you're talking about."

"I usually get up for a glass of water at night... did you know I can see your window from the loft? And there it was, through the gap in the curtains... the same profile. I saw you there..."

"This is absurd."

"You won't even admit it to yourself, will you? You keep Myra caged in this house... just as you keep yourself trapped in that dungeon..."

With an instinct I didn't know I possessed, I turned, just in time to dodge Philip's hand.

It was a glimpse, of something on his face, a mass of distorted flesh that warned me of what would happen next.

"Stop—" I shouted, but Philip lunged again, this time his fingers grasping my jacket. I pulled away, kicking, and leaned forward, lifting myself from Lady, bringing up my hands, shortening the reins. It took another kick for the horse to gallop; I struggled to steer her off the path and onto the field. I'd done this rarely, I could barely hang on, her movements uneven, accelerating. General was catching up, keeping pace. When I glanced back, it was still there, that look on Philip's face. I almost slipped off; I tried to lean forward further, clutching now at Lady's mane. Philip needn't catch me; at any moment, I'd fall and be crushed.

His horse was closer now—I felt the first push, as General galloped into me broadside. Somehow, I managed to stay on.

A second push almost threw me off.

He's mad... I remember thinking... he's mad...

Then, all of a sudden, the world swirled before me, in a cold and endless rush. I didn't know whether it was real or if I was dreaming, sailing through the air for an infinite moment, as though we were flying, or falling. And then a merciful slowing, a loping, a canter, and then a trot. I opened my eyes. I tightened the reins, my breath coming in short, sharp bursts. Despite the cold, sweat filmed my face, my hands.

Lady had almost come to a complete stop.

I dismounted, sinking to the ground. My legs were air. The soil smelled sweet and grassy.

Only then did I hear the whinnying behind me. I glanced back.

In the distance, behind us, General moved restlessly; Philip was lying on the ground.

Slowly, I edged closer; I recognized what it was, the feeling of infinite suspension, Lady had jumped a ditch, but General had halted, abruptly, and thrown his rider off.

———

He was still alive when we reached the hospital.

I'd left my cell phone back in the loft, out of signal, out of battery, so I stood by the road, waiting, wondering if I should attempt to find the nearest farmhouse, a neighboring cottage. Or my way back to Wintervale?

Although I couldn't possibly leave Philip alone. I've never been adequately competent in the face of emergencies; the time I discovered

Nicholas' disappearance, I sat, paralyzed, in the veranda.

Behind me, some distance away, Philip lay on the ground, unconscious, fallen at an awkward angle. Had I read somewhere that an injured party must not be moved? Or did that pertain to about murder victims, a crime scene? I'd edged around him, watching the rise and fall of his chest; the trickling dark stain spreading down his temple.

It rose swiftly, the dark, wide wings of panic.

Yet in answer to a silent plea, a car approached down the narrow country lane; I stepped out and hailed it, waving my hands. The vehicle rumbled to a stop, gravel spitting under its wheels. The couple inside, fair-haired, middle-aged, well-spoken, were assiduously concerned.

"Please..." I asked, "may I use your phone?"

I didn't realize it until I tried to punch in the numbers, that my hands were trembling.

"Emergency, which service do you require? Fire, Police or Ambulance?"

After that, the questions were numerous—which number was I calling from? What was my exact location? With the couple's help, I stumbled through the answers. The ambulance was dispatched and mobile, but I was asked to stay on the line.

"Sir, how many people are involved?"

"One... two... no, one, I'm unharmed."

"What's the age of the patient?"

"About... late sixties... early seventies..."

"Is he breathing?"

Yes, he was breathing.

"Is he bleeding?"

Yes, on his head, slightly. From a surface wound.

Don't move him. Keep him warm.

The lady in the car pulled out a picnic blanket—indecorous in red and white chequered cheerfulness—and laid it over Philip. We pressed her hanky, piteously insufficient, against the cut. We waited, watching, as instructed, for any changes; his breathing, I was convinced, was growing considerably more rapid and shallow.

Finally, the ambulance arrived, along with a police car.

The medical team was small, a paramedic and her assistant, yet briskly efficient. All at once, Philip was monitored, tubed, and braced, his neck wrapped in a cervical support, then carefully lifted and strapped onto a stretcher. The last I saw of him, the familiar outline of his profile, his forehead, the slope of his nose, his mouth, suddenly bereft of all emotion, of everything that had animated them, seemingly moments ago.

Before accompanying the two sombre-faced police officers, I bid a hasty thanks and farewell to the couple. Only when we drove off, me in the backseat, did I realize I hadn't asked them their names. What would I tell Myra?

Myra.

I needed to inform Myra. What about the horses?

"We'll take care of that," said the officer in the passenger seat. He was older than the silver-haired driver, with a stern, tensile face. I couldn't recall her telephone number, but I did know her address. The driver and I sat in silence while he made a call. When he was done, I asked whether we were headed to the house.

"Not yet." We were driving to the hospital first. I must also undergo a check-up.

The officer glanced back. How did it happen? We have so many cases of horseback injuries in these parts, he added.

It was a car, I said. A speeding car, that set the horses off. And I couldn't control mine, and Philip followed.

The words rolled off my tongue.

He was trying... to stop my horse.

I thanked her, and stepped out, looking for Myra.

The waiting room was busy, a child wailed, a youth held a bloodied

rag to his hand, an elderly lady coughed violently into her handkerchief. I filled a plastic cup with water from the dispenser, and sat in
the corner.

Forty minutes later, I asked the receptionist if she had any news.

"Philip... Philip Templeton..."

At a loss, I headed outside. Standing in the driveway was the police
officer who'd brought me here, smoking.

"She's here," he told me. "She left as soon as we informed her."

He exhaled—swirls of smoke and mist.

"You better go in..."

I was shivering, my jacket doing little to keep out the cold.

Around me, the walls of the hospital gleamed gritty and bright, all
steel and glass.

Back inside, I looked for the nurse who'd given me a check-up earlier,
but she was nowhere in sight. The corridors were white and endless, lit
with stark squares of light.

"Nem."

I turned around. It was Myra. Her face colorless as the snow I'd held
in my hand that morning. When I clasped her, her words muffled into
my shoulder: "He's in a coma."

———

One evening, Nicholas explained why he was in Delhi.

"Ananda?" I reiterated.

We were in the garden, past midnight, sitting on the wicker chairs,
our drinks gently perspiring on the table. It was early June, a few days
before I headed home for a month. Outside the gate, gulmohars blazing
scarlet flanked the main road like liveried dancers, while the flower-
beds in the bungalow garden rambled with purple-pink petunias, tissue thin in the heat. Somewhere close by, a champa tree was in bloom;
I couldn't see it, but the air carried its deep, golden fragrance.

Nicholas said the path of scholarly enquiry was strewn with surprises.

"You start out reading about the genesis of the bodhisattva ideal, and end up intrigued by hagiographic literature..."

"Who is he?" Should I be jealous, I added in jest.

Ananda was the Buddha's faithful servant and inseparable companion. A most devout and beloved attendant.

"What scholars find puzzling is his apparent absence within the framework of Gandharan narrative art. He was important to the Teacher... so it's hard to believe he'd be wilfully ignored, or anonymous in a crowd."

Was there much known about him, I asked?

"Buddhist texts offer accounts of their relationship, strange and non-linear as they may be. He was quite an odd figure... sharing this close yet awkward relationship with his master. Despite his devotion, he wasn't a particularly good disciple. He was weak and wavering, slave to his baser nature, persistently giving in to his passions..."

"Why did he choose him then?" I asked. "The Buddha, I mean... why did he choose Ananda?"

Nicholas' eyes were the color of stillness, between water and mist. "Because he was human."

I sipped my drink. The smoky malt filling me with the scent of forests and pine.

"Ananda also knew the dharma best, even if he hadn't reached a state of *arhat*... worthiness or perfection... like the other monks. He alone is credited with hearing Buddha's enunciation of the Doctrine in its entirety: Ananda represents his historical memory."

Seems a bit nasty then, I said, to exclude him from the visual narrative of the Buddha's life.

"Precisely... which is why I don't think that's the case. It's more likely that a criterion of transcodification was used that's now no longer recognizable."

"That makes sense."

"Don't you think? Now if only my supervisors were that easily convinced."

"Perhaps, like me, they have no idea what transco-di-si-cation means."

He laughed. "I could explain... but only if you're truly interest-ed..."

"Tell me..."

What I didn't mention was how this was spurred not by an incipient interest in Gandharan art, but that lately, for me, everything we shared was tinged with a current of urgency. I'd be gone a month, and although I'd return in early July, it seemed endless. Someday, Nicholas too would leave. When, I wasn't exactly sure. I wanted and didn't ever want to know. On the rare occasion I asked, he'd say, mysteriously, that he was staying in Delhi forever. Or melodramatically, that the city had captured his heart. If I persisted, he'd turn impatient. He could be mercurial, quick to anger.

And I? I was uncertain how much time we could claim together, a month or an eternity. Everything I could carry and cherish, every piece of him, his life, must be gathered now.

Later, in the study, as he talked of the elusive Ananda, I remember—not the academic details—but the way his fingers leafed through pages. How a terse line ran along his cheek, down to his mouth. And his hair, dark as a gathering storm.

"Here," he exclaimed, holding a book open. "Vajrapani... Bearer of the thunderbolt sceptre... the Buddha's devoted acolyte. Vajrapani is Ananda. A suffering hero, who through his labors, like Hercules, transfigures himself. Remarkable, isn't it?"

Ananda artworks, he believed, were littered all over; the British Museum, Delhi's National Museum, and further away in Chandigarh. That's why he was here.

In time, all was revealed.

It might have been that night or another, lying half-awake, half-dreaming, when I asked him again about Ananda. Did he gain *arhat*?

Did he finally become worthy?

Nicholas was on his back, bare to the soft swirl of air from the fan. He tilted his head, his chin resting on my shoulder, speaking softly, murmuring like a stream. "After the Buddha's death, the monks gathered to listen to him share the Doctrine... but they thought his narrative faulty, full of omissions. The sole, incompetent heir of the master's words was forced to measure his inferiority in their presence, and they say this burning humiliation pushed him to conquer the *arhat* state. He was greatly tormented... in immense pain, and finally overcome by exhaustion, he fell asleep."

Nicholas placed a palm on my thigh. Unmoving.

His hand trailed up, across my chest, the dip of my neck, my cheek.

"One of few instances... if not the only... where an awakening happens during sleep."

I felt his mouth on mine, at the base of my throat.

My breath was short, barely enough to whisper, "When will you leave?"

"Didn't I tell you... I'm staying forever."

———

The first night Philip was in hospital, Myra and I sat up in the letter room almost until dawn. Elliot was upstairs, sleeping; I presumed Myra didn't wish to be alone. Although in all honesty, I had little inclination to be on my own in the loft—either staring at those rectangles of blackness on the ceiling, or looking out the window at another, darkened now, no longer framing a familiar profile. So we lit the fire, as we did a few nights ago, even though it seemed more distant than ever, sat on the sofa, and cradled our drinks. Tea for her, neat Lochnagar for me.

For long spells, we didn't speak.

My gaze fell emptily on things, the upright Bechstein piano, the sturdy curves of a Georgian wing chair by the hearth, the long, pale fall of floral curtains, undrawn, unable to keep out the night. Here too, as in the larger drawing room, few photographs or intimate memorabilia adorned the mantelpiece. Only a triptych painting, large, and taking up most of the wall opposite us. How did I not notice it the other evening? Perhaps I was occupied with board games, food, wine, and happiness. Some art can only be witnessed when you are bereft.

At first, it looked like an abstract collage of colors, skillful, unfigurative, yet the more I gazed and followed the lines, the more they seemed to swirl into shape. I could discern a figure, up close, painted from the neck down to just below the waist, hands held out and up, as though trying to push through the canvas.

My hands, I noticed, hadn't quite stopped trembling.

Myra pulled her woollen shawl closer, and leaned back, tilting her face up to the blank ceiling. Finally, she said, "How do you think it feels?"

I had no answer.

"Isn't it strange," she continued slowly, "that there's no way of imagining unconsciousness that distinguishes it from a blank in the memory..."

An irreconcilable imbalance.

"There's light and darkness... a contrastive definition that's justifiable since we have experience of both... but with this..." With consciousness and unconsciousness the experience is inevitably, perpetually one-sided.

"Descartes said when we sleep, the soul withdraws from the body."

"Then where is it now?" She looked at me; I couldn't hold her gaze. "And if... and when... he is back, will be remember? Will he have memory? Is consciousness itself possible without memory?"

She stood up and approached the fire, holding out her hands to the warmth.

"I read this strange story once, about a French footballer who was given anesthetic that should have knocked him out for a few hours...

and thirty years later, he's never awoken. He doesn't change, he doesn't age... his wife still looks after him, in a house she named *Mas du bel athléte dormant*... the House of the Beautiful Sleeping Athlete..."

I placed my glass, empty, on the side table. "Myra, there's little chance of that happening. The doctor said your father is physically strong..."

"For his age," she completed.

"For his age," I repeated, moving closer to her. The smell of the hospital still clung to her clothes, her hair. The sharp, nauseating smell of disinfectant. I placed my hands on her shoulders, slight under her jumper.

"He will wake up."

But something in my voice betrayed me. Perhaps it was the memory of that afternoon, played out before us as something altogether distant, a series of events removed by a thin veil of disbelief.

"What does that mean?" Myra had asked.

A ruptured blood vessel, he explained, in the space between the skull and the brain.

And so we had waited, outside closed doors, within pristine white corridors, with figures in light blue gowns gliding around silently as angels. It was, in a way, a church, where confessions spilled behind doors, where there was a steady plunging into secrets—held aloft like birds and stabbed with needles.

Nothing here was delicate anymore.

Was it like this with Lenny?

Did they also rush him to the hospital? Was it already too late? Had he fallen asleep in his bed and never woken up? I remembered my dream, suddenly certain it was a premonition. That somehow, it had been a warning of this eventuality. Sitting on a bench, clutching a paper cup of cold, insipid tea, it wore off—the shock of the chase, the ride, the fall—and the words pierced me, sharp and steely as the silver instruments I'd seen on trays and trolleys.

It was my fault.

We left the hospital sometime after seven, after the surgeon in-formed us the operation had been carried out as best they could. For now, it might be better for us to wait at home. The patient was in a medically induced coma. If the swelling reduced by morning, they'd decide how to proceed.

"Doctor..." Myra had that look on her face again, firm, resilient, "what should we be prepared for?"

In a diplomatic turn of phrase, clinical as our surroundings, he replied that her father was physically strong... for his age. That the situation would look more promising if he pulled through these early days.

All the way back to Wintervale, I waited for Myra to question me on what had happened. Instead she switched on the radio, catching, mid-way, the shipping forecast. She left it on, the nightly litany of the sea, and the forecaster's slow, methodical delivery filled the silence, soothing and hypnotic. *Tyne... Slight or moderate, becoming slight... Fisher... Variable, becoming mainly southwest... Thames... Variable 3 or 4... Sole... Easterly 3 or 4. Moderate. Fair... Shannon... Moderate, occasionally poor in northwest. Fog patches in southeast... Malin... Hebrides... Bailey... Faeroes...*

When it ended, the news began on the hour. Headlines intent on the recent floods. The newsreader's calm, clipped voice of emergency.

"The paramedic spoke to me earlier," said Myra. Her father had regained consciousness, for a short while, in the ambulance, on their way to the hospital. He was disoriented, muttering repeatedly...

"What did he say?"

"I've often told him to be careful with General... that he was a good horse but with a nervous disposition. At first, we tried to train him to jump ditches at home... you know, with poles and black bin sacks, or have him graze near one, but it didn't help, and eventually we gave up..."

I repeated my question, gently.

She kept her eyes on the road. "He kept saying, I knew this would happen..." she added, "Like it was some kind of prophecy."

The next day, I stayed behind at Wintervale.

Myra said she'd call, from the hospital—"If anything happened"—but for now she'd prefer I kept Elliot company at home.

"Are you sure?"

She nodded, slipping on her tweed coat, adjusting her beret.

At the door, I stopped her, my hand on her arm, but the words faded in my throat. "Drive safe."

All morning, we lingered in the letter room, Elliot and I. He stayed well away from the piano, squatting instead on the floor, which he littered with paper and broken crayons.

"Where's Mummy?" he asked once, lifting his head, and looking around as though she might suddenly materialize.

"She's visiting your grandpa... he's hurt, remember? He's in hospital."

"Oh." He stooped back to his drawing, then sat up again. "Will he be alright?"

"I don't—yes... he will be alright."

And, for him, the world slipped back into place.

I was in the wing-back chair by the window, attempting, pretending to work on my article for Nithi. Watching the rain strike the glass with a quiet and relentless fury.

Isn't consciousness memory? Myra had asked. Last night, on the sofa.

Even if we concentrated on merely one thing, we wouldn't be aware of it without memory, since in each instant we'd forget what we were thinking the moment before.

I tried to cleave it before it was born... *Philip may have no memory...* but the thought arose, dissipated, and, like smoke, lingered.

For lunch, Mrs Hammond brought us tea and sandwiches. Egg and watercress, ham and mustard. The tea milky and strong.

"Any news?" she asked. Her usually formal aspect disarrayed by worry.

She was a tall lady, a little stooped, as though to always apologize for her height. Her hands, clasped neatly before her, were large, and elegantly slender.

"I'm afraid not... not yet. I'll let you know if Myra calls," I added gently.

She nodded. "Well, they say no news is good news." For a moment, she stood there, wavering, and then abruptly turned and left the room.

The afternoon passed slowly.

Elliot, I could tell, was growing restless, tired of his drawings and toy soldiers, of being trapped indoors. It was still raining, and we couldn't step out for a walk, or for him to cycle around. "I'll watch TV?" he asked. I didn't see why not.

He skipped to the set in the corner, switched it on, and settled on something colorful and animated. A jingle rang through the room, followed by the sound of something falling, a dramatic crash. Elliot chuckled, immediately entranced.

Despite the feeble signal, I checked my phone, and then again. But if Myra called, she'd do so on the landline. The phone in the foyer, black and archaic, stayed silent.

We had a quiet, subdued meal of mutton and barley stew, bread, and cheddar. Then Mrs Hammond took Elliot up to bed.

"There wasn't much I could do really," Myra told me later in the letter room. "I waited, by his bedside, but he was too weak to talk... I don't think he even knew I was there. I noticed," she added, "he had a stubble and needed a shave. It was strange to see him like that."

I asked her why.

She drew her feet up on the sofa; framed within its leathery depths. "Because as far back as I can remember, my father has always been... immaculate. As though the face he wore for all of us every single day must be as perfectly presented as it could ever be. I used to always wonder what it was like... when I saw my friends' families... or their family pictures... how much more casual their fathers seemed... in their attire and affections. Today, I saw my father unshaven, and I thought how that might be what would upset him most..."

My glance fell on my shoes, the rug. I remained silent.

The phone call came while we were still sitting there; Myra drowsy, reclining against my shoulder. I'd forgotten how it sounded, the shrill, pompous ring of a landline. For a moment, we didn't move.

"I'll get it," she said quietly, and walked out of the room.

Should I follow? That would be rude, I thought. I couldn't assume it was the hospital calling.

"Yes, Myra speaking... his daughter."

But it was.

She was strangely calm. Her voice precisely poised, her words falling like polished stones. "I see... yes... I understand. I'll be in tomorrow morning. Yes... will the doctor be in touch with the coroner? Alright, thank you... thank you."

The funeral was held two weeks after Christmas.

So I watched as the priest blessed the ground where Philip would be laid to rest and saw the coffin being lowered—*Whom I shall see for myself and mine eyes shall behold, and not as a stranger.* The grave filled. The flowers carefully arranged on top. It was too wet to light the candles. Myra, black-clothed, pale but dry-eyed. Elliot, too young to comprehend this, standing beside her in a little black suit, looking up at her in bewilderment.

It was my fault.

The rain fell as hard cold pellets.

At the reception there was little relief.

I lingered at the fringes, picking at cucumber sandwiches and drinking cup after cup of tea. Not from hunger or thirst, but to keep my hands occupied. To seem as though I was somehow part of this communal ritual. I didn't know if it was true, walking through the house, everyone's eyes on me, watching my back, whispering about my role in the tragedy. *He was there. Philip was trying to save him.*

Sometimes, when Myra passed by, she'd grip my hand, gathering something from me—strength, perhaps, some warmth.

I knew no one, apart from her and Elliot, and mostly I sat with the boy in his room.

"Will grandpa come back if I practice the piano everyday?"

"But it will make him happy, and if it makes him happy, he'll come back."

"It's my fault," he said, his eyes bright with tears.

No, I said, trying to reach for him... no, it isn't... but he slipped from my grasp, and ran out crying for Myra.

By the time everyone left, late that afternoon, she looked pale, wrung out by the hours. Mrs Hammond had left soup and sandwiches in the letter room, and bolstered the fire. She'd also placed a bottle of brandy on the tray, and a flask of warm water.

"I don't know what I'd do without her," said Myra, pouring herself a drink. She swirled the dark golden liquor, drank it neat, and then joined me at the hearth.

"Will you sleep here tonight?"

The past few weeks she and Elliot had slept in the hay loft. She couldn't bear it, she said. To be next to a dead person's room. We'd made up a bed for me on the floor.

I gathered her, my arm around her waist. Whatever she wanted...

The silence filled with the crackle of wood, spitting out their secrets.

She looked at me, her eyes edged with firelight. "And you. Thank you for staying."

I shifted on my feet, uneasy. I said it was alright, that after everything that had happened, I couldn't possibly have left.

———

Once, Doctor Mahesar told us a story in class from Plato's Phaedrus, in which Socrates compares the soul to a chariot pulled by a pair of winged horses. While a god was blessed with two obedient animals, a human drove a tame, immortal horse paired with one that was mortal and unruly. One pulled the soul upward, towards goodness and courage, and the other plummeted into darkness and chaos. Within us, they perpetually wrestled.

For the remainder of my winter break, I was at Wintervale.

A Christmas spent, not around the tree, but in drives to the hospital, appointments with the funeral director, and visits to the coroner's office—where I reiterated what had taken place that morning. There isn't a doubt about it, a lie often repeated becomes, for that moment, real. A fabrication woven so intricately it's impossible to unpick.

It set in, a vague discomfort, only after the formalities and paper work were over, and all we needed to do was wait for the funeral.

New Year's Eve was quiet, we stayed home. I cooked an unelaborate chicken curry that pleased them all, even Mrs Hammond, and in the evening, we watched old Lawrence Olivier movies from a pile of DVDs. On Myra's insistence, we opened a bottle of champagne. It was a time—didn't I remember?—of also looking to the future. Else Janus, the two-headed god, would be displeased.

The first week of January, windswept and snowy, saw us mostly holed up inside the house, venturing out only for the occasional walk. To an abandoned water mill, a giant oak tree on a hillock with long, sweeping views of white countryside, even the peripatetic ruins of a medieval castle. Each setting perfect for a confession. For a spilling of secrets. Somehow, I held it all back.

At night, I'd lie awake in the loft, listening to Myra and Elliot, their soft, even breathing. How could I ever sleep? I'd move, restless, on the mattress on the floor, perturbed by the immense silence, by the endless canvas on which I could paint troubled dreams.

On the night of the funeral we walked solemnly up to her room.

It felt like the ceremonial re-enactment of some ancient ritual. The undressing. My jumper, and hers, my belt, her dress, with its line of tiny buttons running from her neck down to the small of her back. The touch. Filled with swift, earthy urgency. The need. At this time, great and pressing, to reaffirm life.

"Do you have to leave?" asked Myra, when we lay later in darkness.

I had no choice. "Term begins on the seventeenth." Santanu and Eva would have texted, or called by now, and been left wondering why I wasn't reachable.

"I'll come visit you..." She ran a finger down my cheek. To my chin. Like Nicholas.

"Myra..."

"Yes?"

I hesitated. "Never mind."

Her eyes searched for mine. "Tell me..."

"I'd like it if you came visit..."

She lay back, and smiled, her skin, uncovered by the sheet, outlined in silver. "That's sweet... but it wasn't what you were going to say, was it?"

I insisted it was, even if, to my ears, my voice rang false. I listened to our breathing. The sudden mute sadness of the house. Somewhere, a pipe gurgling.

She didn't ask again.

She'd closed her eyes, fallen asleep.

———

On my last day there, I was audience to a private recital.

"Bravo! Bravo!" We applauded at the end. He stepped off the piano stool and bowed, beaming.

Then Myra took her place and said she'd play a movement from Brahms' Sonata in E-flat major. She clasped her viola close to her— "Usually, someone accompanies me on the piano... I hope I do justice to this alone..."

The notes rose through the house, soaring, I imagined, as seagulls. Filled with their exhilaration, and loneliness. How it felt to be a bird in a cloudless sky. Suddenly dropping, swooping lower, bolstered by the wind. Lifted, swirling higher, climbing up to the edges, and then drifting further away, growing smaller, fainter.

Eventually disappearing.

At the end of the piece, her cheeks were wet.

Elliot clapped—breaking the silence—and I joined in, giving her a standing ovation.

"Now," she said, laughing, "to the dining room... for a surprise."

She'd requested Mrs Hammond to bake a cake, and she and Elliot had iced it. Loopy letters spelled out "Gool Luck Nehmiah" and a candle burned in the middle, which I permitted Elliot to blow out.

That evening, we feasted on cake, custard and wine, leaving dinner untouched. We played cards and snakes and ladders. Once again, Elliot fell asleep on a cushion.

After we put him to bed, we returned to the letter room. The fire cast a sunset glow on the furniture, deepening the color of the walls.

"Are you alright?" asked Myra.

"Yes... thank you... so much."

She smiled. Her hair, falling loose over her bare shoulders. "I was thinking, if I could get Mrs Hammond to come in over some weekends, I could visit you in London more often... and when there's a concert, I'll have a place to stay. At least, until September."

"Yes," I reiterated, "until September."

"But let's not talk of farewells..."

She walked across to the piano, and lifted the lid, running her fingers lightly over the keys. "Once, when Elliot had just started his lessons, I said... oh, something like, one day, you might play in a quartet like mommy. And my father, sitting there, where you are, said, "unless he's good enough to join the London Symphony Orchestra". It's strange... I walk around this house and it's full of memories of my father... and I try to catch a glimpse of something... happy, but I'm left mostly with this sense of... relief."

She turned to me, "You must think I'm a horrible person."

I reached over, taking her hand. Her fingers icy against mine. "He was a difficult person–"

"Yes, he was..."

"He was also terribly... sad."

She laughed. "You mean he had time for things like that?"

The fire burst and crackled, sending a shower of sparks up the chimney.

"Myra, I know something about your father that I think you don't... that perhaps no one else ever knew..."

Her eyes were sky-pools, edged in black. "What do you mean?"

My mouth was dry. "One afternoon... one Saturday afternoon, in London... I walked into a pub near King's Cross, and accidentally stumbled on this club... a cross-dresser, transgender-friendly place... they had tables and sofas... and these curtained booths... which people could use... for privacy. And one of them..."

"I don't see how this has anything to do with dad."

I looked at her, wondering if it had been a mistake. "He was there... in one of the booths..."

At first she held my gaze, then she looked away, her face drawn in confusion. In hilarity, disbelief.

"You must be mistaken Nem, surely..."

Despite the fire in the room, it was cold, like a window had swept open.

"I don't know if you remember... on my first evening here, I said... I mentioned that I'd seen your father somewhere... that his face was familiar..."

"Yes," she said, quietly, "yes, you did."

"I only realized the night before he... the accident. And all this time, I didn't know how to tell you—"

"Are you certain? How close were you to this... booth?"

I hesitated. "I was on the other side of the room... but it wasn't a large room..."

"You said it was dark..."

"But there were lights from these video screens... and bulbs along the ceiling." I added gently, "I saw him there."

She stood up, pacing, her dress glinting ferociously in the firelight. "Did you go up close? Did you see what he was doing... no..."

"There was a gap in the curtain..."

"No... I don't want to know..."

"I couldn't tell..."

She was on the other side of the room, but I could see her eyes brimming with tears.

"I'm sorry, Myra..."

"If you knew... why didn't you tell me?"

I uttered the only truth I could muster. "I didn't know how."

"Did he... know? That you knew? That you'd seen him there?"

"No."

A space less than a heartbeat.

I moved across, and held her in silence.

———

The world, the next morning, was somehow intact.

I was in the loft, packing slowly. Even then, it didn't take me long— my clothes, a sheaf of papers, my slippers, folded, lined into my suitcase. I checked the bathroom, and picked up my toothbrush, the toothpaste. And then put the toothpaste back, uncertain whether I'd brought it along in the first place. Towels. A pair of socks, rolled up and dusty, under the bed. My pen. It didn't take me long.

While casting a glance around the room before I stepped out, I caught sight of the jade figurine. I'd forgotten it was there. I dropped it into my pocket, and then, by the door, I changed my mind and placed it back on the table, at the very centre, the table cloth under it a field of embroidered snow.

Myra was waiting for me by the car. She was dropping me to the station. Her eyes tired, shiny in the morning air. I placed the suitcase in the booth, and said goodbye to Elliot and Mrs Hammond. To Wintervale.

At first, we drove in silence.

Of the same timbre as the previous night in Myra's room, on her vast, cool bed. I'd glanced at her repeatedly in the dark; she was awake, staring out before her. The light sculpting her face, her neck, the line of her shoulder. Once, she turned, as though she had something to say, but she held her words.

At some point, I couldn't bear it. "I knew I shouldn't have told you..." I blurted.

She remained quiet.

"I shouldn't have..." I sat up. *I would leave. Now. I would leave.*

Her hand was cold on my back; it stayed me. She spoke in barely a whisper:

"All these years, I've spent thinking it was my fault... that he behaved the way he did. I couldn't understand it, where it came from... the bitterness... and so I claimed it. But it wasn't mine... it wasn't mine to claim."

In the car, she lifted her hand from the gearstick, and lightly, for a moment, touched my knee. We drove without a word until we reached. In a silence natural as the one found at wild places, moors and forests and seas.

The small station was livelier during the day, even on this smoke-grey winter morning.

Passengers alighting, leaving. The ticket office unbarred, the gates clicking in importance.

"Thank you," I said, when we'd disembarked.

I left her by the car, her lips briefly on my cheek, her fingers entangled in the collar of my coat. She didn't smile when I glanced back, but lifted her hand, her palm open, her fingers parted. Life is filled with these gestures. The ones that have no equivalence in words. And we carry them away, and we arrange them and we know them as carefully as birds know the pattern of the winds.

I waited on the platform, looking on either end at the vanishing tracks, glittering in the cold white air. At times, there is only one way back, and one way forward. Only a single line, out of so many, that takes you where you were always meant to be. The train slowly drew in, with a gush and a clatter; I found a window seat in a carriage that was almost empty. Motionless, suspended, until, with a slight tilt, we started moving.

As it sped away, the landscape rushed past me like water.

Pulling out of the countryside, my phone came to life, lighting up with missed calls, voice mails and unanswered texts.

"Back. For ages. All well? Ring when you can." Eva.

"Drink? Have you been abducted? By attractive aliens hopefully." Santanu.

I laughed, putting my phone away. This wasn't the appropriate time to reply.

For now, I cast my eyes to the sky, burdened by itself, looking for birds, the sun, anything that could fly.

I thought of Eva, her vast and abiding loneliness. The absence in the shape of a person, endlessly filled by the world. By Tamsin. Of love in the shape of lilies.

Of Santanu. His face when we mentioned the poet's name. The line that separated the ocean from the sky. Sole and many. A perpetual destruction and rebuilding. A love that belonged to no one.

I thought of Myra, lying on the bed. The sunshine through the loft skylights falling on her hips and arms. Hair the color of a lost season. Eyes like water, clear and changing. Our parting marked by something unlike sorrow.

I was filled with a sudden lightness.

All these years, the crevices had carried others, Nicholas and Lenny. Never wholly myself.

I thought of all the train journeys I'd taken, here and in a country across the world.

That led me to and away from people, that pulled me to the past and hurled me into the future. The winter morning lay pearl-grey around me, the clouds in the distance rolling in inky waves, slashed by pale blue, a silver disc edged by radiance, locked by land, and somewhere beyond that, its end. Now I was ready to meet the sea.

EPILOGUE

WHEN I REACHED THE TOWN BY THE SEA, IT STARTED SNOWING.

The winter that had begun before I visited Myra hadn't yet ended. Even though it was early April now, and we should have been well into spring.

It didn't help, no matter how brisk or offended the weather forecasters sounded on the television or radio—"Unbelievable!", "This is outrageous!"—the cold lingered on, befuddling the birds, stifling the trees.

The station my train pulled into was a High Victorian construction, built in the Italianate style popular at the time. Its ceiling a vaulted iron canopy, with ornate pillars and a grand four-faced clock. While the edges were lined with modern contraptions—a WH Smith, an M&S, Upper Crust stall, and AMT Coffee counter. If I took the road in front of the station, explained a kindly officer, it would lead me straight down to the sea.

Outside, I could see it in the distance, a patch of silver-blue between the buildings flanking the sloping street. As I strolled out, passing a Chinese medicine shop, a kebab place, an old-fashioned laundrette, the air around me changed and glimmered. Something—pure, intense, ephemeral—hung like bated breath, and released as snowflakes.

At the end of the road, the sea unraveled before me, a smooth, empty expanse dotted in the distance by a single, white ship. I took a right, away from the giant Ferris wheel, and a desolate pier that looked grievous in this weather, walking past a singularly ugly Odeon, a '60s Brutalist conference hall, and then, in soft, curving contrast, a line of voluptuous Victorian hotels. At the next crossing, I waited for the light to turn green, and strode over, keeping my eye on the ruin in the sea.

I'll meet you by the West pier.

A set of steps took me down to the beach. I walked on the pebbles, crunching beneath my shoes, the snow falling so lightly it barely touched the ground. The sea, topped by small, constant ripples, was darker towards the horizon, a stain of ink growing more dilute, paling into silver. With every lap, it washed over the shore, pushing the sand and stones closer, drawing them away.

From its depths rose the skeleton of an old pier, intricate in its tangle of crossbeams and seaweed. A row of iron pillars, that once had supported the walkway, began on the shore, continued a short distance into the water, and then abruptly stopped, disconnecting the pier from land. It floated on the water like a dream, silhouetted against the sky, circled by swooping sea gulls.

In this weather, the beach was empty. Apart from a couple on the far edge, walking their dogs. A man with a bundled-up toddler. A young girl in a hoodie, sitting cross-legged, headphones plugged into her ears.

It looked like Nicholas hadn't yet arrived.

He'd asked me to meet him there, in front of the old pier.

Or Lenny.

Once, I'd read about a young Dutch artist whose last performance piece was to sail out in a small boat from Cape Cod on a solo voyage across the Atlantic. He called it *In Search of the Miraculous.* He was never found; he never returned.

I like to think that too was Lenny's quest.

Above me, the stony silence of the sky was filled by the swirling flight of birds.

"They say seagulls are the souls of dead sailors."

A figure stepped out from behind a rust-encrusted pillar.

I didn't turn to greet him. I stood and waited. He was a ghost, a figment of my imagination, an apparition.

"Although if that were true," he continued, "they should at least be more careful..." Nicholas pointed to his left shoulder; the black of his coat marked by a splash of watery greenish-white.

"Perhaps it's a curse. It'll happen everyday," I said. "Each time you step outside."

"I have a feeling you may be—cross with me." He stood beside me, also facing the sea.

"I wonder what gave you that idea."

"Remember... Ithaca has given you the beautiful journey." He gestured with his hands, palms upturned and open. It was generous, as though he was offering me the world.

"Has it? To a freezing place by the sea where I'm in danger of being crapped on by birds."

"It matters not where you anchor... etcetera... etcetera... I think you need to revisit some of the poetry we read together."

A brief wind started up, scattering the snowflakes, stirring the waves.

"Before I came here, I thought we had to revisit a lot of things," I said. "Now, I'm not so sure."

We were both silent, listening to the gush and swallow of the tide.

"Did you find it, my builder of new worlds?"

I turned, and looked into eyes the color of the sea at dawn. "What?"

"What you most wanted, of course..."

A chariot of winged horses.

"Why Myra?"

Nicholas sighed. "Because the truth can only be told by someone else. My confession would have been tainted, no matter how hard I'd fought it, by self-preservation."

Behind us, the couple passed us with their dogs; we waited for their chatter and footsteps to grow fainter.

"And now," he continued, looking up, "we meet under a sky that is a blank slate, an empty sheet of paper."

Yet paper carries the marks of the wood that burned, the sky traps all sunsets and storms, the sea cradles every memory of giving life.

"Perhaps..." I said.

The snow was falling lighter. Soon, it may stop, and make way for spring.

"Why are you here?" I asked.

Nicholas smiled. "They have a word for it in Italian... *salsèdine*... the saltiness of the sea. I've always wanted to live by the sea."

In all these years, the flow of time had carved lines across his face, plotting their way around his eyes and mouth. The cartography of him that I used to know so well had changed, shifted between latitudes. He stooped slightly beneath its weight.

"Everyday, when I walk out of my house," he gestured vaguely to the town behind us, "I round the corner, and everything is the same, every aspect of the landscape in its place, yet everything is different. At the coast, I'm greeted always by newness."

"Or the illusion of."

He tilted his head, slightly. "Not here. To love the sea is to long for inconstancy."

The wind rushed at us, suddenly wilder, tugging our coats, pricking my lips, my eyes.

"Why did you leave?"

My words hovered in the air, drifting in slow circles like snowflakes.

"Then, or in a month, or a year, or ten... it had to happen."

"Not in that way."

Very rarely do we have a choice on how to make our departures.

"Not in that way," he repeated.

From high above us rose the cry of seagulls, bright and piercing. They swooped ahead, their grey-white wings held taut and tense, disappearing against the blankness of the clouds. Nicholas walked closer to the water's edge; I didn't follow, not until he turned and acknowledged I was there, and with a gesture, beckoned me over. The pebbles glistened and fractured in the light, wet and shiny, a scattering of a million mirrors catching our reflection, gathered endlessly by the tide.

ABOUT THE AUTHOR

JANICE PARIAT is the author of *Boats on Land: A Collection of Short Stories* (Random House India, 2012). She was awarded the Young Writer Award from the Sahitya Akademi (Indian National Academy of Letters) and the Crossword Book Award for Fiction in 2013. *Seahorse* is her first novel. Currently, she lives in New Delhi, India.

@unnamedpress

facebook.com/theunnamedpress

unnamedpress.tumblr.com

www.unnamedpress.com